NOTHING LESS THAN MAGIC

Books by Stacy Finz

The Nugget Series
GOING HOME
FINDING HOPE
SECOND CHANCES
STARTING OVER
GETTING LUCKY
BORROWING TROUBLE
HEATING UP
RIDING HIGH
FALLING HARD
HOPE FOR CHRISTMAS
TEMPTING FATE
CHOOSING YOU
HOLDING ON

The Garner Brothers
NEED YOU
WANT YOU
LOVE YOU

Dry Creek Ranch
COWBOY UP
COWBOY TOUGH
COWBOY STRONG
COWBOY PROUD

Single Titles
THIS IS HOW IT STARTED
I LOVE YOU MORE
NOTHING LESS THAN MAGIC

Published by Kensington Publishing Corp.

NOTHING LESS THAN MAGIC

STACY FINZ

www.kensingtonbooks.com

KENSINGTON BOOKS are published by

Kensington Publishing Corp.
900 Third Avenue
New York, NY 10022

All Kensington titles, imprints, and distributed lines are available at special quantity discounts for bulk purchases for sales promotion, premiums, fund-raising, educational, or institutional use.

This book is a work of fiction. Names, characters, businesses, organizations, places, events, and incidents either are the product of the author's imagination or are used fictitiously. Any resemblance to actual persons, living or dead, events, or locales is entirely coincidental.

To the extent that the image or images on the cover of this book depict a person or persons, such person or persons are merely models, and are not intended to portray any character or characters featured in the book.

Special book excerpts or customized printings can also be created to fit specific needs. For details, write or phone the office of the Kensington Sales Manager: Kensington Publishing Corp., 900 Third Avenue, New York, NY 10022. Attn. Sales Department. Phone: 1-800-221-2647.

ISBN: 978-1-4967-4763-1 (ebook)

ISBN: 978-1-4967-4762-4

First Kensington Trade Paperback Printing: August 2024

10 9 8 7 6 5 4 3 2 1

Printed in the United States of America

To Jaxon, whose magic makes everything possible

Part 1

I close my eyes, then I drift away, into the magic night I softly say. A silent prayer, like dreamers do, then I fall asleep to dream my dreams of you.
—Roy Orbison, "In Dreams"

Chapter 1

As I stand at the Top of the Mark desperately trying to focus on anything other than San Francisco's spectacular skyline, I'm reminded of how much I dislike heights. Call it a mild case of acrophobia. I can still force myself to fly or visit my uncle's penthouse apartment, but anything higher than three stories makes my stomach pitch.

And the Mark Hopkins's iconic sky lounge is pretty much all glass, making it difficult to ignore the fact that it's nineteen floors up. The whole point of the place is the sweeping bird's-eye view you get of the city, a view I'd feel much more comfortable seeing in pictures. Or even better, from the ground.

But it's the restaurant Austin has chosen, and I have such high hopes for this meeting that my queasiness has given way to excitement.

He wants to talk, which I see as an excellent sign.

The hostess shows me to our table. Thankfully it's at the center of the restaurant, away from the wall of windows, so I don't have to look down. Although it's not as private as I would've liked.

I'm ten minutes late, and Austin still isn't here yet. Nothing new about that. Of the two of us, I'm the more punctual one. If not for my BART train running behind schedule, I would've been here right on the dot of seven. It's a long walk from my office in the Financial District. I probably could've used the exercise, but I ran out of my apartment this morning without a jacket. And we're having an unseasonably chilly October, which is usually shorts weather in San Francisco. It's the summers that are cold and foggy. In any event, it was warmer to take the train. And quicker, even if BART did run late.

I order a martini, which the Top of the Mark is famous for, and examine the 1920s architecture. The story goes that during World War II, servicemen used to come here for a farewell shot before shipping out. Now, travelers come for the skyline.

I'm a little surprised that Austin picked it. He veers toward trendy, and Top of the Mark ain't that. And of course, my heights issues. But it's fine, really. It's a restaurant, not Mount Whitney.

My martini comes, and I check my watch again, letting out a huff. Austin must've gotten held up at the office. He's a divorce attorney, ironic given that I'm a marriage counselor and life coach, helping thousands of couples achieve harmony in their relationships. Whereas Austin helps them cut each other's throats. Okay, a little hyperbole, but the point is that we make odd bedfellows.

I start to text him, then stop myself, afraid it'll come off as naggy. Or needy. One of my first rules to a happy, successful marriage is giving your spouse plenty of space. Then again, Austin isn't my spouse anymore.

We're coming up on our one-year divorce anniversary. A divorce he wanted—not me—and is now obviously regretting. Hence, this meeting. I get a warm tingle just thinking that there is a possibility he wants me back.

I'm not proud of this, but there were times when I didn't want to go on without him. I'm not saying I was suicidal but definitely depressed to the point of having to force myself out of bed most mornings. If it wasn't for work, I probably would've stayed cloistered in my apartment in a stained housecoat, fuzzy slippers, clutching a bottle of wine, binge-watching Ingmar Bergman films. But here I am at the Top of the Mark, drinking a most excellent martini, preparing to reconcile with the love of my life.

Austin is still not here, so I order another drink. Why the hell not? It's not like I'm driving. Besides, I kind of like the gin buzz I'm getting. It helps dull the notion that I'm sitting on top of the San Andreas fault, a bazillion feet in the air.

My server returns with my second cocktail and wants to know if I'd like to order something to eat. I can't tell if he's being accommodating or if it's a subtle hint that the price of two drinks isn't going to cut it. It is a Friday night, and I'm sitting on a prime piece of real estate.

"I'm waiting for my hus—" I stop before I finish, though it's a hard habit to break. For six years, Austin was my husband. Then, out of the blue, he came home from work, packed up his stuff, and said he still loved me, but we weren't working anymore. A year later, and I'm still trying to wrap my head around why. Why weren't we working anymore?

I should know this, shouldn't I? I'm supposed to be an expert on marriage.

The waiter nods, but I can tell he's perturbed. "You know what?" I say, "go ahead and bring out one of those Bavarian pretzel fondue things you're famous for." I'm starved, and something about melted cheese sounds good right now.

I'm beginning to worry that Austin got so caught up in whatever he's doing that he's forgotten our meeting. It's not lost on me that standing up your ex-wife isn't the best start to patching up a broken marriage.

Ah, there he is. He's standing at the hostess stand, searching the crowd for me. I take a moment to look at him. He's wearing the navy blue suit I bought him for his thirty-fifth birthday. They were having a sale at Nordstrom, and the color matched his eyes.

Austin still has the power to take my breath away with his classically handsome good looks. I always thought he resembled a young Jon Hamm. All that thick brown hair and the square jawline.

Secretly, I always wondered whether people thought it strange that he hadn't chosen someone equally as attractive as himself. We all know those couples, the ones about whom everyone says, "Can you imagine how beautiful their children will be?"

I wave to him from across the room, and his face lights up. It's only been a week since I've seen him last, but as he comes toward my table, my heart skips a beat. I notice a few admiring glances from some of the other diners. It's always that way with Austin.

"Hey, Chelsea." He leans over me and gives me a quick peck on the cheek. "Sorry I'm late. I got waylaid by Chuck." Chuck is one of Austin's partners at Blagojevich, Lemons and Rawlins and is a talker. He once held us hostage at one of Austin's work functions for forty minutes, recounting scene after scene of a movie he'd just watched on Netflix. It was excruciating.

"I took the liberty of ordering us an appetizer. You want one of these?" I hold up my martini.

"Nah, I'll wait." Austin shrugs out of his coat and hangs it over the back of his chair and gives me a once-over. "You look great, by the way."

I hope so, having spent most of the previous night picking out my outfit. The sweater is tighter than I usually wear, giving me a boost in the chest department, and the skirt shorter, showing off my legs. They're arguably my best feature. I even managed to persuade Whitney to shoehorn me in this morning for a quick shampoo and blow-out.

Even if I'm reading too much into this date, which I don't think I am, it doesn't hurt to look my best.

"Other than Chuck"—I grin—"how was work?"

"Same old. How 'bout you?"

"Same old," I echo, hoping to dispense with small talk and get right to the point of this meeting. The sooner we reconcile, the sooner we can get back to our old lives when we were together—and happy. At least I was. And I suspect Austin was, too, but it took time apart for him to realize it.

In the last couple of months, he's been super attentive, almost thirsty, as the kids like to say. He texts me nearly every day, and he's come over to the apartment a few times. Although it's always under the guise that he's there to pick up some of the stuff he left behind when he walked out, we wind up spending most of the evening together. I think it's sweet. Almost shy, like he needs an excuse to court me.

The last time he showed up, we wound up in bed together. I don't think that was an accident. And the sex was fantastic, the way it used to be when we first started dating and couldn't keep our hands off each other.

I suspected then that he wanted us to try again but something was holding him back. And now . . . well, there's nothing like the holidays to remind you how lonely the world can seem. October kicks off with what I like to call the fuzzies. You know the drill. When even television commercials for decongestants are filled with happy couples dressed in matching autumn sweaters, taking care of each other. And it only gets worse between Thanksgiving and Christmas.

I warn my followers on social media not to get caught up in all the Hallmark holiday schmaltz, that it's just an illusion created by a billion-dollar industry. But if the season is what it takes for Austin to come to his senses, I'll take it.

The waiter brings our giant pretzel with a hot pot of fondue.

"You sure you don't want a martini?" I ask before the server leaves.

"Nah," he says, surprising me. We've never been huge drinkers, but an after-work cocktail has always been our thing. And Austin did choose a bar for our get-together.

"How come?" I tear off a hunk of the pretzel and dip it in the cheese, careful not to drip on my sweater.

"I don't know." He shrugs. "Just not in the mood, I guess."

Austin has his lawyer face on, the one he uses in court when he's fighting to get his client full custody of a child—or a dog, which is more common than you think. I read his lawyer face, and the fact that he's not drinking, as a sign that he's ready to talk. Really talk. Because to this day, I still don't know what happened that made him leave. He's too young to be having a midlife crisis and too old to be indecisive, or ambivalent. And we were a good team.

Next year, we were planning to start our family. At thirty-seven, we knew our optimal baby-making years were behind us, but we wanted to build our careers to a comfortable place before we brought another human into the world. Besides, women these days are having babies well into their forties.

I have spent much of my life mapping out this future. A beautiful, loving family. A successful profession. A life that is normal and good. Safety.

Of course, this is what almost everyone wants. Ninety-five percent of the couples that come to my lectures and TED Talks will tell you that. But most of them didn't have the childhood I had.

This is all to say that our life was moving along to plan, and then *boom*! He suddenly calls it quits on me.

The server returns, and we order a few more appetizers. Judging from the way Austin keeps fidgeting with his napkin, I can tell he's nervous. I've given a lot of thought to this. Do I make him work for a reconciliation? I mean, he hurt me. A lot of women would force him to pay penance before welcoming him back with open arms. On the other hand, I tell my clients that it's not healthy to play games. They should keep the lines of communication open. That you can't have a fulfilling relationship without honesty.

Austin is laser-focused on something on the other side of the restaurant.

"What is it?" I ask.

"I think I recognize that guy, but I can't place him." He nudges his head toward the back of the room.

I turn to have a look. "Which one?"

"The man sitting alone near the bar."

I shift my focus.

"Don't be so obvious about it," Austin says. "Does he look familiar to you?"

"No." I'm not even sure I'm looking at the right guy. There's at least three men sitting alone in the general vicinity of the bar. "The one in the plaid tie?" I say, because he's the one who stands out the most. The tie, patterned in a series of black and orange checks, is an odd fashion choice. It almost looks like it's part of a costume, or a castoff from a thrift store.

"Yeah."

I try discreetly to have another look, but it means turning around in my chair again. Instead, I scrounge around in my purse for my compact and pretend to fix my lipstick in the mirror, catching a good view of the man's profile. But I can't help but shift my gaze to his tie again. It's the kind of tie that demands attention.

Austin laughs. "What are you, James Bond now? Don't worry about it, he's probably a lawyer or someone who works in the courthouse who I've run into a couple times." He reaches across the table and plucks the compact out of my hand and closes it, sliding it back to me so I can return it to my bag.

The rest of our food comes, and despite being anxious about Austin's and my future, I dig in. Everything smells delicious, and the last time I ate was yogurt for breakfast and a pumpkin spice latte my assistant picked up from the Starbucks in the lobby of my office building.

"Aren't you hungry?" I note that Austin hasn't touched any of the small plates we've ordered.

"My stomach's acting weird." He subconsciously rubs his tummy.

"You want some ginger ale or Seven Up?" I start to flag over our server, but Austin stops me.

"Water is good." He taps his glass, lifts it to his lips, and takes a visual lap around the bar like he's searching for something. Or trying to avoid eye contact. "I thought this would be a good place for us to talk. You know, neutral ground."

A place that neither of us has any sentimental attachment to or a hometown advantage. I talk about it all the time in my seminars. It can be couples counseling or something as simple as a dog park. Just a safe place, where two people can work out their differences, so each of them feels like they're on equal footing.

Except for the fact that I'm afraid of heights and Austin isn't, I'd call the Top of the Mark neutral ground. It was never one of our haunts. Like I said, it's a tourist hangout. And although the lounge is packed, I guess there is some degree of anonymity in a large crowd. In other words, no one will be paying attention to us.

And it is romantic. It's the kind of place you bring your kids for your twenty-fifth wedding anniversary to say, "This is where Daddy proposed." Or in our case, "This is where Daddy begged me to take him back."

"Okay," I say, waiting for him to go on. "What do you want to talk about?"

"Us. I'd like to talk about us."

I nod, because I'm not about to play mediator. In this case, I'm the aggrieved spouse, not a marriage therapist. Still, he's silent, and the anticipation of what he's about to say is killing me. *Just spit it out*, I want to scream.

"I love you, Chelsea."

Finally.

I take a deep breath and reach under the table to take his hand. "I know you do, Austin."

"I've always loved you. Damn, Chelsea, you're my best friend." His blue eyes pool, and he swipes at them with the hand I'm not holding.

This past year must've been hell for him. In all the time I've known him, I've never seen him cry. Not even at his father's funeral. Granted, they weren't close, but still . . . it was his freaking father.

"That's why"—he pauses and clears his throat—"I want you to know how sorry I am for everything I put you through. I just kind of lost all sense of myself. Like I woke up one morning and didn't know who I was anymore. I guess I just needed this time to find myself again."

A million thoughts go racing through my head, none of them charitable. Top among them is you needed to drag us through a heart-wrenching, not to mention expensive, divorce to find yourself? How very self-indulgent of you. But I focus on the mantra of my best-selling self-help book: *Your feelings are valid*. In other words, despite how angry I am with him, Austin is entitled to his pity party.

"I'm sorry you lost yourself," I say, trying to sound like a wife and not do the whole therapist thing, which I recognize may have been one of my overarching problems in our marriage. No spouse wants to be inundated daily with psychobabble. "And I'm so proud of you for doing the work it took to find yourself again." Okay, a little patronizing, but the truth. I am proud of him.

He nods. "It was a long haul with lots of twists and turns on the way. Lots of self-doubt. About me, about us." He smiles softly, sadly.

Seeing him like this, so contrite, makes my heart melt. Every bad word I ever called him is forgotten. All I have is love, so much love that my chest aches with it.

"Oh, Austin." I reach across the table to hug him, already

planning our first Halloween together since the divorce. We used to throw a big party for his colleagues in the clubhouse of our condo. Now my condo, after I spent a bundle to buy him out of his share. Oh well. At least we're back on track, and what was once ours and is now his and mine will become ours again.

Our server returns to the table to see how everything is. His timing couldn't be any worse, and it takes all my willpower not to shoo him away, because Austin and I are finally getting to the good stuff. He wants me back.

Austin's stomach must be feeling better, because he orders a gin and tonic. Perhaps he was nervous that I wouldn't forgive him or at the very least that I would make him grovel. Good. Because after all these years, he should know that I'm not a pushover, even though I am as eager to patch us up as he apparently is.

The waiter leaves, and it's just us again.

"You were saying," I prod, impatient for the grand finale. Then we can go back to my place, our old place, and consummate our reconciliation with a marathon sex session, like we used to do when we first met.

"I was saying what a wonderful friend you've been to me through all this." He is no longer looking at me, instead gazing across the restaurant at that man again. The one he doesn't quite recognize. The one with the distinctive tie.

I clear my throat, and he snaps his attention back to me. His drink comes, and he takes a long sip as I grow ever more anxious.

"And?" I rest my chin on my hands and hold his gaze.

"And"—he blows out a breath—"I have something to tell you. Something . . . well . . . here goes."

I hold my breath, waiting for it, for the words I've been longing to hear since the elevator lurched open on the nineteenth floor of the Mark Hopkins.

"I'm engaged."

I'm already up, ready to throw myself into his arms, when the words hit me like a sucker punch.

I'm engaged.

If it's to me, I'm the last to know. Besides, we already did that song and dance. I want to say, *what the hell are you talking about?* when I realize his lips are still moving but no sounds are coming out. All I hear is a shrill ring. It's either my own fury or a panic attack.

Get ahold of yourself, Chelsea. You misunderstood. Calm down and listen. Really listen.

And just like that, I switch into Dr. Chelsea Knight mode and take my seat, trying to remain serene, even a little removed. "What do you mean by engaged, Austin?" I ask, as if he's just another client.

"I met someone." He takes a moment; then, in a soft voice, says, "Please don't hate me."

I blink a few times, wondering if this is a joke. A cruel joke, but a joke just the same.

"When?" is all I manage to eke out before I completely lose it. "When did you meet this woman?"

His face goes white as he realizes what I'm implying. "It's not what you think. We were in the final stages of our divorce when I met Mary."

So we hadn't even signed on the dotted line of our divorce papers when he was out trolling for the new Mrs. Carter.

"Look," he says, "it just happened. It wasn't as if I was out there, perusing bars to meet women. I was a mess, Chelsea. Devastated. And Mary . . . well . . ."

"Well what?" I want to wipe the pure look of adulation for Mary off his face with my fist. "A week ago, you couldn't get me into bed fast enough. Jesus, Austin."

"Yeah . . . that was wrong. A shitty thing to do." He cocks his head to the side and stares at me with a pair of hangdog puppy eyes that I want to poke out with my fork. "I never meant to send you mixed signals."

"No? How did you think I would take you initiating sex with me?" Because for the first time in his natural-born life, he was the initiator. In the past, I'd always been the one to make the first move in the bedroom. There's nothing wrong with that, and the sex had always been good. But this time, it was all him. Nothing mixed about those signals.

His face falls, and I see regret. Deep-seated regret.

"You know I could never resist you, Chels." He says it with such sadness that I don't know exactly how to take it. Is he sad that he can't resist me or sad that he's a duplicitous jackass?

"You and I have so much history, Chelsea. And I'm having trouble letting you go. Really ending it."

"Then don't." I'm near hysterics, so near that I'm willing to beg. "Don't do this, Austin. We were good together. You said it yourself."

"Ah, jeez, Chelsea, don't look at me that way. You know how guilty I feel about this? I debated on whether to even tell you. But it was bound to come out at some point. How do you keep an engagement secret? And you're the one who is always talking about honesty." He starts to brush a hair away from my face, and I push his hand away. "Come on, don't be like that."

If I hadn't drained my glass, I'd throw my drink in his face. Instead, I simply sit stock-still with my mouth ajar, not knowing what to say or how to react. How is it that one day he's in love with me, and the next he's engaged to someone else? I'm a nationally renowned marriage counselor, for God's sake, and never saw this coming.

"Say something, Chels."

"What do you want me to say, Austin? That I'm happy for you? That I hope you and this Mary woman have a wonderful life together? The life we were supposed to have. What I don't understand is why you led me on all these months? Showing up at the condo. Calling. Texting. Sending me *New Yorker* cartoons." When we were together, we used to cackle over those cartoons, when in truth, half the time I didn't even get them.

"Was I supposed to cut you out of my life?" He holds my gaze, waiting for me to respond. When I don't, he shakes his head. "Jesus, Chelsea, you're my best friend."

"And apparently your fuck buddy."

He motions for me to keep my voice down. "That's pretty low. We were together for nearly a decade. It's only natural that my body still responds to the familiarity of yours."

"Oh, is that what it was?" I laugh, then lean back, fold my arms across my chest, and try to keep from throwing up in my mouth. "Is that what you told Mary? That it was merely the familiarity of my body that you were responding to?"

"Stop it, Chelsea. It's beneath you."

I want to say the only thing beneath me a few days ago was him. But I'm too crushed to go there again. I just want to leave. Run, actually. Grab my purse and take the elevator down nineteen floors until I'm touching firm ground again. But I'm trying to preserve what little dignity I have left. So instead, I'm planning to sit here and eat everything on my damned plate, then stick him with the bill. No, better yet, I'm going to deprive him of the one thing we still share together. The one thing that still means something to him, even if I don't.

"I want the cabin for Christmas," I say, jutting out my chin like a petulant child.

Truthfully, I can't think about Halloween or Thanksgiving, let alone Christmas, right now, because I'll be spending all three holidays alone. It's childish of me, but the urge to lash out is overwhelming, and he loves the cabin. Besides, I don't want him taking his new fiancée there. It was supposed to be the place where we took our children on vacations to make memories, the place he and I would eventually retire to.

"Okay," he says, far too easily. "I'll take it on Thanksgiving then."

"No can do. My sister and her kids are coming up." The closest my sister ever came to sleeping in a rustic cabin in the woods was a five-star ski resort in Aspen.

Austin lets out a sigh. He knows my sister. He knows she and I rarely speak. "Whatever you want, Chelsea."

His breezy acquiescence puts me over the edge. Can he really be this insensitive? This oblivious? This cruel? But more important, how did I not see it? This is what I do, what I've gained a national reputation for. I am the foremost expert on marriage. And yet, I was wrong about everything. The man I married, the marriage itself, even my nonexistent reconciliation. Wrong, wrong, wrong.

I make a show of looking at my watch, because I can't take sitting here one second longer. "I've got to go." I scoop my purse off the floor and rise.

"Ah, come on, Chelsea. Let's talk this out."

That's what I'd tell one of my clients. To talk it out. Instead, I do the exact opposite. "Fuck off, Austin."

I rush out of the restaurant so fast, I forget to shield my eyes as I pass by the restaurant's wall of windows. Now, I feel like retching. By the time I reach the ground floor of the hotel, my heart is racing so fast I can feel it bouncing out of my chest.

Boom. Boom. Boom.

I take the doors out to California Street and start to walk home, hoping the brisk evening air settles me. And clears my head. I'm replaying Austin's and my conversation, thinking about all the mean things I could've said and didn't, as I start to cross to the other side of the street.

It happens so fast that I don't have time to step away. All I hear is the squeal of brakes and people screaming. The crunch of metal. More yelling, horns blasting, and in the distance, a siren rends the air. It's so loud that my head is exploding from all the noise.

Next thing I know, I'm flat on the pavement in excruciating pain. The ground is wet and sticky. And black. Or is it red? The sharp smell of metallic fills my nose, and everything around me seems to have erupted in chaos.

They say you see your entire life flash before your eyes before you die. I see my sister Lolly and me, playing hopscotch on the sidewalk in front of our parents' house just before the shots ring out. The police are there to clear the scene. My uncle, tall, handsome, and sad—so, so sad—comes to whisk us away. Forever.

Next, I see Austin and me on our wedding day, my white veil fluttering in the breeze, as we recite our vows on a sandy beach in Puerto Vallarta. It's there, deep in my chest. Security at long last.

The last thing I see is the man in the restaurant, the one with the orange and black plaid tie, staring down at me before everything disappears.

And then there is nothing.

Chapter 2

"Hey, you'll get eaten alive out here."

I feel warm hands on my shoulders, shaking me. "What? Get off of me." I'm startled awake and my hammock sways, then pitches to one side before I right it without falling out.

"Whoa, whoa." The man holds his hands up in the air and backs away. "I come in peace."

It takes me a few seconds to get my bearings. Then it all rushes back to me in Technicolor. I've come to the cabin to recuperate and regroup. Two weeks of blissful nothingness, where I can pretend that the events of the last week were just a bad dream. That no, my ex-husband isn't getting married to someone other than me.

And no, I wasn't run down by a cable car.

I pull myself up into a sitting position and stare at the man standing in front of me. He looks vaguely familiar, but in my hazy state, I can't quite recall who he is. And we're here . . . alone. The nearest neighbor is a good half mile away.

"Do I know you?"

He tilts his head to the side and looks at me like I'm a little off my rocker before saying, "You hired me to fix your roof." He glances up at the sky, which is clear and blue. "Winter is coming." A slight smile plays on his lips when he says it, and I suspect it's because he's quoting that famous line from *Game of Thrones*, which has sort of become a cliché now, but whatever.

There's also the small issue that I have zero recollection of hiring anyone to fix the roof. Maybe Austin did. Or maybe I've lost some of my short-term memory from the impact of the cable car. I did hit my head, after all.

Regardless of who hired him, fixing the roof is a good idea, because in the last rain, we had two leaks. One over the sink in the kitchen, the other in the middle of the primary bedroom. The latter warped and discolored a few of the floorboards. Now, I have to cover the area with a rug to hide the unsightly damage.

"Um, okay," I say, noting for the first time that he's a rather large man, tall and broad, which alone should be menacing. But for whatever reason, it's not, though a person can never be too careful.

I look around for his car, wondering how he drove up without me hearing anything; then I remember I'm in the back of the cabin, away from the driveway.

The hammock is no easy thing to get out of gracefully, but I manage to do it without falling on my ass. He just stands there as if he's waiting for his marching orders. I walk around the side of the house to find a pickup in the driveway. There's no roofing company insignia on the vehicle, just a few dings and a ladder strapped to the top of the truck's utility rack.

I turn around to find that the guy is a few feet behind me.

"What roofing company are you with again?" I ask.

He squints at me, and I can't tell if it's from the sun or if he's confused. Confusion ultimately wins, judging by the way he's staring at me, perplexed.

"I've been doing work around your cabin for the last three years." He raises his arms in the air. When I don't say anything, he presses, "A few months back, I installed the new front door."

I shift my eyes to the cabin's entrance. One of the reasons I fell in love with the house is the wide front porch. That first year after we bought the place, Austin and I searched high and low for the perfect Adirondack chairs so we could sit out front when the sun's glare off the lake was too blinding. We wound up buying recycled plastic ones at Costco, of all places, because Austin said they would last longer. To this day, I hate them.

Sure enough, there's a new red Craftsman door where the old oppressive oak one was.

The man folds his arms across his chest as he watches me take in the door, and I let out a sigh.

"You'll have to excuse me," I tell him. "I was in an accident a few days ago, and I'm apparently not myself." I leave out the part that I was run down by a cable car, because I suspect this guy is starting to think I'm a nutjob, and most people don't realize just how dangerous those streetcars can be. All anyone associates with them is that they're iconic San Francisco. Or it reminds them of the annoying Rice-A-Roni jingle or the Tony Bennett song about little cable cars climbing halfway to the stars. When in fact, dozens of people are maimed, even killed, by streetcars a year, if you believe the statistics.

"Sorry to hear that." He gives me a wary glance, then switches his gaze to the roof. "You still want me to do the work?"

"Yes," I say, though I was hoping for peace and quiet and anticipate that the roof work will cause a good amount of racket. "You're . . ." I wait for him to say his name, because for the life of me, I can't remember it, only that his face is starting to register.

He gives me a hard look like he doesn't believe me and finally says, "Knox." Just Knox, no last name.

I don't know why, but I have the sudden urge to say, "Knox, Knox, who's there?" but don't. We're already getting off to a shaky start.

He unfastens the ladder from the utility rack and lifts it up like it weighs nothing, then carries it to the back of the cabin. I consider whether to return to my hammock, but Knox is right. This time of year, the mosquitoes off the lake will eat me alive.

Since there's little chance of me getting much rest with the noise from the roof, I decide to go to town and stock up on supplies. Knox is strapping on his tool belt when I find him.

"I'm taking off for a while; you don't need to get in the house, do you?"

"Doubtful. But just in case, is the key still under the flowerpot?"

I wonder if Austin leaves it there, because I don't remember ever leaving a spare key anywhere. I don't even remember us having a flowerpot.

"Uh, let's take a look," I say, then wait for him to lead the way to this alleged flowerpot.

Sure enough, it's on the front porch, next to the new door, and there is a shiny copper key underneath it. Knox slides the empty pot back over the key and bobs his head at me as if to say, *we're all good.*

"Okay, then." I shove my hands in my pockets and make a mental note to plant something in the pot. Orange mums or marigolds, maybe. "See you when I get back."

I'm halfway to my car when I realize I need a jacket. It's like fifty degrees out, and my cheeks feel chapped from the cold. I run inside the house and grab a fleece, then on second thought, a hat and scarf. October in the mountains is usually milder, somewhere in the sixties or even seventies. Here in Northern California, summer doesn't start until August and lingers well into mid-November. Not this year, though.

Knox is on the roof. I can hear him banging around up there, confirming that my decision to get out of Dodge was the right one. On my way out, I notice the leaves have turned shades of bright yellow, red, and orange. And the sheer beauty of the trees and the mountains in full fall regalia catches in my throat.

When we bought the lake cabin, it was summer. The house needed work and still does. But it's about as close to perfection as it comes. It's nestled in the trees, and it took us forever to find it, especially because our budget was modest, at least by California standards. For months, we toured every house near a body of water, because we'd decided that a lake or a river view was imperative to improving our mental health. It was only our second year of marriage, and our lives had become so immersed in our respective jobs that we didn't know how to relax anymore. We'd convinced ourselves that if we bought a vacation home, we'd use it to slow down, go kayaking and swimming until our skin turned brown in the hot summer sun, or just read a book by the water. The kind of things normal couples do on their days off.

We were well-intentioned at first, packing up our busy city lives on the days we were here, sleeping in and lazing around the lake. But it didn't last long. Austin always had a legal motion that needed researching or a needy client who monopolized his time on the phone. I had an entire company to run or a book to write, or a lecture to prepare. Eventually, when we managed to make it up here, the cabin became an extension of our offices.

When it came time to divide everything up in the divorce, we told ourselves the cabin was too good of an investment to sell. But honestly, we knew we'd never find another place like it and decided to share custody, each using the little house in the Sierra foothills on alternate weekends and holidays.

And secretly, I thought we'd work our way back to each other, and the cabin would stand as a symbol of our enduring love.

These are the things I'm thinking about as I take the meandering two-lane highway to town, gazing out at the breathtaking trees and their vibrant autumn colors. I'm still trying to decide whether I ever took the time to just look and take in all that there was to see. The sad truth of the matter is I can't remember, and I don't know if it's because I hit my head when I got run down by the cable car or if the answer is simply no. No, I never took the time to really look, because I was too busy being Chelsea Knight, the brilliant marriage therapist who was too stupid to realize her own marriage was in trouble.

Ghost has a population of fourteen thousand people, not tiny by any stretch but hardly a sprawling metropolis.

The story goes that the town got its name during California's Gold Rush and from the bloody massacre of the Ramsey family.

James Marshall and John Sutter had just discovered gold in a streambed on the American River in Coloma. Word spread, and prospectors flocked to California from all over the world to seek their fortunes.

Such was the case of Charles Ramsey. Charles, his wife Jane, and their four-year-old son William came from Oregon, down the Siskiyou Trail on a covered wagon to try their luck in the goldfields. But after a year, defeated and exhausted, they were ready to go home. That's when they got an offer to join a dozen other families from the Pacific Northwest to branch out down the mountain in Bear Creek, where the land was still rough, fertile, and virgin territory. According to prospector legend, the fields near the creek were bursting with gold. But only if you had the grit and fortitude to stake your claim without catching cholera, getting robbed, or killed first.

When the Forty-Niners arrived, they set out to dig deep shafts along streams and riverbeds. They toiled for days in the hot sun, panning for gold in the silt deposits of the riverbed. It was backbreaking and dangerous work, and Charles didn't know how much longer he could ask his family to put up with the squalor and violence of the camps.

But then one day, it happened. Charles struck gold. At first, it was small flakes that he found at the bottom of his pan. Then, with a pick and shovel, the flakes grew to lumps and eventually nuggets. The others in their group calculated that it was a small fortune, enough to buy land, build a house, and raise livestock. Enough for a good life.

But three days after Charles staked his claim, bandits murdered the couple and little William while the trio slept, and stole their gold.

Deciding that mining was too dangerous, the other twelve families wound up settling in a verdant hamlet in Bear Valley, selling supplies and food to a new influx of prospectors. They called their new town Ramsey to honor their murdered friends. But when the specters of Charles, Jane, and William haunted the prospectors at night as they worked the goldfields, the town simply became known as Ghost.

The name was reaffirmed in 1883, when the gold was depleted and residents abandoned the place for greener pastures, literally making Ghost a ghost town.

It wasn't until after World War II and California's housing shortage that a small developer from Sacramento decided Ghost was the next frontier and began building modest homes for returning GIs and an influx of immigrants. Just an hour away from the state capital and rich in agricultural land, Ghost attracted a new fortune seeker.

And the Gold Rush lore of the Ramsey murders has only added to the town's mystique. Tourists flock here for the sole purpose of coming face-to-face with Charles's or Jane's ghost or to hear little William wailing in the middle of the night.

That's why I'm not surprised that there's no parking in the lot across from Main Street. Halloween is only a week away, and I suspect visitors want an early start to getting their Ghost on. In the past, Austin and I avoided Ghost around this time of year for this very reason. If we wanted crowds, we could get them in San Francisco.

I find street parking a couple of blocks away and make my way to Main Street, joining the clusters of people window-shopping and eating at the restaurants. Two years ago, the city got a state grant to turn Main into a pedestrian-only street. And while it makes driving through town a bit convoluted, I have to say it's a nice touch. Now, café tables and market umbrellas spill out onto the street, and in summer, there's live music on the weekends.

For Halloween, it's safe to say Ghost goes for broke, judging by all the decorations. I marvel at the jack-o'-lanterns hanging from the streetlights and the orange and black luminarias that line the rooftops. Someone gussied up the communal firepit to look like a witch's cauldron and replaced the old wooden benches with straw bales.

But my favorite so far has to be the scarecrows that dot Main Street. According to a placard, each of the town's civic organizations is responsible for creating its own original one. I wander down the street, examining each display.

The Cattleman's Association did a cowboy. Cute, but not terribly original. The local 4-H club made one completely out of garden vegetables, which seems to defeat the purpose of a scarecrow. But still, clever. The Kiwanis did a ghost, because someone had to. But it's the Soroptimists for the win. Their Minion scarecrow blows it out of the park and looks just like the animated character from the movie.

I head to Flacos for a carne aside burrito. Austin and I didn't eat out much when we came up on weekends, opting to cook at home. But when we did, we always went to Flacos, a hole-in-the-wall taco shop that makes better burritos than the places in the Mission District, which are famous for their burritos. I think it's the fact that at Flacos, they don't put rice in the burritos, which in my opinion overwhelms the rest of the ingredients and adds a texture that doesn't really need to be there. But I'm hardly a food critic. I'll pretty much eat anything that's put in front of me.

As soon as I walk in the door, I'm flooded with memories of Austin. How we used to hold hands as we walked along Main Street. How we used to share a basket of chips, even though every time we went, I would emphatically announce that I was swearing off chips. How we used to laugh at the weird folk dolls on the wall and make up names for them. "That one looks like a Hazel," Austin would say, to which I would respond, "What does a Hazel look like?" "Like that." He would point to the doll, and we would bust up laughing.

It wasn't like any of it was the stuff of romance novels or swoony rom-com movies, but it was us. And I liked us. I loved us.

And yet, I have to wonder if I imagined that we were a better couple than we really were. If maybe there were signs that I somehow wasn't enough and that Austin had tired of me. Because I certainly hadn't tired of him. I loved him as much as the day we met, the day my old boss set us up on a blind date. We both laughed about it later, because who goes on blind dates anymore? But there we were at a British-style pub at Fifth and Mission, eating bangers and mash, complaining about our college loans, and planning how we were going to pay them off. By the time he walked me home, I was smitten. By the time he called me the next day, I was hearing wedding bells. And by the time we set a date, I was convinced we'd be the couple to beat all the odds. And look at us. We didn't even make it to the seven-year itch.

If Lolly was still talking to me, she'd have herself a good, hard laugh. So perhaps it's for the best that she and I are no longer speaking. But the thing is, I miss my baby sister. I miss her even more than I miss Austin. And that's a lot.

We used to be two peas in a pod. When we were kids, our late mother even dressed us the same. Even though I'm three years older than my sister, people always mistook us for twins. Not anymore, I'm sure. Now, we live in two different worlds. And the only thing they have in common is that they're a long way from the modest San Fernando Valley neighborhood where we grew up. Far from the idyllic life we once had before everything blew up.

I take my burrito to go, because I don't want to eat alone,

which is ridiculous, because I eat alone nearly every day. Half the time at my desk at the office, the other half when I'm traveling on a speaking circuit. It's either a hotel restaurant or room service. Today, it's in my car.

Afterward, I swing by the grocery store and buy enough food to last the two weeks I'm staying. If I'm forced to eat alone, I'm going to do it in the comfort of my own home.

On the way out of the market, a woman with two youngsters in tow stops to smile at me. "Hey, Chelsea, you up for the weekend?"

I think she's mistaken me for someone else, because I don't know her from Adam. Then I remember that she said my name.

I stutter, "Yes, I am" as I try to figure out who she is. I'm positive I've never seen her before.

"Well, it's great to see you." One of the kids, a boy with a mop of red hair, starts to pull her toward the cereal aisle. "Let's grab coffee if you have time." The boy drags her away before I can respond.

My whole way home, I rack my brain to figure out where I know her from, eventually concluding that my lack of recall has got to be short-term memory loss from head trauma. I worry that I may have serious neurological ramifications that weren't detected by the MRI the night of the accident and make a mental note to book an appointment with a specialist.

I don't give the exchange another thought as I keep my eyes on the road. The cabin is only ten minutes from town, but today the drive feels longer.

The days are getting shorter, and in a few hours it'll be dark. I'd like to get everything put away and have a fire going before the sun sets.

My mind shifts to tomorrow, the twenty-fourth anniversary of my parents' death.

For the first time in a long time, I wonder what Lolly is doing, whether she's thinking about tomorrow, too.

Chapter 3

Knox is back. I'm in my bathrobe, drinking coffee at the kitchen table. He waves to me through the window. I open the top of the Dutch door and ask him if he wants me to top off his thermos.

"Sure."

I go to grab the pot, and when I turn around, he's standing in my kitchen.

"Oh, let me get dressed." I hand him the pot and dash off to the bedroom. I wasn't expecting him to come in the house.

The cabin is tiny, just a two-bedroom, one bath that Austin and I winterized after we bought it. The previous owner was a widower, who used the place on weekends and holidays for fishing trips, relying on the woodstove for heat. We had plans to add a second story at some point and to expand the kitchen and living room, which currently is a cramped space with dated appliances. What sold us was the location and views. You can see the lake from every room in the house, and the light is magnificent, even though the property is covered in large oak and pine trees.

We furnished the place with a few good pieces—a leather sofa from Ethan Allen, an overstuffed recliner Austin took from his office, and a cannonball bed we got at an antique store in wine country. But other than that, we've left the place mostly as is. At least aesthetically. Unfortunately, upkeep has been a constant money pit. Between replacing the old pipes and all the failed windows, we blew our budget for the good stuff, like replacing the hideous '80s faux rock around the fireplace and the wagon-wheel light fixture that hangs over the dining room.

But I'm not complaining. From the day the real estate agent showed us the place, I knew it was magical. The coziness of the cabin. The fact that I can toss a stone from my back door to the lake. The constant smell of fresh air, the deer that graze in my front yard, the birds, the trees . . . well, it's just majestic.

I hurriedly dress in a pair of jeans and an oversized sweater, swiping a brush through my hair on my way out, not even bothering to check my reflection in the mirror. It's a relief not to have to dress up while I'm here. Don't get me wrong, I like clothes. I like makeup and having my hair done. I even like shoes that kill my arches and squish my toes if they make the outfit. I may not be a fashionista like Lolly, but it's always been important to me to keep up appearances and look the part of a successful woman. But here, I'd look pretty silly in a suit.

I return to the kitchen to find Knox is still here, sitting at my table, drinking coffee. I half expected—and half hoped—he'd be up on the roof, banging away. I'm not exactly in the mood for company. *Then why'd you open your big mouth about coffee?*

He looks up from his phone and gives me a thumbs-up. I have no idea why, but I self-consciously pat down my hair.

"The coffee," he says, and may as well roll his eyes. "It's good. Where did you get it?"

I think for a second, because it's probably been here a while, and I didn't bother to look at the label while I was scooping beans into the grinder. The bag is in the pantry, and I pull it out, look at it, and put it down on the table.

Knox studies the packaging, then slides it back to me. "Not from around here, I can tell you that."

"It's from a small roaster in San Francisco. If you like, I'll get you some." I'd offer him the bag, but it's all I have.

"Nah, I'll stick with Yuban."

"Okay." He's the one who brought it up, but whatever. "How's the roof coming along?"

"It's coming, but it'll take me a couple of days. It's a multi-stage process. Luckily, there's no rain in the forecast."

At least something is going my way.

Knox drums his fingers on the table. "You still doing those TED Talks?"

He catches me off guard with that one. I am surprised he knows anything about my lectures. Sure, I've built a large following with my seminars and books, but it's not like I'm a household name.

"You've been to one?" I ask.

"No, but I've seen you on YouTube."

I surreptitiously glance at his ring finger. There's nothing there, not even a band of pale skin. My TED Talks are about marriage, how to improve them, how to maintain them, how to compromise so that everyone is happy. Needless to say, the vast majority of my clients are married couples. Or couples on the precipice of divorce, desperately trying to save their marriages.

"Did you find it helpful?" I ask Knox, because the absence of a ring doesn't mean he isn't married or that he's not trying to improve or save a relationship.

"Not in the least," he says.

Again, I'm taken aback. Not just because of his bluntness, but because I'm good at my job. So good at it, that I don't even see patients anymore, just lecture and write books full time. Next year, I have a line of calendars with aspirational sayings coming out. We're also working on a marriage journal for couples to track their good and bad days.

"Oh, I'm sorry to hear that," I say.

"Why?"

"Uh . . . because the whole purpose of my talks is to help."

"Okay, then can I get a refund?"

"I thought you said you watched it on YouTube." I shake my head, wondering if he's intentionally trying to provoke me. "What didn't work for you?"

"All of it, meaning none of it. Nothing you said saved my relationship. In fact, it probably made things worse, and they were pretty bad to begin with."

My first inclination is to argue with him, tell him he wasn't putting in the work, but I realize how insensitive that would sound. "I'm sorry. The death of a relationship is very painful, and it's tough that you had to go through that." It was my stock response when I was seeing recently divorced patients.

He holds my gaze, and I can see it in his eyes. He's laughing at me.

"No offense," he says, "but you should probably work on your delivery. It sounds a little rehearsed. There's nothing to be sorry about, anyway. It was for the best; otherwise, we would've ended up miserable."

It's on the tip of my tongue to ask him what happened, but I'm here to relax, to recuperate, not to analyze him or give counsel. Besides, I'm clearly not as good at my job as I thought I was, evidenced by my own marriage—or lack of one. The last thing I want to do right now is remind myself of that fact.

Still, I'm curious about Knox, intrigued by this mystery relationship of his. Or maybe it's just true what they say, that misery loves company. Though why I assume he's miserable is probably projection on my part. I really don't know anything about him.

Knox rises to his feet and refills his thermos with the last of the coffee, signaling that our conversation is ended.

"What did you say your last name was?" I ask.

"I didn't." But on his way out, he calls back to me, "It's Hart."

What an odd fellow.

I clear my breakfast dishes and clean out the coffee machine, weighing the wisdom of brewing another pot, ultimately deciding against it. I've had enough caffeine for one morning. A quick glance at my phone shows there are no new emails or texts. Knowing Ronnie, my assistant and gatekeeper extraordinaire, she's forwarded all communiqués to her own phone, so I can rest.

I had sort of hoped Lolly would call. Pretty unrealistic. But putting our grievances aside for one day—this day of all days—doesn't seem too much to ask for. It's not like we couldn't pick up where we left off of not talking to each other as soon as we finished memorializing our parents.

You could always call her, I remind myself. But what's the use? She'd either ignore her phone or hang up on my face. Frankly, I don't need the rejection right now.

Instead, I decide to do a little reconnaissance on Austin's fiancée. It won't be easy, because other than her first name, I don't know anything about her. I get my laptop from the bedroom and set it up at the kitchen table. We're lucky in that we get decent Wi-Fi here. Not all the neighbors do, but for whatever reason, we get a strong signal. It was one of our conditions for buying the cabin.

I jump onto Google and search "Austin Carter and Mary." No last name, just Mary. I get more hits than I know what to do with, so I add "San Francisco" and "Attorney" to my search in hopes of winnowing down the results. The first thing that comes up is Blagojevich, Lemons and Rawlins. I scroll through the firm's staff pictures to see if there is a Mary there, because it makes sense that Austin would've met her at work. It's safe to say that the dating pool is deeply diminished after thirty.

There's no Mary, so I soldier on.

Austin doesn't do social media, the obvious place to look. And there doesn't appear to be an announcement of their engagement in any of the local papers. I hoped that perhaps they'd attended a newsworthy event or benefit (something he and I would occasionally do) and I could find a picture of them on the social pages. But so far, nothing.

After an hour of searching, it becomes clear that Austin's fiancée is as elusive as cheap rent. I slam the lid of my laptop down, chiding myself for being childish. What kind of marriage expert spies on her ex-husband? *Hey, it's only natural to be curious*. Besides, if I see them together, it'll give me closure, I further rationalize, realizing this internal argument I'm having with myself makes me sound like a loon. Okay, *loon* isn't an official term in the DSM-5, but we all know if I keep this up, I'll be bordering on one.

Knox pounds on the roof as if to agree. I flip him the bird, even though he can't see it.

I decide that getting out of the house will make me forget about Austin, Lolly, and my parents. The sun is shining off the lake, and it seems like a good day to take the boat out, except I don't know how to clip the electric motor to the battery. I should've paid more attention when Austin did it.

What the hell, it's nothing I can't learn from a YouTube video. I grab my phone and a jacket and head to the dock. There's a whisper of a breeze, and the scent of pine needles fills the air. But the sun tricked me into believing it was warmer than it actually is. Still, I don't let the chill dissuade me from going out on the water. A nice bracing ride will do me good.

Austin was supposed to pull the boat out of the lake on his last visit and store it before the rain comes. We are below the snow line but will occasionally get flurries that coat the ground, making it look pretty before it quickly melts. But lucky for me, Austin forgot. The aluminum boat is still tied to the dock, rocking in the gentle current.

I lug the battery, which weighs as much as a small cow, from the boathouse and manage to drop it onto the floor of the boat, then go back for the motor. I'm sitting on one of the captain's chairs, studying how to hook everything up, struggling with which wire goes where, when I realize I forgot my life jacket. The lake is as calm as an empty parking lot, and I'm a good swimmer, but I'm coming off a concussion and shouldn't take any chances. What if I have a blackout on the water and fall out of the boat? These are the things I think about.

I make the trek back to the boathouse and snap myself into one of the vests we purchased when we first got the cabin. Austin isn't much of a swimmer, and neither of us started out as boat enthusiasts. The first time we attempted to get in kayaks, we wound up in the drink. I've mostly mastered getting in and out now, thanks to a fancy failsafe launch. Because what's the good of living on a lake if you never use it?

Once I figure out that red goes to positive and black goes to negative, I try to attach the motor to the mounting bracket. This is no easy feat. The electric motor doesn't want to stay and keeps falling off the bracket. My frustration is growing to the point where I'm considering giving up and going inside. I punch the motor, which only hurts my knuckles, and let out a curse, then scream when I realize there's someone on the dock behind me.

"Jesus Christ, you nearly gave me a heart attack."

"I couldn't stand to watch you any longer." Knox steps into the boat like he's been doing it his whole life. He doesn't even grab the edge to steady himself the way I do every time I get in, afraid I'll be pitched over the side. Nope, he just climbs over me, and on the first try fits the motor into the mounting bracket and tightens the bolts. I don't know whether to be thankful or to hate him for making it look so easy.

He hops out of the boat with the same dexterity as when he got in.

"Thanks," I say, and to prove I know what I'm doing, I rev the engine and accelerate. When I say *engine*, you have to understand that we're only talking about thirty pounds of thrust, meaning this thing tops out at five miles an hour. Still, it jolts alive like I'm on the high seas and lurches forward. I'm moving now, though it feels like I'm dragging something behind me. Something heavy.

Knox shouts for me to turn off the motor. But instead of rotating the dial to stop, I accidentally turn it to the top speed. There's a horrible creaking noise, and when I turn around, I see a section of the dock coming loose.

"You're still moored," Knox is yelling, grabbing onto the rope that's tied to the cleat. It's a risky endeavor. The engine may not have much torque, but there's still the risk that if I keep going, he'll be pulled overboard.

I quickly fumble with the dial, and after what seems like an eternity, manage to turn it to the off position. I take a deep breath as the boat bobs up and down on the water only a few yards from where I started. Knox pulls me in.

"Your first time driving?" he says in that laconic drawl of his that I'm starting to recognize as sarcasm.

"Is the dock busted?"

"You pulled one of the anchor poles out. It should've been in the ground deeper anyway. I can fix it. Next time, untie the boat before you take off."

I nod, feeling incredibly stupid. "It's the accident," I tell him. "I'm still not myself."

"Let me guess. You were the one behind the wheel." He glances at the boat, then offers me an arm to get out. Yes, it seems sensible to leave boating for another day.

"I got run over by a cable car." Why not tell him? Better the truth than letting him believe I'm a bad driver.

His brows wing up. "How did that happen?"

"It's a long story," I say, then do an about-face and decide to tell him the whole story. Why not? It's not like I know the guy well enough to humiliate myself any more than I already have. "My ex-husband had just announced that he was engaged. I was despondent over the news and wasn't paying attention when I walked in front of a moving cable car."

Knox doesn't say anything, but his silence speaks volumes.

"I guess that must confirm for you what a lousy marriage counselor I am."

"I didn't say that." He crouches down to re-knot the boat rope around the cleat, then points to the pole. "I'll bring a post driver tomorrow. Why were you despondent over an ex-husband?"

"I was hoping to patch things up. I actually thought we were on the road to reconciliation when he dropped the whole engagement thing on me. Some woman named Mary. His one true soulmate," I say, not even trying to disguise my disdain.

"Why'd you want to patch things up?"

The answer seems obvious, but I realize that Knox is asking the same exact question I would've asked one of my patients when I still had my practice. *Why are you drawn to a person with whom you are divorced?* I look at him to see if he's doing it intentionally. If he's mocking me. But his expression is absent of ridicule, neutral even. If anything, it's mild curiosity I'm seeing.

"He left me," I say, even though I could be setting myself up for professional embarrassment, because if word gets out—the real word, not what my publicist and I cooked up for the world in a written statement when Austin and I parted ways—it could blow up my career. "I want . . . wanted to work things out. I thought we were on the same page, but I was wrong."

"Oh," Knox says blandly. "I'm sorry. But if he left you, why would you want him back?"

"I don't know how to answer that; it's a long story. More important, though, are you a psychotherapist disguised as a handyman?"

"Definitely not. You want to go back to the house? It's getting cold."

I note that he doesn't have a jacket on.

"Thank you for averting disaster," I say, and start for the cabin.

"I was too late for that."

I give him a sideways glance. "Way to make me feel better. Look, I admit that I'm not that boat savvy, but my old self never would've pulled away from the dock while I was still tied to it." The truth is, I'm having trouble distinguishing what my old self even was.

"Does your old self know how to make a sandwich? I forgot my lunch today." As if on cue, his stomach growls.

Chapter 4

I'm fast asleep when the phone rings. At first, I decide it's a dream and roll over to drown out the sound of my cell vibrating on the nightstand. But the noise doesn't stop, and I bolt upright, realizing it's real and not a dream at all.

I glance at my alarm clock. It's two in the morning. No one calls that early unless it's an emergency. I reach for my phone, but it stops ringing. Before I can check who the missed call was from, the ringing begins all over again.

Lolly.

"Hello."

There's no response, but I know she's there. I can hear her breathing.

"Cut the shit, Lolly."

"What are you doing?" she finally says.

"What do you think I'm doing? I was sleeping."

"You know what day it is, right?"

The day was yesterday, but I don't correct her. Who am I to quibble over a few hours. "I do."

"I went to the cemetery."

I take a moment to absorb that, surprised. Then I wonder whether I'm a bad daughter . . . a bad sister . . . because I didn't go, too. But even twenty-four years later, I'm angry. I'm still so damn angry.

"Did Uncle Sylvester go?" I assume he's the one who suggested it.

"No, just me."

"Why?" I ask. "You've never gone before."

"I don't know." Her voice is quiet, almost contemplative, if Lolly can ever be contemplative. "I guess I just thought it was time to let it go, to let them go."

"Did it work?"

"I don't know." She lets out a sigh.

She was only nine when it happened. I don't think it scarred her as much as it did me. But it's wrong of me to compare. Everyone experiences pain differently. At the time, the deaths of our parents traumatized both of us. How could it not?

"What was it like?" I ask.

"What do you mean what was it like? It was Forest Lawn, two headstones in a sea of graves. I stood there for forty minutes like an idiot not knowing what to say, trying to feel something other than contempt."

It's more than I could ever do, and I'm supposed to be the evolved one. "It's good that you did it, Lolly. I'm proud of you."

"Save me the psycho mumbo jumbo, Chelsea. I pay a king's ransom for that. It would've been nice if you'd come with me. They were your parents, too."

"You didn't ask me," I say, knowing full well that even if she had, I wouldn't have gone.

"You're always too busy to take my calls."

That isn't true, but arguing the issue is fruitless. Lolly believes what she wants to believe. "I'm taking your call now, aren't I?"

Lolly lets out a not-so-nice laugh. "Why do you think I called at this god-awful hour? I knew you'd have no choice but to pick up the phone."

I squeeze the bridge of my nose, tired of this. Tired of the animosity between us. We used to be so close; then sometime after college, Lolly started running hot and cold where I was concerned, but mostly cold. First, she thought I was being a bitch because I didn't approve of her marriage to Daddy Warbucks. Then it was because I didn't spend enough time with her kids. Her biggest complaint, though, is that I'd become too big for my britches (my father's favorite phrase) and had left her behind, which simply isn't true.

"For once, can we not fight?" I say. "I've had a bad week."

I wait for her to tell me her week was worse, because that's how it usually goes with Lolly. But instead, I get a long pause, then, "What happened?"

"I got run over by a cable car."

She laughs, as if it's a joke.

"I'm not kidding," I say. "I literally got mowed down by a cable car." I tell her about my meeting with Austin and how he's engaged to someone else now and how I walked in front of the streetcar before it had time to stop.

"Are you all right?" She sounds genuinely concerned, which surprises me.

I was expecting her to downplay the accident and gloat about Austin, whom she never really cared for. Why? I don't know. Austin was never anything but nice to her. But I suppose we're even, because I like her ex, Brent, about as much as I do leukemia, which is to say not much, though I never gave him a lot of thought, to be honest. And other than being my niece's and nephew's father and Lolly's bottomless wallet, he's out of the picture, so I don't have to like him.

"I'm fine," I say. At least physically I am, although that's debatable, too. I'm seriously starting to suspect I have brain damage. Still, I refrain from telling her about the incident with the boat and dock or how I've stopped recognizing people. Why scare her?

"You should get a good lawyer."

"For what? Austin and I worked out the settlement for our divorce nearly a year ago."

"Not Austin, for the cable car. You should sue the city."

I lie back down, pulling the covers up to my neck. "It was my fault, not the conductor's. I wasn't watching where I was going."

"He could've killed you, Chels."

"Well, he didn't." I quickly change the subject. "What about you? How are the kids?"

"They're spoiled little shits and take me for granted, but other than that, they're great."

I can hear a smile in her voice. "You should come to the cabin, Lolly. Bring them. The town is decked out for Halloween, and there's a big parade. They'd have a ball."

She sighs. "They're in school. Besides, I give you and me ten minutes before we're at each other's throats."

I want to say, *whose fault is that*? That's the other thing. She's never completely forgiven me for going away my freshman high school year to boarding school. But I thought we'd moved past that and all my other infractions, until a few years ago when she found a new perceived slight to be angry over. And instead of telling me all the things I've done wrong so we can hash it out like adults, she's been giving me the silent treatment. It seems like our relationship went from bad—but tolerable—to worse in the blink of an eye.

I know how to pick my battles, though.

"At least think about it," I say.

She doesn't say no, so I take that as a win. Progress.

"I have to go now."

Before I can say goodbye, she's gone.

I roll over and go to sleep, only to be awakened at seven in the morning by the patter of rain on the roof.

The roof!

For the second time this morning, I bolt upright, then rush out of bed to inspect whether there is a swimming pool in the middle of my cabin, padding first into the living room and then into the kitchen where the original leak was. But all appears dry.

It's coming down in sheets now as I stand at the window, staring out at the lake, watching the rain make ripples in the water. I hear the crunch of gravel in the driveway and rush into my room to shower and dress.

Thirty minutes later, I find Knox in my kitchen and coffee brewing. The smell makes me instantly happy. I reach in the cupboard for two mugs and place them on the counter next to the machine, impatient for my first cup.

"It's too wet to work on the roof," Knox says. "But I can fix your dock."

"Sounds good." The rain isn't as hard as it was before, but it's still falling fast enough to make puddles on the deck outside the kitchen window. "I didn't see rain in the forecast."

Knox shrugs. "Me neither. But I knew it was coming, that's why I tarped the roof yesterday." He gazes out over the backyard and lets out a breath.

The coffee is ready, and I pour us each a mug, then grab a carton of milk from the fridge. "You want eggs or something?"

"Nah, I ate before I came."

It dawns on me that I know very little about Knox Hart. Not where he lives or whether he has any children, or if he can support a family, picking up handyman jobs. I'm guessing we're similar in age, though he's definitely more fit than I am. He's a nice-looking man in a rugged sort of way, in the way men look around here. Austin used to joke that the guys in Ghost single-handedly keep the plaid industry afloat. It is true that Pendletons are the uniform of choice here.

I grab a bag of cookies from the pantry and take them and my coffee to the table. "Where do you live, Knox?"

"A few miles from here on my family's farm." He joins me at the table and snags a cookie from the bag.

"What kind of farm?"

"It used to be a goat farm. Now it's just where I live."

"And do you have a family?"

"Yep. A one-hundred-and-twenty-pound Great Pyrenees."

"Why don't you ever bring him . . . or her?"

"Not everyone likes dogs."

I may be in that camp. But I don't know, because I've never owned a dog . . . or a cat. Growing up, Uncle Sylvester didn't allow us to have pets. Not because he was an ogre, it just wasn't practical in a high-rise apartment in Century City. And when I went out on my own, the opportunity for a pet never arose.

"So no wife, huh?"

"No wife. Why? You interested?"

I laugh. "Would it disappoint you to hear that I'm not?"

He grabs his heart. "I guess I'll have to muddle along without you, then."

I laugh again. "How did you become a handyman?"

"I didn't. I'm a biophysicist."

I start to say, yeah, good one, but something tells me not to. "Wait, you're not joking, are you?"

He shakes his head. "Nope, not joking. We biophysicists are humorless. I'll prove it to you. What's the fastest way to determine the sex of a chromosome?"

I shrug.

"Pull down its genes." He waits for a laugh, and when he doesn't get one, says, "See what I mean?"

"That was actually kind of funny." I lock eyes with him, because I'm still not sure if he's pulling my leg. "Are you out of work, then?"

"Out of work? Oh, no. I'm on sabbatical to write a book."

"Then why are you fixing my roof?"

"Have you ever written a book about plant-based biofuels?" He hitches his brows, then pops a second cookie in his mouth.

"Can't say I have. Boring stuff, huh?"

"Not boring, the opposite of boring. Try mind-blowing. So mind-blowing that sometimes my brain needs a rest."

"So you swing a hammer?"

"I swing a hammer."

"Never once while writing one of my books have I felt the need to swing a hammer," I say.

"It's a process. It doesn't necessarily work for everyone."

"Or maybe I'm doing it wrong. Maybe you're onto something."

"Could be." He steals a glance out the window, where the rain seems to have let up. "Let me see what I can do about that dock of yours."

He's nearly at the back door when he does an about-face and swipes the bag of cookies off the table. "I'm taking these for the road."

After three tries, I manage to get a decent fire going. It has rained off and on all day, and I feel as if there is a dampness in my bones. I drag a chair in front of the wood-burning stove and try to get warm.

I spent most of the day under the covers, reading. What I wouldn't do for a little television right now. But the satellite is down, so it's up to me to entertain myself. I consider calling Lolly and picking up where we left off but know it's futile with her. Besides, she's probably at Pilates or yoga or pole dancing, or whatever they do in Malibu to keep in shape. I could call Uncle Sylvester, but he's probably on a set or in a meeting, or deep into a script somewhere, too distracted to be good telephone company.

Instead, I while away the hours surfing the web, searching for news of Austin and Mary's pending nuptials. I would tell my clients to stop, that it's not helpful and even destructive. But I do it anyway. Once again, I find nothing.

I switch over to my email. Nothing there worth reading, either.

I may as well go to bed, but it's only six and I'm not the least bit tired. If it wasn't dark and wet outside, I'd stroll over to the lake and watch the geese duck in and out of the water. I wonder what Knox is doing alone in his farmhouse, if he's working on that book of his, or if he's bored like I am. I'm tempted to drive over there just to see, but I don't have his address. Probably for the best. Last thing he needs is me showing up, uninvited. I could go to town, but what would I do once I got there? There's a bar in the Ghost Inn, a gorgeously remodeled building from the 1800s. I heard somewhere that the new owners spent nearly a million dollars on furnishings alone.

And just like that, I have a burning desire to see it for myself. I quickly change out of my sweats into a pair of jeans and a presentable sweater and hop in my car. Twenty minutes later, I'm sitting on a stool, waiting for a Fool's Gold, a jumped-up version of a margarita with mezcal and jalapeño-infused tequila.

The place really is spectacular. Dark and moody, with lots of cow rugs and brick walls. There's a roaring fire in the big stone fireplace, and Miles Davis is playing on the sound system, which seems somewhat incongruous with the whole Old West vibe of the town. But sophisticated is okay by me.

The bar is pretty quiet, just a couple canoodling in the corner and a few men—who, judging by their plaid shirts, are local—at the other end of the bar. At this rate, it'll take a century to recoup the million bucks the owners sunk into the renovation. But maybe it's too early. Maybe the real action starts after eight. No doubt the hotel and bar will be packed to the gunnels next weekend for the Halloween crowd.

My Fool's Gold appears, and I order the chips and guacamole, even though I made myself a frozen pizza for dinner before I came.

"You on break from the old ball and chain tonight?" asks the bartender, a woman in her mid-twenties with a bough of flowers tattooed across her chest and flaming red hair not found in nature.

"Uh, I'm divorced."

"From Austin?" She does a double take. "When did that happen?"

It's on the tip of my tongue to say, *Do I know you?* She doesn't look even a tiny bit familiar. The only time I've been in the Ghost Inn was to have a peek while contractors were gutting the place. Austin and I had gotten burritos at Flacos, and I was curious about the work, so I popped in and wandered around until someone told me the hotel was closed for renovations. That was at least two years ago.

There's a chance she saw one of my talks or read one of my books and thinks she knows all about me. It's not at all unusual with public people. And while I'm not Jay-Z or Beyoncé, I have touched a number of lives.

She reaches across the bar and squeezes my hand. "Let me get those chips and guac for you, and I'll be right back."

One of the men on the other side of the bar flags her over, and she's gone, leaving me alone to enjoy my drink.

The couple in the corner have gone from canoodling to arguing. They're trying to keep their voices down, but I'm still able to catch snippets of their conversation, which is getting exponentially louder.

She wants him to stop something, and he swears he will but that she should stop nagging him. I never get to find out what the "something" is, because the bartender returns with my chips and another drink, making it impossible to eavesdrop.

"From Calvin and the guys," she says, and motions down the bar at the men in plaid. "They heard about you and Austin and are really sorry."

By "heard about," I assume she means she told them, along with who I am and what I do for a living. I'm sure the irony of it wasn't lost on them, either. Don't get me wrong, the drink is an incredibly sweet gesture, but I'm mortified.

"I shouldn't have come here alone," I say, realizing that I've said it aloud. But I don't want these guys getting the wrong idea that I'm here, looking for a hookup.

The bartender laughs. "Of course you should've. We're your friends, Chelsea. I mean, we love Austin, too. But we want to be there for both of you."

Friends? To be honest, I don't have too many friends, unless you count Austin, which I don't anymore. And while Ghost makes a good chunk of its change off tourism, the townies don't exactly love us flatlanders, who've flocked here from the Bay Area, hiking their once-affordable housing into the stratosphere. *Don't love* may actually be an understatement; they hate our guts.

And now the bartender is acting like we're all the greatest of pals. I don't even know her name. I swivel in my barstool and give Calvin and the plaid shirts a thank-you wave, then turn back to the bartender, who has parked herself in front of me on the other side of the bar.

The angry couple is leaving, and the man mutters something to the bartender about putting their tab on their hotel bill. He calls her Katie, which is helpful.

Katie follows them with her eyes as they leave the bar. "Looks like they could use a couple of sessions with you. I give them a year max."

"I only caught snippets. What were they fighting about?" I don't know why I ask. I'm on vacation and not looking for a busman's holiday. I suppose there's something soothing, though, about focusing on someone else's dumpster fire of a relationship instead of my own.

"He's been day trading, using the kids' college funds. The

wife found out about it from their financial planner, who noticed some discrepancies in their bank accounts." Katie pulls a face. "First-world problems, if you ask me."

"How'd you get all that?"

"I have supersonic hearing, not to mention mad lip-reading skills."

I chuckle. "So basically, he's a compulsive gambler."

"Sounds like. She thought a weekend getaway would work as an intervention. He thought a weekend getaway was going to get him laid. Neither is getting what they came for."

I withhold my opinion but think Katie is one heck of a perceptive bartender.

"Hey, when you two are done gossiping down there, maybe you could get us another round," Calvin calls from the other end of the bar.

Katie gives him the finger, then draws four pints and delivers them to the plaid shirts.

"Put it on my tab," I tell Katie, who then shouts, "This round is on Chelsea."

The four men salute me and go back to talking amongst themselves.

"Knox told me he's working over at your place," Katie says as she wipes down the bar, a gorgeous live slab of wood that's been epoxied to a high shine. "At this rate, he'll never get his book done. But that's Knox for you."

Clearly Knox is the reason everyone seems to know who I am. Small towns; people talk. I don't hold it against him. But I am curious how Knox and Katie fit in together. She seems a bit young for him.

"Are you two an item?"

She seems startled by the question. "Ew." She looks at me long and hard. "Knox said you were in some kind of an accident. Must've banged your head."

Obviously, I'm missing something here. But when one of the plaid shirts calls, "Hey, Hart, how about some of those smoked chicken wings?" I put it together. I don't know why I didn't see the resemblance before. I guess I was distracted by Katie's bottle-red hair. But she and Knox have the same hazel eyes, same crooked smile.

She disappears into the kitchen and returns a few minutes later with a plate of hot wings large enough to feed the entire town of Ghost, then wanders back over to me. "You want anything from the kitchen?" She eyes my barely eaten chips and guac. "We're slow tonight, so they're closing early."

"I'm good. Is it usually this slow?"

"It can be in the offseason. We're booked solid for Halloween, though. Everyone coming up to see the ghosts of the Ramseys." She laughs, but it's clear as a local, she finds the fascination with the legend of the town tedious. "You going to the parade?"

"Yeah, sure." Why not? I've got nothing better to do, and in the five years we've owned the cabin, I've never been to Ghost's annual Halloween parade. I'm sure it's hokey as hell but when in Rome . . . right? "How about you?"

"I'll be here, serving the likes of them." She tips her head to the plaid shirts. "Come in and say hi. The rush won't start until after the parade when the flatlanders want their martinis and cosmopolitans." Katie snorts.

It's funny that she isn't counting me as a flatlander. I don't know when I became a local, but I like it. I like sitting here in this bar, having human contact with people other than paying clients or colleagues I'm trying to impress. I like talking about something other than marriage and how to keep it alive. Perhaps now that Austin is out of the picture, I should start finding some balance in my life.

"I will," I say. "I invited my sister, but I'll probably be flying solo."

"I didn't know you have a sister. Knox never said anything about her."

"We're sort of estranged. But I really miss her. We used to

be close." It's not like me to talk about Lolly, especially to a stranger. But Katie doesn't feel like a stranger.

"Well, you should work things out with her. Life's too short to hold grudges or to hang onto a lot of meaningless bullshit. She's your sister. Whatever came between you can never erase that."

She's right, of course. I only wish Lolly would see it that way. But she thinks I deserted her, and she's not the type who forgives and forgets. It doesn't take a psychology degree to know that both she and I have abandonment issues because of our parents dying when we were young. And while Uncle Sylvester tried, he wasn't much of a surrogate.

I used to think it was Lolly more than me. But I'm starting to wonder.

"I'm trying," I tell Katie, but honestly, I haven't tried very hard. How many times did I prioritize a lecture or symposium or a looming deadline over Lolly and her family? How many times did I blow off one of her kids' birthday parties or weekends at Uncle Sylvester's getaway home in the desert?

"Try harder," Katie says.

On my drive home, I make a pact with myself to do it, to try harder.

Chapter 5

It's odd, but my assistant Ronnie hasn't responded to my last email. I want to make sure everything is in order for my lecture next month. It's in New Mexico, and she is seeing to all the details, including my lodging. Ordinarily, I'd book it myself, but I'm not supposed to be thinking about work while I'm at the cabin. I'm supposed to be recuperating from my accident, though I feel fine if you don't count the short-term memory lapses. I'll take care of that problem as soon as I get home. For now, I just need time to heal from the past year and figure out a way to move forward.

I prop my laptop on my knees and fire off another message to Ronnie. It isn't like her to forget or ignore me. She's usually on top of everything. In fact, she's so good at her job that she often knows what I'm going to say before I even think it. I hope she's not sick or having personal problems. A few weeks ago, she was complaining about her roommate, who was always late paying her share of the bills, which, unfortunately, are all in Ronnie's name.

I can hear Knox on the roof. And here I am, still in bed. There's coffee. I can smell it wafting under my bedroom door from the kitchen.

My phone lights up, and a second later, it rings. Austin. I

let it go to voicemail. He's called a couple of times. I presume he found out about my incident with the cable car and is checking to see if I'm okay. It's kind of him, but I wish he would go away and leave me alone.

I drag myself out of bed and into the shower. Those Fool's Golds last night did a number on my head. It was probably the mezcal.

There's still a half pot of coffee left when I make it into the kitchen, and I don't waste any time mainlining a cup. It's good stuff. Any trace of yesterday's rain is gone, only blue skies. The leaves on the trees keep changing color. From here to the lake, it's a sea of orange and yellow.

Knox comes in, nods his head at me in greeting, and refills his thermos. The man seems to live on coffee.

"I saw your sister last night."

"Yeah, she told me."

"She thinks you're procrastinating and won't make your book deadline."

"Katie talks too much. She should spend more time worrying about her own life, which is a train wreck, if you ask me."

"How's that?" You can never really know a person after only talking with them for a few hours—or in Austin's case, a multitude of years—but Katie seems to have her head on straighter than most.

"She spent six years getting an advanced degree in urban planning and works tending bar."

"Oh, you mean like a biophysicist who fixes roofs?"

He shoots me a look. "Did I mention I'm on the faculty at UC Davis? Roofing is just something I do in my spare time."

I don't bother to point out that he doesn't have spare time, that what he has is a book deadline.

"And why is it, in your opinion, that Katie doesn't want to work in her chosen field?" As soon as the question leaves my mouth, I regret it. First, it's none of my business. And second, I sound like a douchey therapist.

And why is it, in your opinion, that Katie doesn't want to work in her chosen field? Who talks like that?

"Because she likes wasting her life serving people drinks."

"That sounds like a judgment call on your part. Perhaps Katie doesn't think bartending is a waste." I can't seem to help myself.

"Yeah? Then she should stop asking me to float her so she can make her rent."

"Have you had that conversation with her?" Here I go again.

"About a million times. Look, if she doesn't want to be an urban planner, that's fine. But she needs to find a vocation and stop pretending she's still in college."

He has a point there. "Then you have to set boundaries. No bailing her out when she can't make her rent."

He warms his hands on the thermos and holds my gaze. "I'm working on it. But it's hard. I don't want my baby sister living on the street."

My heart melts, even though I try to stay neutral with patients. But Knox is not my patient, and I'm supposedly off duty, so to speak. I'm allowed to just feel. And today, all the feels are swishing together. Regret over the fission between Lolly and me. And the sweetness of Knox's love for his sister.

I must be wearing my heart in my eyes, because Knox looks away right before his cheeks turn pink.

"Break's over," he says on his way to the door.

A few minutes later, I hear him up on the roof again. I make myself a couple of eggs and some toast and wash it down with the rest of the coffee. As I'm sitting at the breakfast table, my phone pings with a text. Hoping it's Ronnie, I reach for it, only to see that it's from Austin.

"I've desperately been trying to reach you. Please call me."

I debate whether to respond or ignore his message. There's no time like the present to cut the cord with him, I tell myself. It's not like we have children that require us to stay in communication with each other. The only thing we still share is this cabin and all its expenses. For that, I can easily send him a bill without having to talk to him. It's healthier that way.

Yet, I continue to stare at his text as if it's a lifeline, my finger hovering over the telephone icon at the top of my screen. It would be so easy to tap it. So easy to assure him that despite my close call, I'm fine. It would be the grownup thing to do, I rationalize.

"What are you doing?"

I jump at the sound of Knox's voice. "I thought you were on the roof."

"I forgot my coat." He removes a denim jacket that's hanging from the back of the chair across from me and shrugs into it. "It's cold outside." He bobs his head at my phone. "Emergency?"

"No." I put my phone down on the table. "It's my ex. He wants me to call him. I suspect he heard about my accident and wants to make sure I'm okay."

"So?"

I hitch my shoulders. "I'm grappling with whether to do it. On the one hand, what's the big deal? I call him, tell him I'm fine, and hang up. On the other hand, why do I owe him a status report? He's no longer my husband, and he's a lousy friend." Real friends don't lead you on and sleep with you while they're in a relationship with someone else.

"There you go; sounds like you have your answer."

"Which one?" I ask, because each of my reasonings hold merit.

He gives me a look. "You know which one. But you could split the baby, send him an impersonal text. You know, 'I'm good. Thanks for your concern but kindly fuck off.' "

I laugh. "I do like the ring of that. I'll think about it."

"You're welcome." He heads for the door and calls over his shoulder, "I'm knocking off early today."

I wonder if it's so he can get some writing in. But before I can ask, he's gone, leaving me alone with only the stillness of the cabin to keep me company. I decide to take a walk and commune with nature. That's why I'm here, after all.

I grab a thick down jacket from the closet, put on a pair of tennis shoes, and start for the lake. The ground is still muddy from yesterday's rain, and the smell of wet grass clings to the air. When I get to the dock, I find the bottom of the boat ankle-deep in water. There's an old watering can in the boathouse that I use to bail out the puddle. It's a long process, but I find the monotony of it soothing, almost meditative. The next time Knox is here, I'll ask him to help me drag the boat out of the water and carry it to the boathouse.

The geese are loud today, honking as they fly over the lake, then splashing as they make crash landings into the water. My favorite is when they dive headfirst beneath the surface with only their butts in the air.

I get the boat as dry as I can, then head to the trail that wends around the lake. Knox was right; it's cold. I can feel my entire face turn numb. There's a wad of tissues in the bottom of my jacket pocket that I use to wipe my nose, which is runny. Still, it's nice to be outside. At work, it's a rare occasion when I have time for fresh air. I'm on the lecture circuit half the year, and the only things I see are the insides of airports, hotels, and auditoriums. The other half of the year, I'm either absorbed in building the small empire I've started or promoting it. It doesn't leave a lot of time for recreation or friends. I've always told my patients to create a life of balance and yet, I didn't take my own advice. Hell, I wrote the book on how to have it all: a perfect marriage and a life filled with fulfillment. And here I am, the opposite of fulfilled. What kind of woman my age has no family, no friends, and no social life? Even my success has been predicated on a myth. I can see the headlines now: FAMOUS MARRIAGE GURU IS A FRAUD.

At least the view lifts my spirits. Mist hovers over the lake like an ethereal cloud, and instead of it looking eerie, it's dreamlike and beautiful. It reminds me of a loch in a fairytale. Even the trees with their colored leaves seem brighter and more varied in shade, like a rich mosaic.

I get halfway around the lake and am so winded I have to sit on a log to catch my breath. When did I get this out of shape? My head is spinning, and I have to hold back from retching as strobes of light flash before my eyes. It seems like a weird reaction to a leisurely forty-minute stroll. Then I remember the accident and remind myself that it could take a while before I'm at a hundred percent again.

I close my eyes to block out the searing light but have to force myself not to fall asleep. All of a sudden, I'm exhausted. Even though last night I slept like the dead, I can't seem to stay awake. Just a little nap, I tell myself. And there, in the distance, is a bed of moss under an old oak tree. It takes all my energy to crawl to it before curling up. I pillow my hands underneath my head and let myself trail off into sleepy land. Still, something niggles at me, something that says that I shouldn't let myself go too deep. That I should keep one eye open.

I awake to find a red fox sniffing me, or at least sniffing the air around me. He's about two feet away. Rabies is the first thing that comes to mind, and I freeze, searching my brain for anything I might've read about how to fight off a rabid fox or just a hungry one (are they even carnivorous?). Do I make noise, wave my hands in the air, or play dead? If it was a bear, I'd know what to do. Lord knows I've studied enough guidebooks about the black bears that roam the area and what precautions to take if you cross an angry one. But nothing about foxes. I always assumed they were harmless. That is, until they were only a nose away from my jugular vein. In a fit of irony, it occurs to me that I may have survived a 15,000-pound cable car only to be killed by a fox smaller than my neighbor's border collie.

He seems to realize that I'm awake or not dead and is contemplating his next move. I don't recall ever seeing anything in the news about a fox mauling a human. But it doesn't mean it hasn't happened. Then again, perhaps he's as freaked out by me as I am by him.

"Hi, little fox," I say in a singsongy voice.

His head jerks up; then he goes stock-still. A few seconds later, he howls, but it comes out like a high-pitched scream that makes the hairs stand up on the back of my neck.

Shit.

I should search for a rock or something I can use as a weapon, but I'm too scared to move my hand. He's staring at me, his beady little eyes alert, feral. And just when I think he's going to pounce, he backs up and runs away.

As soon as my heart stops pounding, I come up into a sitting position. That's when I realize it's almost dark. And so cold, I can see my own breath. The scent of woodsmoke swirls around me, and it takes me a while to realize that it's coming from someone's chimney. It's got to be close to four or even five o'clock, judging by the lack of daylight. I've been out here for hours.

I get to my feet, anxious to go home, where it's safe and warm. But I've sort of become disoriented, and I'm still a little dizzy. Still, I manage to find the trail and follow the lake until I come to my cabin. It's not until I get inside that I see that my clothes are covered in moss, leaves, and dirt. There's even a mat of twigs in my hair.

I strip down in the laundry room and take a hot shower, which helps the leftover throbbing in my head. When I get out, I put on the warmest pajamas I own. They're red flannel with little Christmas trees that I ordered nearly a year ago from a catalog I found in the mailbox addressed to the previous owner. They looked soft. And the one thing I hate is scratchy lace. The bright spot of sleeping alone is that I never have to wear uncomfortable lingerie again. Lolly would not approve. Not only are these on the garish side, but they're also pilling from wear.

I go to the kitchen and throw together a sandwich with the rest of the deli meat I got at the market and wolf it down with a tall glass of water. I don't know if I'm more thirsty than hungry. All I know is the sandwich doesn't fill me. I scrounge through the pantry, looking for something sweet, and curse Knox for filching my cookies. I rummage around until I find the Halloween candy I purchased for the trick-or-treaters, who I know will never come because the cabin is too off the beaten path, and rip into the bag.

I spend the rest of the evening eating bite-sized Snickers and Baby Ruth bars in front of the television. If I didn't feel so lousy, I'd go visit Katie at the Ghost Inn, where I'm sure she's bartending tonight. Instead, I nod off after my fourth *Law & Order* rerun, only to be awakened by my phone ringing.

It's Austin. The man never lets up. I let it go to voicemail. But as soon as he disconnects, he starts calling again.

I finally relent and answer, trying to sound as composed as possible. "Hello, Austin."

"I heard what happened after you left the Top of the Mark. Jesus, Chelsea, are you okay?"

"I'm fine. Just a few cuts and bruises." I don't tell him about the headaches and my loss of memory. What's the point? As soon as I return to San Francisco, I'll see a specialist. I'm sure there's medication I can take or some other remedy. Modern medicine.

"Why didn't you call me?" he says. "I could've come to the hospital. I could've made sure you got home all right. For God's sake, Chels, you don't have . . ."

"I don't have . . . What, Austin? What don't I have? Spit it out!"

"I just meant . . . well, a person who's been badly injured shouldn't be alone."

"I'm not alone, Austin. I've got plenty of friends up at the cabin. And Lolly and the kids are coming. Uncle Sylvester, too."

There's a long pause. Then, "You don't have to put on a brave face for me. Say the word, and I'll come up and make sure you have everything you need."

"That's very kind of you," I say between gritted teeth, because what I want to tell him is I wouldn't be in this position in the first place if it wasn't for him. But that's not really fair. I'm the klutz who walked into a cable car. I should've been paying attention. "But it's unnecessary. I'm getting all the care I need."

"Are you sure?"

Even though I don't want him to come, I'm angry that he's given up so easily, which is incredibly passive-aggressive of me. It's something I spend a lot of time discussing in my courses and books. How damaging and unhealthy passive-aggressive behavior is. How instead of confronting anger, you let it fester just beneath the surface, thwarting any hope of resolution.

"Absolutely," I say. "Well, thanks for calling." I start to disconnect, but he stops me.

"What's the big hurry? Can't we talk for a few minutes?"

"I'm tired, Austin," which is the truth, despite having slept a good portion of the day away.

"But it's not even ten o'clock yet. I thought you were feeling fine?"

"I was out last night and got up early this morning to go on a long hike."

"Out last night? Where?"

I'm about to take a page out of Knox's instruction book and tell him to "kindly fuck off" but decide it's better to be an adult about it. "The Ghost Inn."

"The Ghost Inn? Why?"

"I popped in for a drink."

"You go to random bars now?"

"Random bars? You make it sound like I'm a barfly. It's a beautiful hotel, and the lounge is lovely. My friend is a mixologist there." I don't know where the mixologist part came from, but I want Austin to know that we're not talking about some saloon at the O.K. Corral.

"Chelsea, it's not like I don't know the place. I'm not casting aspersions at the Ghost Inn, for God's sake. It's just out of character for you to hang out at a bar, any bar, is all I'm saying."

"Oh, is it? Did you ever think that maybe you don't know me anymore? We've been divorced for a year. A lot has changed, including how I choose to entertain myself."

"I'm surprised is all. There's no need to get pissy about it."

I modulate my voice, as if I'm talking to one of my clients. "Do I sound pissy? I don't think I do, Austin. Perhaps you're hearing what you want to hear."

"Look, Chels, I'm not trying to turn this into a fight. I called because I was worried about you. When you didn't return my calls, I became even more concerned. Now that I know you're all right, I feel better. I'm glad you're at the cabin, safe and sound. And I hope you enjoy your stay there. Okay?"

"That's very kind of you, Austin." It's all I can do to keep from saying, I hope you and Mary choke on your wedding cake. "Thank you for calling and good night." I hang up before he can get the last word in.

Now I'm wide awake and angry. To make matters worse, I'm a little sick from all the chocolate I've eaten, and my headache has returned with a vengeance. I go in search of a bottle of Advil and stub my toe on the console. Dammit! I wish I'd never answered the phone.

I find the bottle in my nightstand drawer and wash down

three tablets with water from the bathroom sink. It's funny, I think as I catch a glimpse of myself in the mirror, that the swelling and bruising in my face is gone. My skin looks the same as it did before the accident, which I take as a positive sign. It means I'm a good healer.

I plop down on the sofa and switch through the TV channels while I dissect every word of my conversation with Austin. Who knew he was so judgy? What's it to him if I want to hang out in bars? It's not like he and I painted the town red when we were together. Most nights, we were too tired to have an in-depth conversation, let alone grab a drink at the cute Irish pub down the street from our condominium. Maybe I'm making up for lost time.

Then it occurs to me that the one thing he didn't ask me about, the one thing that would've meant the most to me, is about the twenty-fourth anniversary of my parents' death. While there's always been a pact between us that we don't talk about it (my rule, not his), he knows the date as well as I do. He can set his clock by it. Every October it's the same. The melancholy sets in around the twelfth, and on the actual day of their death, I basically go MIA. No speaking engagements, no book signings. No professional or social interactions whatsoever.

And to ease my pain, Austin sends me a bouquet of white calla lilies, my mother's favorite. It's his way of silently commemorating their death with me, so I don't have to talk about it. Even last year, in the midst of our breakup, the flowers came.

But this year, nothing. Not so much as a simple note like, *I know today is difficult. Thinking of you.*

It should convince me that he's moved on, that we're truly over. But instead, I find myself making up excuses for him. FTD doesn't deliver this far out. He was distracted by my accident and forgot about my parents.

But the reality of it is he's with someone else now. It would be disrespectful to Mary. How would I feel if my fiancé was still sending flowers to his ex-wife?

And for the first time, I let it sink in. Really sink in. I'm alone now, truly alone.

Chapter 6

Knox doesn't come today. I keep expecting to hear the whir of the coffee grinder or to smell the scent of fresh brew coming from the kitchen.

I get up and make my own coffee and listen for any sign of him up on the roof. But other than a woodpecker tapping on the side of the cabin, it's quiet. I peek out the front window for his truck, but the driveway is empty.

The man could've at least called. I take solace in the fact that there's no rain in the immediate forecast.

It's a good day to go to town, I decide. Though for the life of me, I don't know what I'll do once I get there.

I dress warmly and grab a coat and hat on the way out. A slight breeze ruffles my hair, and I let myself inhale the crisp air. It'll be good to be out and about, rather than stuck inside the cabin all day.

The driveway is rutted with big potholes from all the rain we've been having, and I make a mental note to add it to Knox's honey-do list. That is if he still wants the work. I suspect he's playing hooky from me today to dive into that book of his, which is good. Procrastination is more stress than it's worth.

I skip the shorter route, a two-lane highway, for Miner's Lane, a winding country road that acts as a detour to town.

It's more scenic, and there are fewer cars—not that Ghost has traffic. But since I don't have anything to do today, I may as well take my time.

In the five years of owning the cabin, I've gone to town this way many times. Today, the lighting is almost dreamlike, awash in brilliant sunlight with pink and white stripes brushing the sky. Lush, green incense cedars dot the mountainsides, making me think of a Christmas card. And the water in Bear Creek is so clear that if I wasn't paying attention to the road, I'd swear I could see the fish swimming all the way down to the rocky bottom.

There is definitely something to that old adage about taking time to smell the roses. Just a brief drive in the country has me humming along to the music on the radio. It's a local station that plays everything from the Rolling Stones to Kacey Musgraves. Today, it's Linda Ronstadt.

On the rare occasion Uncle Sylvester was home, he would play her music in the kitchen while making Lolly and me scrambled eggs and bacon. It's one of the few memories I have of the three of us together. For the most part, Lolly and I were cared for by a string of nannies and babysitters. It wasn't Uncle Sylvester's fault. He hadn't asked to be a father. But he'd stepped up when no one else did and took on two orphaned, traumatized little girls. He did the best he could.

I head to the public lot and park my car with no idea what to do next. Ultimately, I decide to stroll Main Street and window-shop. There's a flurry of activity, city officials and volunteers making last-minute preparations for Saturday's Halloween parade. Crowd-control barriers are being unloaded and stacked in an alleyway at the end of the street, and shopkeepers are changing out their window fronts to pick up on the themes of the scarecrow displays. It's so small-town and quaint that it's easy to forget that Ghost is only an hour away from the state's capital and two hours away from San Francisco.

There's a sweets shop on the corner that I don't remember from previous visits. I'm still recuperating from last night's chocolate binge, but it doesn't stop me from going in for a look-see. Rows of bins offer up a variety of old-fashioned candies, and a series of glass showcases line the store with homemade fudge, chocolate-dipped fruit and pretzels, and at least ten different kinds of truffles. A freezer counter stands on the other side of the store with ice cream and gelato.

A pretty teenager in a pink-striped uniform that reminds me of the Hot Dog on a Stick cashiers at the mall Lolly and I used to frequent when we were kids wants to know if I'd like to try any of their two-dozen flavors.

"No thank you," I say, but don't leave empty-handed. On my way out, I buy a big bag of caramel corn, which I snack on as I slowly amble down the street, taking in all the activity.

The stores are a mishmash of touristy gift shops with the usual bric-a-brac and T-shirts, utilitarian mercantile that sells everything from kitchen gadgets to farm equipment, and clothing boutiques with designer jeans and three-hundred-dollar handbags. It's that last one that offers the greatest clue that Ghost is transitioning from unassuming cow town to a chic vacation enclave for the wealthy. It's happening all over rural California; Ghost just took a little more time to catch up.

Calvin, the guy who bought me a drink at the Ghost Inn the other night, waves from across the street. I turn to see if his greeting is meant for someone else, but there is no one behind me, so I wave back. He's helping a group of men line the sidewalk with more straw bales, presumably so the parade spectators will have more places to sit close to the action.

A woman in an orange apron is arranging carved pumpkins on a small antique table outside a floral shop called Flower Power.

"Hey, Chelsea, you up for the weekend?"

"I am," I say, even though I don't recognize her. I'm learning that it's just better to go with the flow. Besides, I rather enjoy feeling like I'm part of the fabric of this town. In San Francisco, I couldn't pick my neighbors out of a police lineup. Other than the crazy lady who walks her cat on a leash and likes to complain about her various allergies, I haven't said more than a few words to any of the residents in my building. Everyone is always in a rush.

"Beautiful pumpkins." I crouch down to have a closer look at the intricate carvings of sunflowers, sprigs of wheat, and a fruit cornucopia, all backlit with battery-operated lights. Adorable.

"Thank you, but the credit goes to Ginger. She did the carvings." The woman straightens and rests her hand at the small of her back. "Katie says Knox is working over at your place. When he's done, send him over to mine." She laughs.

"Actually, he didn't show up today. I think he's working on his book. But I have something for him. You wouldn't happen to know the address of his family's farm, would you?"

"Well, of course I do. It's out on Old Ranch Road. Come inside, and I'll draw you a map."

I follow her into the shop, which smells like a combination of eucalyptus, apples, and cinnamon spice. The wall behind the counter is filled with autumn wreaths made with tiny pumpkins and colored leaves.

While the woman goes in the back room to find a pen, I look for a trash can to toss my caramel corn, which wasn't as tasty as it looked.

I've never been in the floral shop (I didn't even know Ghost had one) and take the time to explore. It's lovely and clearly does a brisk business, judging by the refrigerator case filled with floral arrangements of all kinds.

My face is practically pressed to the glass, counting the bouquets and vases, when the woman returns. "We've got two weddings, and all the hotels and restaurants in the area want flowers for the parade."

It makes sense, given how many people will flood the town this weekend, many of whom will stay the night and eat here.

"You do good work," I tell her.

She beckons me over to the counter, where she's drawing a rudimentary map on the back of an old receipt. "It's a little hard to find. Do yourself a favor and don't use your GPS. Otherwise, the dang thing will get you hopelessly lost. Best to follow the map."

"Okay," I say, though her map is unintelligible, just a series of squiggly lines. To be frank, I don't even know where Old Ranch Road is.

She slides the scrap of paper across the counter at me. "Look, we all know about you and Austin. I'm very sorry, but I can't say I'm surprised." She looks up at me and lets out a breath. "Am I being too forward? My husband is always telling me that I need to shut my mouth."

"You're not being too forward." She is, but I'm too curious to care. "Why weren't you surprised?"

"Because every time I saw the two of you together, you seemed perpetually unhappy. Miserable, actually."

Unhappy? Miserable? Ha, I don't bother to tell her that Austin is the one who dumped me. Until then, I was blissfully happy. Okay, *blissfully* may be an exaggeration. But I loved him. Sure, there were times I felt lonely, even unseen, but I've studied enough marriages to know that's perfectly normal. Every day can't be a honeymoon. All that mattered was we were well on our way to having the life we'd carefully planned. In my marriage courses, I call it the three *S*s. Stability, safety, and satisfaction. That's what it takes for a successful marriage.

And I thought we'd knocked it out of the park, made it look easy. I guess I was wrong.

"Hon, when you've been married as long as I have, you know what the face of misery looks like. I see it every morning in the mirror."

"Then why do you stay?" I ask.

She hitches her shoulders. "Kids, guilt, the hope that if I hang on, I won't be seen as a failure."

But there's more. I see it in her eyes. Desolation, hurt, betrayal.

"You should attend one of my lectures."

"I read one of your books once." She makes a face that says she was less than impressed.

"I take it it wasn't helpful."

"The picture of you on the jacket was nice, though." She smiles and points to my ponytail. "You ought to wear it down, like it is on the book, more often."

I should be crushed but oddly appreciate her candor—about my book, not my hair.

"I'm sorry it didn't work for you," I say.

"Hey, you win some and you lose some. How long are you up for?"

"At least a week." I have another nine days before my lecture in Albuquerque.

"Nice. If you find yourself with nothing to do Wednesday night, a few of us ladies meet for happy hour at the Ghost Inn. You should join us."

"I might just do that," I say, but probably won't, because I don't even know her. "Thank you for the invite."

Before I leave, I buy one of the autumn wreaths to hang on the cabin's front door, then head back to the car. A few minutes later, I'm on a dirt road in the middle of nowhere, worried that I made a wrong turn. I pull over on the shoulder and study the map, not even sure if I have it turned the wrong way. Reading maps is not one of my skill sets, and this one is more like hieroglyphics on the side of an ancient monument than something you'd find in Rand McNally. But I see a mailbox up ahead that looks similar to the florist's diagram, so I persevere, tempted to ignore her advice and turn on the GPS.

I make out the name Hart on the mailbox, and the address matches the one the woman gave me. Apparently, I'm in the right place, but I don't see a house or anything that looks remotely like a farm. Just green rolling hills dotted with oak and pine trees. It's quite pretty, but there's no sign of life, not even a lone cow. Or a goat. Didn't Knox say it was a former goat farm?

I pull away from the mailbox and keep going, hoping I'll eventually reach some form of civilization. The dirt road is bumpy and windy, and I'm still unconvinced that I'm in the right place. By now, I've driven at least a few miles. If this is all Knox's land, it's vast.

Up ahead, on the top of a knoll, I spot a structure. I'm too far away to tell if it's a house or a barn or some other kind of outbuilding, but it seems promising. Halfway there, a polar bear jumps in front of my car, and I slam on the brakes to keep from hitting it. That's when I realize that it's not a bear but a very large, white dog. Knox's Great Pyrenees.

I roll down my window a crack. "Good doggy. Please move."

But he just stands there, staring at me with big, inquisitive eyes, eyes that say, "Who the hell are you and why are you here? And if you don't leave soon, I will eat you." He may even be growling.

"Nice doggy." I quickly roll up my window, because the doggy doesn't seem so nice. In fact, I like my chances better against yesterday's fox than this behemoth. And I can't move until he does.

I tap my horn, hoping that does the trick. But he doesn't budge. I'm about to give up, when I see Knox coming down the drive in some kind of an all-terrain vehicle. It looks like a cross between a dune buggy and a three-wheel motorcycle. Heavy on the Mad Max vibe.

He pulls up alongside me, so I roll down my window again. "Call off your beast."

"Bailey, come!"

The dog trots over to Knox, his tail wagging so hard I fear it'll do damage to my car.

"He's a gentle giant," Knox says.

"I don't know how gentle he is. He looked as if he wanted to rip my throat out."

Knox rolls his eyes. "Are you lost, or are you pissed that I'm playing hooky?"

"Not lost and not pissed if you're working on your book."

He grins. "I was feeling inspired. Wrote two thousand words without breaking a sweat."

"That's wonderful."

"So if you're not lost and not pissed, what brings you out to the farm?"

It's a valid question, one I should've asked myself before I came. I guess I've come to enjoy his company and missed it. "When you didn't show this morning, I wanted to make sure everything was okay. The florist lady in town gave me directions to your place."

"Which one? Ginger or Sadie?"

"Uh . . . Sadie, I think."

"Great," he says, heavy on sarcasm, but I get the sense that it's mostly for show. That in his own gruff way, he's happy to see me. "Come on up to the house."

Before I agree, he takes off in his dune buggy, as if it's been decided. Bailey shoots off after him, and I slowly follow behind, taking the rutted dirt road up the hill. The structure on the top of the knoll is indeed a home, a weathered old farmhouse that could use a sanding and a paint job. At one time, though, it was probably quite stately, with its deep wraparound porch and copper cupola.

He waits for me at the front door as I stand in the driveway, shielding my eyes from the sun, taking it all in. "Nice place you have here."

I join him at the top of the stairs, and he ushers me inside, which is in even more disrepair than the outside. Yet, it holds a certain charm that only an old house can. The floors, some kind of oak, and the millwork and high ceilings are spectacular. And everywhere I look are windows with views of the rolling hills and the Cascade Mountain Range in the distance. A place like this in the Bay Area would go for a mint. Even here, it's probably worth a small fortune.

He leads me to the kitchen, an airy room that hasn't been updated since the 1920s. Even the stove is one of those vintage Stewarts with gas burners and a separate baking oven and broiler. As far as cabinetry, there are a few Hoosiers with built-in bins, and that's it. Despite its datedness, it's homey. And unlike the other rooms I walked through to get here, neat as a pin.

"You want tea, coffee, or milk?"

"Tea, please." I'm not a tea drinker, but it feels appropriate in this house, in this kitchen. I can somehow visualize white lace tablecloths, dainty porcelain cups, and ladies serving cake off a green Carnival glass stand after church.

Knox, not so much. For him I envision something more rustic. A log cabin, a Craftsman, even a treehouse. I think about tattooed Katie and her flaming red hair and can't see her here, either.

Knox puts a kettle on the ancient stove and pulls two mugs out of one of the Hoosiers.

"So you had a good writing day, huh?"

"Yep. But no worries, I'll be back tomorrow to work on your roof."

"What about the book?"

"It can wait. More rain will be here before you know it."

That's probably true, and it will give me peace of mind to batten down the hatches, so to speak. Then, apropos of nothing, I say, "Let me ask you something. What about my TED Talk did you find unhelpful?"

"All of it," Knox says without hesitation.

"Wow." He couldn't even candy-coat it just a little.

"Some relationships just aren't worth saving," he says.

The kettle begins to whistle, and Knox gets up to make our tea.

"But you must've thought yours was, or you wouldn't have watched my TED Talk in the first place."

He returns to the table with the two mugs and takes the chair across from me. "Let's just call it a last-ditch effort, even though deep down inside, I knew it was over."

"So there wasn't anything at all you could glean from my message that was worth trying?"

He shakes his head, then looks deep into my eyes. "Where's this all coming from?"

I start to tell him about my conversation with Sadie at Flower Power and stop. Even though I'm not her therapist, I don't want to divulge anything she may have told me in confidence. "I'm starting to think I'm not very good at this."

"I don't know about that. All I know is that it didn't help me. Anyway, isn't the whole inspirational industry a bit of a crock? Smoke and mirrors to separate consumers from their money?"

I should be offended, but a part of me has asked myself the same thing. At least at his comment about it being a crock. There is no magic bullet, and yet a lot of my marriage advice hinges on the generic. "There's no smoke and mirrors about what I do. I'm using sound psychological theory."

He pins me with a look. "You're the one doubting yourself. If it makes you feel better, consider me an outlier."

I sip my tea and cross my arms over my chest. "Who was she, and what happened?"

"She was my fiancée, and she dumped me for my best friend. There, are you happy?"

"No, of course not. I'm sorry, Knox."

"Don't worry about it. Like I said before, it was probably for the best."

"Why is that?" I add a teaspoon of sugar to my tea and give it a good stir.

He gives a half-hearted shrug. "It wouldn't have worked out anyway. We were too different. Opposites may attract, but they don't stick."

"What about the best friend?" I raise a brow in question.

"Yeah, him. Let's just say we're no longer acquainted."

"How long ago was this?"

"About a year. They're married now. Probably have a kid on the way."

I don't detect any bitterness, but some people are better at hiding it than others. "I told you that my ex is engaged, right? He met her after he left me. Or at least that's what he says."

"You think he was seeing her while you two were still together?"

"I have no idea. I've never known Austin to be a liar, but it seems awfully pat, don't you think? Out of the blue, he says he doesn't want to be married anymore, and next thing you know he's met the love of his life."

"Stranger things have happened."

"Yeah," I say. "Don't tell anyone, okay? People here seem to talk."

"You can say that again. Between Sadie and my sister, they don't need a newspaper in this town. Your secret is safe with me."

"It's not a secret, it's just that . . . Well, I'll just say it: it's not terribly great for my professional reputation."

Knox leans across the table and winks. "Gotcha."

"What? You think I'm being duplicitous?"

"No. If people are stupid enough to dish out good money to hear you tell them how to live their lives, they deserve to have the wool pulled over their eyes."

"For the record, I don't tell people how to live their lives. But you're entitled to your opinion." There's no sense arguing with him. As long as he doesn't blab my dirty laundry all over Ghost, we're good.

"Gee, thanks for letting me have my own opinion." He gets up and disappears inside the pantry, only to return with a package of cookies, which he slides across the table at me. "I owe you."

They're the same brand of vanilla wafers he took from my house. "You can keep them. They look better on you than they do on me."

He gives me a once-over and grins. "They look fine on you."

"You're a real charmer, you know that?"

"Said no one. Ever."

"I don't know, Knox, you have your moments. I better get going." I unloop my purse strap from the back of my chair and rise, debating on whether to accept the cookies or not. They are my favorite. "Okay, I'm taking these."

The corner of his mouth hitches up, and I have to admit he's undeniably attractive.

"I'll walk you out," he says, and leads the way to my car, Bailey tagging along beside him.

"I hope it was okay that I barged in on you like this."

"It's fine." He opens my door, a playful grin playing on his lips. "Try not to make it a habit, though."

I get behind the wheel. "Knox, you really could use a filter," I say, then drive away.

Chapter 7

When I get home, there's a Mercedes SUV in my driveway that I don't recognize. Austin and I were never into showy cars. Even though our combined salaries put us in a high-income bracket, we were always practical with our money, stashing it away for that proverbial rainy day.

I go in search of the vehicle's owner and find Lolly sitting on my back porch. She looks like a vintage Hollywood post-card with her big white sunglasses and Hermès scarf tied around her head, reminding me of Grace Kelly.

"You're here!" If it wasn't her in the flesh, I wouldn't believe my eyes.

"I'm here." She offers a weak smile.

"Where are the kids?"

"With their father." Lolly turns to the cabin. "So this is it, huh?" Her tone and expression are flat. She's clearly unimpressed.

"Did you walk down to the lake?"

She leans back in the lounge chair and lifts one foot in the air, showing off a designer shoe with a four-inch heel.

"I have some hiking boots you can borrow."

She scowls in distaste. "It's cold."

"Well, come inside. I'll crank up the heat and make a fire."

"Do you have Diet Coke?"

"No, but I have coffee and tea. We can go to the market later."

She trails after me, showing the same enthusiasm for the inside of the house as she did for the outside. I leave her in the living room while I head to the hallway to turn up the thermostat.

"Where did you get this furniture?" she calls, and before I can answer, says, "Chelsea, you're filthy rich, and this stuff looks like it came from the Goodwill."

I plop down in the chair across from her. "First of all, I'm not filthy rich. I work hard and make a good living. There's a difference, you know? If anyone is filthy rich, it's your ex-husband. As far as the cabin, it's the whole point. It's supposed to be comfortable, relaxing, a place where you can put your feet up, not a designer showcase."

"No risk of that," she says, looking around.

"Should I put a pot of coffee on?" I get up and take the five steps to the kitchen.

Lolly is right behind me. "It's like camping, not even glamping." She opens and closes a few of the cupboard doors, then takes a seat at the table.

"Are you hungry?"

"No, I stopped in some godforsaken town on the 5 and got a sandwich."

I can hardly believe she's here. "What time was that?"

"I don't know. Noonish, I guess. The drive took forever. By the time I got to Sacramento, I was ready to book a hotel."

"Are you tired? Do you want to take a nap?"

"I'm fine. What is this you've got going?" She points at me and moves her finger up and down.

"What?" I drop my chin to have a better look. "My clothes?"

"Chels, hon, you need a stylist."

"This is the country, Lolly, not Rodeo Drive. Part of being

stylish is dressing appropriately. Jeans and a sweater as opposed to . . ." I turn my finger on her and mimic her up-and-down gesture. "Hermès? Prada? Is that jumpsuit Prada?" I may not be as familiar with designer labels as my sister, but I know Prada when I see it. "Really?"

"Had I known it was going to be this . . ." She stretches out *this*. "I would've worn my overalls. Oh wait, I don't own any overalls."

The overalls comment is funny, but she didn't say it as a joke. In fact, from the moment I found her sitting on my back deck, I could feel the hostility coming off her in waves. She's trying to pick a fight, and I don't want to fight. I want us to be best friends again.

"Let's not do this, Lolly. You came all this way. We should try to have a good time, make the best of our weekend together."

The coffee maker signals that it's done brewing, and I pour Lolly a mug. Hopefully coffee will warm her up.

"I have cookies in the car." I race out to get them.

"None for me," Lolly says when I return, waving the package of vanilla wafers in the air. "Carb overload."

That's when I take the time to look at her. Really look. She's thin as a rail, and her face is hollowed out so that she's all cheekbones and pumped-up Botox lips. If I didn't know my sister better, I'd worry that she was sick. No, her waifish appearance is quite intentional. Her obsession with weight started when she met Brent, her now ex-husband, and apparently hasn't subsided with her divorce.

"Well, they're here if you want one." I put a few on a plate and place it in the center of the table, then catch Lolly looking at them with hungry eyes. But I know better than to insist. That'll only make it worse.

"I'm disappointed Taylor and Luna couldn't come. Besides getting to see them"—I say that pointedly—"they would've enjoyed the parade. Ghost goes all out for Halloween."

"It's Brent's weekend, and he would've thrown a tizzy fit if I'd asked for them. He was an asshole husband, but when it comes to the kids . . . he loves them." She turns away, staring out the window.

"I'm sorry, Lolly." Though I don't know what I'm sorry for. We all knew she'd tire of him eventually.

"Yeah, well, what are you going to do?" She plays with the handle on her coffee mug. "So, Austin is getting married, huh?"

"Yep." I let out a breath.

"Are you going to try to get him back?"

"Why would I do that? He's in love with someone else."

"Are you still in love with him?"

"If you'd asked me a week ago, I would've said yes. But now . . ."

"You're not so sure?"

I lift my shoulders. "Sometimes I think I'm living in an alternative universe. Anyway, what do you say we don't talk about Austin this weekend?"

"That's fine by me," Lolly says. "I never much liked him anyway."

I start to say her dislike of Austin isn't fair, but we'd just agreed to not talk about him anymore.

"Would you like to go out to dinner tonight? I'd love to show you the town and this newly refurbished hotel that has an amazing restaurant that I know you'll appreciate." It's about the only thing in Ghost that is up to Lolly's impossible standards.

"I don't know. Maybe."

"Where's your stuff?" I don't remember seeing any luggage.

"It's still in the car."

"Let's get it and you can unpack, get comfortable, and later we can decide about going to town."

Lolly totters all the way to the car on her four-inch heels. We'll have to look for a good shoe store.

She's brought enough bags to stay for a month, but I bet nothing she's packed is practical for the country. That's my sister for you. I help her carry them into the house, then show her to the guest room.

"Where's my bathroom?"

"There's only one," I say. "We'll have to share."

My sister scrunches up her nose.

"Lolly, we grew up sharing the same bathroom. It won't kill you to do it again for a few days."

"It might." She glances around the cramped room and zeroes in on the tiny closet. "Oh, boy."

"There's room in mine." I take her to the primary bedroom and shove my clothes to one side of a closet that is only slightly larger than hers.

"Where's the bathroom?"

"You passed it when we came in here," I say through gritted teeth.

She's intentionally being difficult, but I vow to keep my cool. I'm thrilled she's here and don't want to do anything that'll make her leave. It's a delicate balance with us.

She grabs two toiletry bags from her suitcases and hogs all the space on the sink vanity. "Honestly, I don't know how you live this way."

"Don't be so melodramatic, Loll. It's a vacation cabin, not Folsom Prison."

She lets out an aggrieved sigh. "Whatever, I'll make it work."

"Thank you. It means a lot to me."

She studies me to see if I'm being facetious, which I sort of am but am trying not to be.

"Where were you earlier?" she asks.

"I went to town, then drove over to my handyman's farm. He's actually a biophysicist who's on sabbatical from his teaching job to write a book. But he's fixing my roof."

She doesn't seem to find that odd in the least and nods. "Why were you over there?"

The real answer is, I don't know. His unfiltered opinions should be a blow to my already fragile ego, but strangely, I find them refreshing, even liberating. "He didn't show up today, and I wanted to make sure he was okay."

"Maybe you should get a more reliable handyman."

"Perhaps," I say, not wanting to argue with her. "Finish unpacking and meet me in the living room."

"Where is it?"

I shoot her a look. "If you have any trouble finding it, text me."

While she's in the other room, I build a fire, then scroll through my emails. Still nothing from Ronnie. What in the world is going on with her? This is so unlike my assistant. Before I can dwell on it, Lolly makes her grand entrance in a pair of jeans, albeit designer ones, and a cashmere hoodie. The four-inch heels have been replaced by a pair of furry boots that she probably bought at an over-the-top ski shop on one of her annual treks to Park City.

"Look at you," I say. "Apparently, you do know how to dress for a weekend in the mountains." The mountains of St. Moritz, but she's at least making an attempt.

She plops down on the sofa, grabs the throw blanket off the back of the chair, and wraps herself in it.

"Between the heat and the fire, you should be warm in no time." I want to say, if there was a little more flesh on your bones, you'd realize it's sixty-eight degrees in here.

"How'd you find this place, anyway?" She stares up at the open-beam ceiling.

"Austin and I had been looking for a long time. Originally, we wanted something in wine country, but even a shack was over a mill."

"First off, this is a shack. And second, the two of you are loaded."

"Would you stop saying that? I'm not loaded. Yes, I make good money, but San Francisco is an expensive city. And if this was a mansion perched on a cliff above the ocean in Carmel, I wouldn't love it more than I love this."

"You're just like Dad," Lolly says. "Beer taste on a champagne budget."

"Dad was a cop, Lolly. Mom was a housewife. Their budget was hardly champagne, unless you count Cold Duck."

"You know what I mean." She waves her hand in the air.

And the thing is, I do. Dad took perverse pleasure in driving the same car for twenty years, in eating the same leftovers five days in a row, and in wearing a pair of jeans until they were threadbare. It wasn't because he couldn't afford new ones; he just didn't believe in waste. I suppose a similar ethos rubbed off on me. Not Lolly, obviously.

"There's nothing wrong with being frugal," I say.

"I much prefer the way Uncle Sylvester lives. Now there's a man who likes fine things."

"Is he still driving that Maserati?"

"Nope, a Porsche Cayenne."

"At least it's a grown-up car. Ridiculously ostentatious, but grownup. The Maserati was embarrassing."

Lolly laughs. "Yeah, kind of. I think Freud would say he was compensating for something."

"Eww. Don't make penis jokes about our uncle."

Lolly tucks her legs under her. "You think Mom would've wanted us to go to Uncle Sylvester?"

"I do. Grandma was in no shape to raise two young girls, and Dad's people . . . well, that wouldn't have gone over well."

"No, I guess not." She pauses, letting the room fall silent, letting it say all the things we won't. "And Uncle Sylvester loves us."

"He does." That was never a question.

"You think our lives would've been different if it never happened, if they didn't . . . die?"

"How do you mean, different?" I ask.

"I don't know. Like, would you have become a therapist? Would I have married a man twice my age?"

It would be a lie to say I don't ask myself the same things. Did I study psychology in search of closure? Did my sister settle for an older man she never loved to fill the gap my father left behind?

As kids, we'd planned to become detectives, which was obviously influenced by my father's law enforcement career and probably one of the silly TV shows we used to watch. We would spend hours playing "detective" in our bedroom. Dad would give us a make-believe crime to solve, and three or four suspects. Lolly and I would work through the clues, presenting our theories at the dinner table. Looking back on it, it was sort of a weird game for two little girls to play. But we got lost in the challenge of it, Lolly standing on her bed, acting out each scenario.

It's no wonder that in high school, she joined drama club. I'd always thought she'd become an actor. But when she met Brent, any aspirations of having a career seemed to fade away.

So, would we have chosen different paths if our parents hadn't died? "I wish I could tell you the answer to that. But I can't. No one can," I say.

"Loll, what's got into you?" I don't recognize this side of my sister. The contemplativeness, the visit to our parents' grave, her willingness to bury the hatchet for a weekend and come all this way to see me is so out of character that, frankly, I'm worried.

"Nothing has gotten into me." She unfolds her legs, stands up, and stretches. "Let's go to dinner."

"Okay." Her sudden shift throws me, but if she wants to

go to town, we'll go to town. "I hope you brought a coat." The nights can dip down to the thirties.

"Can I borrow one of yours?"

Of course she didn't bring one. It's always warm in sunny Los Angeles. I rifle through the coat closet until I land on something Lolly will find acceptable and grab a down jacket for myself.

"Here you go." I toss her a shearling coat I splurged on last winter when I was going through post-divorce-stress syndrome.

She puts it on and goes in search of a mirror.

I shake my head and yell, "It's on the back of the bathroom door. Meet me in the car."

It takes her ten minutes. "I had to refresh my makeup."

"Unless you care about impressing a bunch of men in plaid shirts and beer guts, it was unnecessary. But you do you."

"I always do. What kind of food do they have at this place? I'm a vegan now."

"Since when?"

"Why do you have to act like that, Chelsea? If you bothered to spend time with me, you'd know that I've been a vegan for a long time, now."

I don't bother to correct her. "I'm sure they have plenty for you to eat."

I take the highway this time, saving the scenic route for tomorrow, when it's lighter outside and Lolly can better enjoy the view.

Lolly's purse rings, startling us both.

"It's probably one of the kids." She pulls her phone out of her bag and with one look at caller ID her whole face lightens up and time melts away, making her look fifteen years younger.

That's the sister I want back. The happy, loving sister. The sister without armor.

It's Luna. It's clear from their conversation that my niece is angry with her father for something he won't let her do. Lolly is patient but stern. After Lolly talks Luna off her ledge, she tells her she loves her and hangs up.

"What was that about?" I ask.

"Brent won't let Luna watch an R-rated movie."

"Ah. It sounded like you were taking your ex's side."

Lolly sighs. "For the sake of the kids, we need to be on the same page. He's stricter than I am. I probably would've let her watch the movie. I've seen it, and it's a silly rom-com with some bad language and a few kissing scenes. Nothing she doesn't hear and see at school. But Brent is from a different generation. What am I talking about? He's old as shit. The bottom line is it's not going to do Luna and Taylor any good if we contradict one another."

"That sounds sensible," I say, impressed.

"They're good kids. I only pray that our divorce doesn't screw them up."

I know she's thinking of our parents and the toll it took on us. "It's not the same thing, Lolly. Mom and Dad are not you and Brent."

"No, they actually loved each other."

I can't disagree. In the end . . . well, who knows what was going through my father's mind? But there is no denying that they loved each other. They always had.

We both become quiet, having said more than we usually do on the topic of our parents. From a young age, we learned to compartmentalize our memories of them, especially the last ones. I'd be the first to say it isn't healthy, but it's less painful.

I pull into the public lot and cut the engine. It's dark, but the streetlamps throw off enough light that it's an easy walk to the hotel.

"See all the scarecrows?" I stop so Lolly can get a better look.

"They're kind of creepy, don't you think?"

"What are you talking about? They're cute."

"They remind me of a Chucky doll," Lolly says.

"You're nuts."

I open the door to the Ghost Inn and am welcomed with a din of voices. It's crowded tonight. Everyone up from the city for the weekend's festivities.

"I hope we can get a table. I should've called ahead for a reservation."

Katie is behind the bar, sees me, and flags us over. "It's crazy. The hotel is completely full. I heard they're even booked at the Prospector." She makes a face, because the motel on the other side of town is a little long in the tooth.

"This is my sister, Lolly. She's visiting me for the weekend."

"You guys staying for dinner?"

"We'd like to, that is if we can get a table."

"Let me see what I can do." Katie comes out from behind the bar and whispers something to the hostess.

Next thing I know, we're getting whisked away to the back of the restaurant and seated at a table next to the fireplace.

"Your friend the bartender came through," Lolly says, surveying the place. "Is it always like this?"

"No. It's because of the parade tomorrow. People come from all over to celebrate Halloween. Because . . . you know . . . Ghost."

"People are morons. Hand me that menu."

Katie brings us tonight's cocktail special. "A little creation I cooked up called the Ghost Ghoul. It's basically a Moscow Mule with tequila instead of vodka. Tell me what you think."

"Clever name," I say.

Lolly takes a sip. "It's good."

I test it and nearly choke on the tequila. "Whoa, how much booze did you put in here?"

"Too strong?" Katie swipes mine off the table. "I'll make you another one and be right back."

Lolly smirks. "You're a lightweight."

"What I'm not is an alcoholic. Slow down there, girl."

"It feels good to have a night out." She leans her head back and takes in a deep breath. "You were right, this is a fun place."

"It is, isn't it?" I turn away so she doesn't see the tears shining in my eyes.

We've been so distant for so long, I didn't know if we could ever get back to the place where we were each other's everything. Sister, mother, survivor. But today feels like progress. Maybe, just maybe, we can put the past behind us and start to heal.

Katie returns with a revised Ghost Ghoul, then rushes back to her post behind the bar. I glance around and note there isn't a plaid shirt in the house. Tonight, it's a sea of city wear. Lots of sweaters in dark colors.

"What's good here?" Lolly is studying the menu.

"To tell you the truth, all I've had here are chips and guacamole. Pretty hard to mess that up. But the menu looks interesting."

When the server comes, we order a variety of small plates to share. It's not until later, when we're in the car, that I say, "You do realize that absolutely nothing we ate tonight is vegan?"

"Uh-huh, the brussels sprouts were."

"They were dripping in butter."

"Oh well," Lolly says, and stifles a giggle. Those Ghost Ghouls have made her slightly drunk.

But when we get home, we polish off a bottle of wine, getting good and soused. Lolly passes out on the couch, and I practically carry her into the guest room, convinced that she'll be less hung over in the morning if she sleeps in a bed instead of the sofa.

I tuck her in, the way I used to do when we shared a room in Uncle Sylvester's penthouse apartment, and wait in the dark, watching the steady beat of her heart, trying not to remember.

Chapter 8

There's a giant pumpkin balloon floating over our heads. When I say giant, I mean Goodyear Blimp giant. It's attached to the cupcake float from Rolling Scones, one of the local bakeries in Ghost.

Lolly and I have claimed a small swath of sidewalk for our folding chairs to watch the parade. While it's not Macy's Thanksgiving Day, it's less amateur than I'd imagined. Some of the floats are quite elaborate with moving parts and sound effects. So far, my favorite is the Bank of the West's haunted mansion float, a replica of the Gold Rush Museum in downtown Ghost. The float designers took some creative liberty, embellishing the old Victorian with flying bats, ghost holograms, and shrieking noises.

Even Lolly is entertained and hasn't complained once since we got here, which has to be some kind of a record. She's been taking pictures and texting them to Taylor and Luna.

"Let them see what they're missing."

I hide a grin, because it's so unlike her not to be snarky. Not one single Mayberry joke out of her mouth. She genuinely seems to be enjoying herself. And I can't remember having this much fun since . . . I can't remember.

"Are you hungry?" I ask over the Ghost High School band's rendition of "Monster Mash." It's not terribly good, but I give them an A for enthusiasm. Their dance moves are a feat in and of itself.

"I could eat," she yells over the music.

It appears to be the tail end of the parade and a prime opportunity to beat the crowds. "Mexican?"

I wait for her to remember she's a "vegan." Instead, she gives me a thumbs-up. We fold the chairs, take them to the car, and walk to Flacos. The place is empty. Lolly grabs a two-top in the corner, while I put in our orders.

We're just about to eat when none other than Knox walks in.

Lolly swings around in her seat to see what has my attention, then turns back to me. "Who's that, and why are you blushing?"

"Oh please, give me a break. That's Knox, my handyman."

"The one who's a scientist or whatever you said he was?"

"A biophysicist."

She turns again to have another look. "He's hot."

"Shush. He can hear you."

But he's absorbed in studying the menu board and seems oblivious to the fact that Lolly's ogling him. We're like a couple of teenagers, or at least Lolly is.

"Stop." I tug her sleeve to face forward, away from him.

It takes a few minutes before he notices us, then bobs his head in greeting. After his food is up, he snags the table next to ours.

"This is my sister, Lolly."

"Yeah, Katie told me she was visiting." He shakes Lolly's hand. "Up from Los Angeles, right?"

"Yep." She's still ogling him, and I have to surreptitiously nudge her to stop.

"Were you at the parade?" I ask Knox.

"Got there towards the end, then decided to cut out before the crowds migrated to Flacos."

"Good move."

"Well, I'm taking mine to go." He holds up his bag. "I've got another thousand words to bang out."

"Nice seeing you."

"Yes, very nice seeing you," Lolly says in a lascivious voice that makes me want to strangle her.

Luckily, Knox doesn't seem to notice. He gets to the door and calls over his shoulder, "I'll be over tomorrow to work on the roof."

As soon as he's out of earshot, I kick Lolly under the table. "What are you, fifteen?"

She laughs. "Jeez, Chelsea, have a little fun, would you?"

And the thing is, I am. I'm not even trying to; it's just so easy. And suddenly I wish I could live here forever. With Lolly. With Taylor and Luna. And Knox and Katie and even no-tact Sadie. In my head, I know it's the buzz talking, not that I've been drinking. It's the buzz I'm getting from being with my sister again, from getting to share this special place with her, this place where, for the first time in my life, I feel like I belong.

"You're crazy, you know that, right?" I poke her in the arm.

"Don't get mad, okay?" she says, and I know instantly that it has nothing to do with her making goo-goo eyes at Knox.

"What?"

"Austin called and asked me to come."

I'm stunned silent, letting it sink in. My ex-husband and my estranged sister have been conspiring. "Since when do you and Austin talk? You like him even less than you like me."

She puts her fork down and meets my gaze. "You're wrong. Not about Austin but about you. But I'll give him this, he's worried, Chels. He says you could've been killed."

"You're here. You see me. Do I look near death?"

She shakes her head. "You look good, happier than I've seen you in a long time. But I thought you should know."

"So that's the only reason you came, because you thought I was dying?"

"I thought you might need me. And when has that ever happened?" She looks away, unwilling to make eye contact. What she's not saying is that when she needed me, I wasn't there.

"I've always needed you, Lolly."

"You have a funny way of showing it."

The parade crowd has already started to descend on the restaurant. There's a line at the counter, and a group of kids are chasing each other in and around the tables.

"If we're going to do this now, if we're going to hash out what's been going on between the two of us, let's not do it here," I say.

"Okay, but we're stopping first to get a couple of bottles of wine. No way am I doing this sober."

We make a pit stop at the market, where at the last minute, Lolly decides that margaritas are in order and spends half an hour picking out a top-shelf tequila. Mind you, the grocery store only has three (more than I would've thought). But Lolly deliberates over which one to choose, as if she's buying her first car. I'm betting it's a stall tactic, but whatever. She takes an equally long time to peruse the produce aisle for limes and strawberries, and maybe mango. "Because who doesn't love a mango margarita?"

I advocate for one of those premade lime juice mixes, but Lolly isn't having it. I don't know when she became the Barefoot Contessa.

Three grocery bags later, we hit the road. But halfway home, Lolly gets a call from Brent. It appears dire. From her side of the conversation, I deduce that Taylor has come down with a bad case of stomach flu and wants his mommy.

"Do you really have to go?"

"Nah, I'll just let my kid die while I drink margaritas with you."

"Lolly, it's a stomach flu, not malaria. Can't Brent deal with it?"

She pierces me with a condescending look that says I know nothing about motherhood. Or kids. Or her or Brent. "He's useless in situations like this."

She's out of the passenger seat before I have time to activate my emergency brake in the driveway, then rushes from the car to the house. When I get inside, she's throwing her clothes in her suitcases and packing up her toiletries.

I follow her to her vehicle, and we hug like we can't let go, our visit cut ridiculously short.

She pulls away from me, looks at her watch, and hops in her car. As she drives off with her window down and her middle finger waving in the air, she yells, "Don't drink all the tequila, bitch."

Even Knox's incessant banging on the roof can't sour my mood. Lolly and I have made significant headway in patching up our tattered relationship. Though we never said as much, I can feel a shift between us. I can feel us coming closer together.

I roll over on my side and send her a quick text to make sure she made it home safely. A few seconds later, my phone pings with a picture of her and Taylor, hugging the toilet, pretending to barf in the bowl, and a message that reads, *It must've been a 24-hour bug. Catastrophe averted. #BrentIs-Incompetent.*

I smile and get out of bed. It's late, well past the time I usually wake up. Last night, I slept like a rock. Without Lolly, there's plenty of hot water, and I stand under the shower head until my skin turns red, then dress and go in search of coffee. As per usual, Knox has left me half a pot.

As I sit at the table, sipping and scrolling through my phone, Knox comes in and refills his thermos, then scrounges through my pantry for the cookies he gave me. It's on the tip of my tongue to say, *Just make yourself at home*. But honestly, I've come to enjoy him making the coffee in the morning. In the city, I don't bother with it at home, instead sending Ronnie out for Peet's or Starbucks, or whatever is convenient.

I hold up my cup and say, "Thanks."

"Don't mention it. Where's your sister?"

"She had to leave early. Her kid was sick."

"That's too bad. You two looked as if you were enjoying yourselves."

It's true, we were, which in and of itself is a minor miracle. "The parade was really good this year," I say, though it's the only one I've attended.

"Yeah? Seemed like the same old crap as every year."

"You don't like it?"

"I love it. But it never changes. That big pumpkin balloon. Bank of the West's haunted mansion. The high school band. Let's just say variety isn't the spice of life here in Ghost."

"Why don't you leave, then?"

"Because I like it."

"It doesn't sound like it." He grins, and my insides do something funny. "You're a weird guy."

"I'm told that a lot." His mouth slides up again. "What's your plans today?"

"I don't know. Why?"

"It's going to get noisy." He looks up at the ceiling. "Maybe you want to go out for a while."

"Okay," I say, but don't have anywhere to go. It's too early to hit the Ghost Inn for a cocktail and too chilly to go out on the boat. Plus, that didn't work out too well the last time. "Any suggestions? I've run out of things to do in town."

"You ever been to the farmers' market? It's at the grange hall every Sunday. Nice produce. Lots of artisan foods. Definitely worth checking out."

I don't remember a grange hall, but Austin and I never fully explored the place, sticking mostly to home and town. "Where is it?"

Knox grabs the pencil behind his ear and draws me a map on a napkin. "It's easy to find."

After Knox climbs up onto the roof, I clean up the dishes and go in search of his farmers' market. His map takes me on a windy, two-lane road that overlooks Fall Lake, a large reservoir enjoyed by water-skiers and wakeboarders from all over Northern California. Austin and I looked at homes near the lake but ultimately decided that the vibe wasn't for us. Too loud from the motorboats and too rowdy from the perpetual summer parties at the sprawling campground on the south shore of the lake. Though I'm vaguely familiar with the area, I've never been on this road before and am worried that I may have gotten lost. Still, I'm enjoying the ride. There's not another vehicle around, so I take my time, pulling into a turnout to take in the view. The reflection of the trees off the water looks like a painting. And unlike summer, when the lake is filled with throngs of people and their water toys, there's only a lone kayaker and miles and miles of clear, blue water.

I wish Lolly was here with me to see it. When we were little, our parents used to take us to Big Bear, where we would sometimes rent paddleboats and paddle our way around the shore, hoping to see fish jump out of the water. Before I pull back onto the road, I snap a picture of the view and text it to her.

It takes me another ten minutes, but I finally find the grange hall, an old barn dating back to the early 1900s that, according to the sign, was rehabilitated in 1998 and now serves as a community center. Despite the empty road, the farmers' market is bustling. Lots of people spilling out from the big white church across the street.

There's a lady selling handmade market bags at one of the stalls, and I buy a pink and gray one made from woven straw. It's rather beautiful in its simplicity. As I stroll down each aisle taking in rows and rows of colorful squash, pumpkins, artichokes, cauliflower, mushrooms, and cabbage, I'm left wondering why I never came here before. Besides the beautiful food, the place is brimming with life.

There are so many things to see that I try to be methodical, resisting the temptation to go off in a different direction whenever a flash of vibrant color or an interesting shape catches my eye. No, I stay the course, stopping to browse at each stall.

My first food purchase is a loaf of olive and rosemary bread, which I put in my new basket. My next, a package of fresh pasta and a container of alfredo sauce. Then I pick through rows and rows of produce for a salad to go with my fettuccine dinner.

"Hi, Chelsea." A woman waves to me, then crosses the aisle to join me.

I recognize her from that first day at the grocery store. The harried woman with the two children. One of the boys had an unruly head of red hair.

"Oh, hey," I call back. "Where are the kiddos?"

"Judd has 'em. After yesterday, they're all sugared up, the little monsters. I needed a break. You coming to happy hour on Wednesday? Sadie said you were in."

I'd said I'd try, but now I'm game for anything. "Yep, I'll be there."

"Let's make time to talk," she says, and I nod, because I don't know what else to do. Or say. It's all so odd.

"I've gotta dash before Judd goes nuts. But I'll see you on Wednesday."

"Wednesday." I wave goodbye, then continue to the handmade soap stall, where everything smells like lavender, lemon, and peppermint.

I buy a bar of the olive oil soap for Lolly and a bar of basil soap for Ronnie. For me, I get a bar of the lavender, because I can't resist the scent. I'm just about to move on, when I decide to get another bar of the lavender for Katie. I have a feeling it's something she'd really like, though I don't know why.

In the next row of booths, I run into Sadie, who is selling wreaths and bunches of fresh flowers. I remember that I never hung my wreath on the front door. It's still in the back of my car.

"How's business?"

"You just missed the rush," she says. "Everyone wants Thanksgiving wreaths and arrangements. Ginger and I have our hands full. But I guess it's better than having no business. Poor Rhonda had to close up her knitting store because everyone's shopping on the damned Internet. We brick-and-mortar people are a dying breed."

I suppose she's right, but you'd never know it from the farmers' market. There's almost as many people here as there were at the parade.

"Where's Ginger?" I ask, as a line begins to form at Sadie's table.

"She's managing the shop, while I work the market." Sadie pulls a wreath off one of her displays for a couple who is interested, while simultaneously taking payment from a young man who is buying a bouquet of flowers for his grandmother. Sweet.

"You need some help?" I have no floral expertise whatsoever but can probably work a cash register.

"If you wouldn't mind."

Before she can show me what to do, she's pulled to the other side of the stall by a woman who wants to special order a cornucopia centerpiece.

"Excuse me, how much is this?" asks a man holding a small square vase with an arrangement of orange roses, bronze mums, and red daisies.

I search for a tag, only to find a price list tucked under Sadie's purse. He hands me two twenties, and I count out his change. For the next thirty minutes, there is a steady stream of customers. Sadie does the heavy lifting, but I hold my own, even putting up new displays as the old ones blow out the door. Let me tell you, the floral business is a license to print money. Sadie's stand has to be one of the busiest in the entire market.

If someone had told me a week ago that I'd be peddling flowers at a farmers' market, I would've laughed my ass off. It's a far cry from giant lecture halls or bookstores in Times Square, but oddly, I'm enjoying myself. I'm finding it immensely satisfying to be talking with people instead of talking at them.

Finally, there's a lull, and Sadie and I both take a deep breath.

"Is it always like this?"

"It's usually pretty good, but this is holiday season, girl. Never a dull moment. Thank you, my dear. But you should get to going while the going is good. Otherwise we'll get another rush, and I'll have to pay you." Sadie laughs, but it sounds more like a cackle.

"You sure?"

"Honey, this ain't my first rodeo. Go ahead and enjoy yourself."

"All right. But here's my number if things get crazy again." I reach out for her cell and punch in my digits. "Don't hesitate to call; I could really use the cash." I wink to show her I'm joking.

I pick up where I left off, visiting a rancher selling grass-fed beef, a local pot dispensary—which is even busier than Sadie's shop—and a woman named Misty, who claims to be a fortune teller. She's certainly dressed for the part in her Stevie Nicks getup, a tiered velvet dress and lace-up ankle boots. She is the only person here not doing a brisk business. I take pity on her and plop down in her chair just for shits and giggles. Her table is covered in a pink velvet runner, and there is a stack of business cards in the corner and a deck of tarot cards fanned out in the center. They look well-worn.

"How does this work?" I ask.

"You tell me," she says, then looks me over like I'm the prized calf at the county fair. "You want your palm read, or your cards done? Or you can tell me a little about yourself. Maybe I can help. Because, hon, you seem a little lost."

"Lost? I'm not lost."

"Okay." She shrugs, placating me. "Let's do your cards, then."

"I'm a marriage counselor. Well, I'm more like a motivational speaker, kind of like a life coach, but I focus on relationships," I blurt, because now I'm questioning the wisdom of doing this. For some reason, I feel like I'm playing with fire.

"It sounds like you and I are in the same business, then," she says, brushing a stray gray curl away from her face.

I hold her gaze to see if I've just been insulted, if she's trying to tell me that we're both charlatans. But I don't see either laughter or malice in her eyes.

"Well, not exactly. I have a graduate degree in psychology. I've written books and you know . . . I'm pretty well-known in my circle."

"Me, too."

"You have a graduate degree?" Now I'm just being mean.

"I do. I'm a nurse practitioner. Or I was a nurse practitioner. Now I do this." She waves her hands over herself, then juts her rather pointy chin at me. "Shall we get started?"

"By all means," I say with false bravado.

She places a wooden sign on the table that says WITH A CLIENT, gets up, and walks to the back of her stall, motioning for me to follow her inside of a makeshift tent. I take one of the purple velvet chairs while she closes the patchwork flaps to give us privacy. The setup is pretty elaborate for a farmers' market—if not a little odd—but interesting. I'll give it that. She takes the seat across from me at a folding table that's been draped with more velvet and clutches both my hands.

Her eyes are closed, and it takes all I have not to burst out laughing at how ridiculous she looks. Oh, if Lolly could see me now.

"I see the ocean," she says, her eyes still tightly shut, like she's concentrating or traveling to another dimension. "It's green, no, blue. Very blue." She opens her eyes and holds my gaze. "Do you live by the water?"

"I live next to a lake."

"No, it's not a lake. It's most definitely the sea."

"I can see the San Francisco Bay from my condo in the city."

"Not the bay, the sea."

"I don't know what to tell you." There is only so much I can humor her.

"I'm also seeing shells. Seashells." Her eyes are closed again, and she's deep in concentration. "Have you taken a trip to the ocean recently? Somewhere on a beach?"

"Nope."

"Wait." She pauses. "Shells. Then sea. Shellsea. Ring a bell?"

She knows damn well it's my name. She has to. "My name is Chelsea."

"Chelsea, Chelsea, Chelsea," she chants. "You're recuperating from something. It's either your head or your heart."

That covers a lot of bases. I figure it's a good go-to for any fortune teller. I mean, isn't everyone recuperating from something? A vacation, a cold, a bad night's sleep.

"I was in an accident more than a week ago," I say, again willing to humor her. "Got a minor concussion."

"Yes, I see it. It was on a big street. Lots of people. A man. There was a man there."

"There were a lot of men there." An entire paramedics crew.

"Just one. I'm only seeing one."

I hitch my shoulders, but she can't see me through her closed eyes.

"You were running from something. I see your heart. No, I see your head."

"Like I said, I suffered a minor concussion."

"I see sadness. Your heart again. No, it's your chest."

Oh, for goodness sake, why doesn't the woman name every one of my body parts? Eventually she'll touch on something. Isn't this the way it works with so-called soothsayers? Aren't they supposed to be just vague enough that everything is open to interpretation?

"My chest is fine. It was only my head," I say, not even trying to disguise the skepticism in my voice.

"Your pride was hurt. Yes, that's what it was. You were running from your pride."

I'm silent.

"There's the man again." Her eyes squeeze tighter, like she's desperately trying to make out the shadowy figure in her trance or whatever state she's in. "No, this is a different man. A handsome man, who is having his own difficulties."

I lean in. "Like what kind of difficulties?" I tell myself I'm only playing along.

"He's holding on too tightly. Very tightly. Like a death grip. He's afraid. Yes, I think he's afraid. Wait, he's running toward something. Somebody. A woman."

"Is it me?"

"I can't tell. It's smoky. Misty. A fire maybe. No, water. Lots of water."

I let out an exasperated breath. "It wasn't a fire or water! It was a cable car!"

"That's not what I'm seeing." She releases my hands and splays her palm over my heart. It's as if she's trying to read my mind through my pulse.

"The other man. The other man is torn," she continues.

"He's holding on, too. He can't seem to let go. He keeps going back and forth, pacing. No, he's vacillating. He's stuck, frustrated. Sad."

"Who is he?"

"I don't know. I can't quite make him out."

"Is his name Austin?"

"Who is Austin?"

"My ex-husband."

"I don't know."

"What does he look like?" It's unbelievable that I'm even asking. It's all nonsense, a charade, I tell myself.

"I can't see him clearly enough," she says. "But he's there. He's by your bed, kissing you. There's a woman there, too."

That makes zero sense, unless my future holds a threesome. Not interested.

"She's all in white," Misty says.

"A wedding gown?"

"No, I don't think so. But it's hard to tell. I see another woman. She's angry. No, not angry. Lonely. Confused. She doesn't know."

"She doesn't know what?"

Misty moves her palm lower, almost to my midriff, then higher, back to my heart. "I'm not sure. All I know is that no one has told her yet."

Oh, for God's sake. "Told her what?"

"Not sure. It's murky."

I want to ask her if people actually pay her for this.

"No, wait, she's getting a phone call. She's sobbing. I can feel her pain."

"Is she me?"

"Not you. Definitely not you. But she looks a little like you."

"Lolly?"

"Who's Lolly?"

"My sister."

"Maybe."

My heart stops. "I just spoke to her this morning."

"Then it's not her. But there's someone else, too. She feels distant. Like she's no longer here. Where is your mother?"

"Dead."

"It's her, I think."

My immediate reaction is to shut this down now. But I can't. Even if it's all bullshit, an act, I still want to know. "What is she saying?"

"She's telling you to go back."

"Go back where?"

Misty shakes her head. "Unclear."

"Ask her if she's angry that we buried her next to Dad."

"She's not angry."

"Did she say that?"

"No, but I can feel it."

Yeah, right. "Tell her we're fine, that Lolly and I are fine. That she's a grandmother."

"She knows. She loves you very much."

I'm shaking, beside myself. Initially, I thought this would be fun, even amusing. A way to pass the day and something I could giggle about with Lolly later. But it's no longer a game. I should've listened to my intuition when it told me that this wouldn't end well. Because tears are streaming down my cheeks, and I'm sobbing uncontrollably.

Misty opens her eyes and reaches across the table for a box of tissues, then slides them toward me. "We're done for now."

But I have the strange sense that we've only just begun.

Chapter 9

"Do you know a Misty?" I ask Knox when I get home. He's in my kitchen, cleaning the coffee pot. "I didn't catch her last name, but I think she's local. She's a fortune teller, used to be a nurse practitioner."

"Can't say I do. Why?"

"She was at the farmers' market. I don't know . . . she seems interesting."

"How so?"

"She really played the part, right down to the Witchiepoo lace-up shoes to the closed eyes, while she pretended to see my future."

"Did she have a crystal ball?"

"She may as well have."

He chuckles. "Not a crystal ball as in a prop. I was being sarcastic."

"You? Sarcastic? Never. Do you mean a literal crystal ball? Because that would've been a little over the top, even for her, though I wouldn't put it past her."

"What I mean is did you want her to tell you your future? I was using crystal ball as metaphor. That's all.

"A *metaphor*? You're getting kind of professorly on me."

"All I'm saying is if only life was as simple as a crystal

ball? If only we could all be assured that tomorrow will be better than today." He gives me a meaningful look that I can only guess has more to do with me than it does with Misty.

"What if today is already outstanding?" I challenge with a smug grin.

"It can always be better, right? My point being that if we all had a crystal ball telling us that five years down the road, we'd be winning the mega millions of life, we could put up with a lot of crap in the meantime."

It's true that if we all knew tomorrow would be better than today, it would make today more palatable. And less heart-breaking. "Yeah, if only I had the power to predict those things for my clients."

"That's the point," he says. "You don't. No one does. And if you did, it would take the element of surprise out of life."

"I could live pretty happily without the element of surprise. In any event, I can't tell if she's a fraud or not."

He cocks his brows, as if to say *Of course she is.*

"Okay, I'm not saying she can really see into a person's future or past. As you've already established, we both know that's a crock. But I think she actually believes she can."

"Does that make it better or make her any less of a fake?" he asks.

"It's a good question. No, it doesn't make her any less of a fake. But if she really believes in what she's doing, it makes her less of a con artist, I suppose."

"Is this about her or about you?"

Knox is more perceptive than I want to give him credit for. Still, I stop to ponder his words. "Do you think I'm a con artist?"

"No, I don't. I do, however, think the one-size-fits-all approach doesn't work. But, hey, if you can give people hope, even if it's only a glimmer, there's a little bit of magic in that, right?"

I think about what Knox says long after he's left. Is there really magic in giving people hope or is it just the opposite? A curse.

For dinner, I throw together the salad fixings I bought at the market along with the pasta and bread. It's a veritable feast for one person, with plenty of leftovers. Tomorrow, I'll see if Knox wants some for lunch.

I build a fire, curl up on the couch, and call Lolly.

"Hey."

"How's Taylor?" I ask.

"As good as new. Kids today, they bounce back fast. What's up with you?"

"I spent my day at the local farmers' market. It was a real kick." I swipe the throw blanket off the back of the sofa and wrap myself in it. "Have you ever gone to a fortune teller before?"

She laughs. "Don't tell me you did."

"I did. Her name is Misty, and she was something straight out of central casting. Flowy dress, Victorian boots, long, curly hair, the whole nine yards. It was weird. Sometimes I thought she was making it up as she went. Other times, it was as if she was actually seeing things, real things."

"Like what?"

"My name, for one."

"Aren't there billboards all over the place with your name and face?"

"Billboards, Lolly?"

"Okay, maybe not billboards, but you're a *New York Times* bestseller. There's a pretty good chance she knows who you are."

"That's what I thought. But she also seemed to know about my accident."

"Did the news cover it?"

"Not that I'm aware of. And she knew about you, or at least we think it was you. And about Austin. She said I was running from my pride when I was hit by the cable car, not a broken heart. Do you think that's true?"

"Only you can know that. What else did she say?"

I take a moment, wondering whether I should tell her, whether it'll only pick at old scabs. "She talked about Mom," I say reluctantly, waiting to take Lolly's temperature.

"What did she say about Mom?"

"That she wasn't angry that we buried her next to Dad. That she loved us and knew she had grandchildren."

"Do you believe her? Misty, not Mom."

"I guess I want to. Do you?"

"How would I know? I wasn't even there. But if you want to, then believe it."

"It doesn't work that way, Lolly."

"It can if you let it. You're the one who went to a freaking fortune teller in the first place, so clearly you believe in it on some level."

"I did it because I thought it would be fun. The truth is, I did it because it was something you would do."

"So now you want to be like me?"

"More spontaneous, yes."

"Since when?"

"Since I had a brush with death." It's an exaggeration, but there's also truth in the fact that getting dumped by my ex-husband, getting hit by a cable car, is a wake-up call of sorts. A wake-up call to mend fences with my sister. A wake-up call to make friends. A wake-up call to have balance.

A wake-up call to get a life.

"I wish you would come back and talk to her," I tell Lolly.

"The fortune teller? What in heaven's name for?"

"To vet her."

"Chelsea, you're the brain trust in the family, not me. If anyone knows whether this Misty woman is full of shit, it would be you. Did you Google her, look up her reviews?"

"Do you think there are reviews for fortune tellers?" The idea of it sounds absurd.

"Why not? There are reviews for everything else. Have you ever looked at your own?"

"No, I never even thought of it."

"Well, I have."

"Really? For me? Were they good?"

There's a long silence.

"Lolly?"

"They were a mixed bag. But who cares? Even Adele gets bad reviews."

"You're contradicting yourself. What's the point of reading someone's reviews if you don't believe them?"

She laughs. "You're too literal, Chels. Lighten up. All I'm saying is you can get a feel for this Misty woman's credibility by reading her reviews. For example, if the vast majority say she was busted for check kiting a month ago, she's probably not too reliable."

Her logic may be twisted, but oddly enough, I see the wisdom in it.

"My personal trainer is here, so I've got to go. Chels, try to relax, okay?"

"I'm doing my best."

"Do better." And with that, she hangs up.

I go in search of my laptop, curl up again on the couch, and search for Misty the fortune teller. Believe it or not, she's got reviews. Lots of them. And they're pretty good, a 4.5 out of 5. I scroll through the reviews, reading.

"*It was as if she could see straight inside of me.*" *—Nick C. of Nevada City.*

"*Misty said good news was on its way. And boom, two days later, I found out I was preggers.*" *—Josephine R. of Ghost.*

"*I've seen Misty on three different occasions, each time I was in a slump in my life. She helped me narrow down the source of my unhappiness and see into a bright future. I highly recommend her to anyone who is feeling a little lost." —Carol M. of Auburn.*

"Misty told me my husband was seeing another woman. Who does that? Seriously, who the hell does that? If I could give her zero stars, I would." —Sandy T. of San Francisco.

I click out of Yelp, having seen enough. Before I close out altogether, I consider looking at my own reviews, then quickly shut my laptop down.

It's only seven o'clock, though it feels later. It's pitch dark outside, not even a sliver of light from the moon, which is hidden behind the mountains. Most nights, I can see even a partial moon glowing off the lake like a beacon. But tonight, the darkness is eerie, even foreboding.

I tell myself I'm being ridiculous and pick up the phone again. Uncle Sylvester picks up on the first ring, which catches me off guard. Usually, I get his answering machine.

"Chelsea, how are you? I've been meaning to call, honey, but my phone never stops ringing. Did Lolly tell you I'm casting the new James Bond movie?"

I don't think she did, but I say yes anyway. "Who's going to be the Bond girl?"

He chuckles. "That's classified. But that's not why you called. What do I owe the pleasure?"

If I didn't know better, I would think he was taking a jab at me for being MIA this last year. But between Austin leaving me and my tense relationship with Lolly, it's been hard. Sadly, Uncle Sylvester and I don't have a whole lot to talk about. His world is making movies, and mine is saving marriages. The two rarely collide.

"Lolly went to Mom and Dad's grave for the anniversary," I blurt.

He doesn't say anything at first, then, "I know. She told me. After the fact, otherwise I would've gone with her."

I could take that as another jab, because I should've been

the one to go with her. But he doesn't mean it that way, that much I know. He's never pressured us to do anything we weren't comfortable doing.

"Do you think we made a mistake burying them next to each other?" I ask. "Was it cruel? Or worse, was it denial?"

"Honey, you were twelve. Of course you were in denial. Thank God. No kid should ever have to go through what you and Lolly did."

"But was it wrong of us to bury them together?"

"They were dead, honey. All that's in those graves are their bodies. Their souls are long gone. Burial is for the living, not for the dead. And that's what you and Lolly wanted. It gave you peace, and that's all I wanted. I wanted you girls to have peace."

"If it was just you, though, would've you done it that way? Would you have buried them side by side?"

"Yes," he says without hesitation. "Because they loved each other. Even in the very end, they loved each other, and I believe that's how your mother would've wanted it. Why are you doing this to yourself, Chelsea? Why now?"

"I guess it's the anniversary. It brings it all back, everything about that day."

"I've always told you girls to focus on the good, to remember the happy times. There were more of those than the bad ones. For a long time, I couldn't forgive your father for what he did. But I always knew that my sister would've wanted me to. And eventually, I did forgive him. That's the way you've got to look at this, Chels. You've got to forgive and let go." He takes a long pause. "Lolly and I are so proud of you. You channeled what happened with your parents into something good. You turned all that pain into something productive."

It's definitely why I became a psychologist, a marriage counselor. I suppose I thought I could save people from the same trauma my parents couldn't save themselves from. But somewhere along the way, it became more about me than me helping people.

"I miss them," I say.

"I miss them, too. And I miss you. I know you and your sister have your problems, but it would be nice to see you every once in a while."

"Did Lolly tell you about my accident?"

"What accident?"

I tell him about being hit by a streetcar, leaving out the stuff about Austin.

"Chelsea, you need to slow down, take a vacation. All this constant work is grinding you down. It'll kill you if you let it."

I let out a snort. "Now isn't that the pot calling the kettle black?"

"I didn't get hit by a cable car, kid."

"Touché. If it's any consolation, I'm on vacation now. Up at the cabin." I start to tell him that Lolly came for a visit, but this thing between my sister and me is still tenuous. I don't want to jinx whatever progress we've made.

"Good. I still have to see that cabin of yours. It sounds like a special place."

"My door is open twenty-four/seven," I say. "I love you, Uncle Sylvester."

"I love you, too."

Our call leaves me a little melancholy but at the same time, a little consoled, if it's even possible to be both at the same time. Twenty-four years is a long time to hold on to guilt over something I insisted on when I was twelve. Something that, as my uncle pointed out, could only matter to my parents' survivors.

At the time, I believed that my parents would forever be soulmates, even in the afterlife, despite what my father had done. Despite that he'd shot my mother three times in the heart before turning his service weapon on himself. I believed they needed each other as much in death as they needed each other in life.

Was it the romantic delusion of a young girl to help her sleep at night? Or was it something only a child of their DNA could intuit? I no longer know what I once so solidly understood about them, about their love for each other. Age has a way of making you skeptical. It has a way of making you question yourself.

But Misty said my mother wasn't angry. Misty. The woman is either wanted in fifty states or a complete nutjob.

I go to the kitchen and make myself a cup of chamomile tea. Supposedly the herb binds to the benzodiazepine receptors in the brain and makes you sleepy. I travel with a box whenever I'm out of town, because I find it difficult to sleep in strange places. Who knows if it really works? I remind myself to ask Knox about it. It seems like something a biophysicist might know about.

Tonight, the tea is useless. I don't nod off until well after midnight, and it's a fitful sleep, filled with bizarre dreams. I see the fox again. This time, it's curled up at the foot of my bed on top of my feet. When I try to kick it away, it bares its teeth.

The big orange pumpkin balloon from the parade is hovering above me, clinging to the ceiling. Every time I reach for its string, the balloon moves, its candy-corn mouth laughing at me. I laugh back. Soon, both of us are giggling until we're gasping for breath.

Austin is here. He keeps kissing my forehead and my cheek, which is wet from my tears. The fox growls at him, and he starts to sob. A woman in white, maybe Mary, tells him if he doesn't get a grip, he has to leave. And I feel at once grateful and sad.

Uncle Sylvester is here, too. He's on his phone, pleading

with someone. I think it's the new Bond girl, because she's so pretty.

The only one I want is Lolly, but she's nowhere to be found. I keep calling her, but she doesn't answer.

Then I see my mother, my beautiful mother. I reach for her, but I can't move my arms; they're too heavy, like bricks. My father is here, too. He's in his policeman's uniform, more handsome than I even remember. I try to talk to him, tell him I forgive him, but my mouth is so dry, no words come out. Just squeaks.

They're leaving, and I want to follow them. Maybe if I follow them, we can be a family again. Mom, Dad, Lolly, and me.

"Wait for me," I say, but no one hears me but the fox. Its ears prick up, and it cocks its head to one side before running off into the forest.

I try to get up to go with Mom and Dad, but my body won't move no matter how hard I try. I look down at my feet, willing them to carry me away, but they are blue, and I can't see my toes. I start to cry, but no one notices.

Then out of nowhere, Knox is here. He's holding my hand and I feel better, safer.

"I want to go with my parents," I tell him.

"Not today," he says.

"Misty says it's okay," I whisper back.

"No, she doesn't. She wants you to stay. Please stay."

That's when I wake up in a cold sweat.

Chapter 10

In the morning, I go to the lake to sit with my cup of coffee. The sun hasn't quite come up yet, and the sky is awash in color. I wrap the wool blanket I brought from the house tightly around me, trying to keep warm and ward off all the weirdness of the previous night.

I'm not the kind of psychologist who studies dreams, but Freud would probably have a heyday with mine. There's a noise coming from a nearby bush, and I sit perfectly still in hopes of seeing my friend the fox. But it's one of the Muscovy ducks that roam, or rather waddle, along the shoreline. I don't think they're native here. One of my neighbors says they are from Mexico or South America. My guess is someone originally brought them to the lake as pets, where they reproduced and thrived. They're funny-looking creatures, black and white with red faces, and half the time sound like they're having an asthma attack. The same neighbor says the sound is normal, though the first time I heard one, I wanted to rush it to the nearest vet.

I watch as it grubs for insects, immune to the cold. I should go inside and make a fire, but I need the air and the open space for a few more minutes. And the lake is so tranquil this time of the morning, it would be a shame to miss it as it wakes up.

So I wait for the sunrise, pulling my blanket tighter as I lean back in one of Austin's plastic Adirondack chairs, making a decision to buy real ones today. Perhaps I can persuade Knox to pick them up in his truck.

I'm down to the last of my coffee when I hear him drive up. It only takes him a minute or so to spot me in the chair. He waves, goes inside, only to join me a short time later.

"Kind of cold," he says, and plops down in the chair next to me.

"Yeah. I had a rough night, needed some fresh air."

He looks me over. "What happened?"

"Nothing really. I just had trouble sleeping. How 'bout you—get any writing done?"

"I was in the zone till about one in the morning. Then Katie called. Her car wouldn't start, and she needed a ride. Same old crap, different day."

"Her car breaks down a lot?"

He laughs. "I think the question is when does it run? I guess I'm going to lend her money for a new used one."

"That's nice of you."

"Nothing nice about it. It's purely self-serving. I'm tired of chauffeuring her around."

"It's wonderful how close you two are. My sister and I used to be like that."

"Why aren't you still close? What happened?"

I stare out over the lake into the distance, deciding how to answer, because it's complicated between Lolly and me. I suspect it would be complicated for any family with our background. "She thinks I deserted her."

"Did you?"

"I didn't used to think so, but on further reflection, yeah, I probably did. We had some unpleasant stuff happen to us in our childhood, and I suppose the way I escaped it was to leave behind the people I loved most." *Unpleasant* may be my best euphemism yet, but talking about my parents' murder-suicide has never come easy. “First, I got caught up with school, then trying to build a practice, then a business that put me on the road most months out of the year. I thought I was doing good work, but maybe I was running away.”

“Or it could be you were doing both.”

He takes my hand, lacing his fingers through mine, and for a long time, we just sit there like that, staring out over the lake, reveling in the sounds of nature, his big, warm palm in mine. And just like in my dream, I feel safe. The real kind of safe. Protected for the first time in my life.

“But it’s better now, right?” Knox is the first to break the silence. “You and your sister have mended your broken parts.”

“I don’t know. My sister can be mercurial. But I think we’re on our way back to each other.”

“That’s good,” he says.

“Very good. What about you, Knox? Why did that woman leave you for your best friend?” I can’t wrap my head around it. People leave all the time. Look at Austin and me. Look at what my father had done. But Knox . . . there’s something so captivating about him, something that makes you want to stick, at least to me.

“She said I wasn’t fun.”

I laugh, even though I shouldn’t. It was a hurtful thing to say. “She was wrong.”

“Yeah?” He grins. “I can be a pretty fun guy when I’m in the mood.”

“Did she break your heart, Knox?”

“At the time, I thought so. Now . . .” He shrugs. “She and I wanted different things. Eventually, that would’ve become a sticking point. But you’re the expert.”

“I suppose it would’ve depended on how much the two of you were willing to compromise. Marriage is always a series of compromises.”

"You put that on a sticker somewhere?"

I laugh. "It's on my inspirational calendar. But seriously, were you willing to compromise?"

"On some things, sure. But probably not on the things that mattered most to her."

"Like what?"

"Like money. She wanted a lot of it. As long as I have a roof over my head and food on the table, I'm fine. It's more important to me to have a good life."

"And what does a good life look like to you?"

He turns in his chair to face me and holds my gaze. "Are you trying to shrink me, Chelsea Knight?"

"Shrink you?" I arch a brow. "Maybe. Just answer the question, Hart."

"A life that's good is me doing exactly what I'm doing. Living on my family's farm, teaching classes at UC Davis, writing the occasional book, and fixing roofs, using my hands." His was still in mine.

"What about yours?" he says.

"Same. Doing exactly what I'm doing. Changing lives and giving people tools to a successful marriage."

Perhaps it's my imagination, but he seems disappointed by my answer, like somehow I got it wrong, like somehow I like the sound of it more than the thing itself.

"Well, as much as I like sitting here with you, I should get to work. That roof isn't going to fix itself." He untwines his hand from mine, and the urge to pull it back is overwhelming.

We walk together to the house, where we go our separate ways, me inside and he up the ladder.

I shower, then check for my itinerary from Ronnie. Still nothing. I'll call her later, after I come back from town. But right now, I'm on a mission.

Instead of the scenic route, I take the highway to Ghost, park, and climb the hill to the florist shop. Sadie is behind the counter, and a red-haired lady, who I presume is Ginger, is removing thorns from more than a dozen long-stemmed roses at a table in the corner.

Both women greet me like we're the oldest of friends. I still haven't gotten used to how warm and chatty everyone is.

Sadie and Ginger are deep in conversation about a local boy who rescued a dog from drowning in the river and nearly got swept under himself. At the last minute, he managed to hang onto a branch until help arrived. Apparently, it is headline news in the *Ghost Advocate*, in which the boy is being hailed as a hero.

"I'd whoop his ass if he were my kid," Ginger says. "Risking his life like that for a damned dog. Boy ought to have his head examined."

"That dog is probably his best friend. Wouldn't you save your best friend?" Sadie looks over at me with a conspiratorial smile. "What's a matter with you, Ginger? Grow a heart."

Ginger gives a dismissive swat of her hand. "You people and your dogs. Give me a cat any day."

Sadie shakes her head. "What brings you in today, Chelsea? Because if you're looking for something to do, Ginger and I will put you to work."

"Not today. I was actually hoping you could help me with something."

"What's that?"

"I'm looking for someone. Her name is Misty, and she had a booth at the farmers' market yesterday."

"What was she selling?" Sadie asks. "The name isn't familiar."

"She does palm readings, fortune-telling, that kind of thing."

"I know her," Ginger says, and makes the crazy sign with her finger. "Used to work up at the hospital when I was taking Floyd in for treatments. Now she does the woo-woo thing. Nuts, if you ask me."

Sadie shakes her head at Ginger. "Don't listen to her. Why are you looking for this woman?"

"Uh, we got to talking at the market, and she seemed interesting, that's all."

The door chimes, and a customer walks in, pulling Sadie away. The client wants a fall assortment to give as a hostess gift, and Sadie is rattling off a list of flower options.

"She has a place up on the ridge," Ginger says. "An old bungalow that's about ready to fall down, where she keeps office hours." She shakes her head. "I use the term *office* lightly. I can give you directions if you want."

"Yes, please."

Ten minutes later, I'm taking a grade so steep above Ghost, I keep one hand on my emergency brake. Had I'd known Misty's bungalow was this high up, I would've waited for the next farmers' market. I'd turn around if there was a place to do it, but the road is so narrow and twisty, my only option is to go full-bore ahead.

Don't look down.

If I do, I'll make myself sick. I try to distract myself by searching address signs. Ginger thinks Misty's is in the 900s. Two minutes ago, I passed 640. Not too much farther, I tell myself.

I bet it's pretty up here; I bet if I were brave enough to look down, I'd see the whole valley stretched out before me. Lakes and rivers, even irrigation ponds that dot the landscape like freckles.

Keep your eyes on the addresses.

I only have a vague description of what I'm looking for. A decrepit bungalow, which may or may not have Misty's shingle hung out front. Ginger wasn't altogether sure. Most of the homes are perched above an ancient stone retaining wall covered in green moss. I'm sure the views are spectacular, but who the hell builds on the side of a mountain?

I follow the switchback and hold my breath as I ascend

even higher. This has got to be the universe thumbing its nose at me. As the road starts to plateau, I see it on the right. Misty's shingle, a wooden sign that says MADAM MISTY, UNIVERSAL DIVINER.

There's a small, empty driveway and I pull into it, taking a moment to collect myself before cutting the engine. As soon as my pulse returns to normal, I grab my purse and head up the driveway. Ginger wasn't kidding; the place is a dump. The front porch alone should be condemned.

I take the steps gingerly and ring the bell, which doesn't work, so I try the knocker, a bronze mermaid. The fact that there is no car in front (I did not see a garage) tells me there's no one home. But I stand there waiting anyway, not ready to get back in the car. I'm never making this drive again.

I'm just about to give up when the door flies open, and it's her. Misty. She's wearing a pair of leggings and a poet's blouse, her hair pulled back in a messy bun held together with a giant clip.

"Sorry to just drop in like this." I stand there awkwardly, wishing I'd rehearsed something better to say.

"Come in," she says, and ushers me across the threshold into the front room, which is surprisingly charming.

"I couldn't find your number on Google, but a friend knew where you live."

"Have a seat. Would you like something to drink? Tea, juice, coffee?"

"I'm fine, but thank you." I try to decide between a wing chair upholstered in tapestry covered in cat hair or the . . . I guess you would call it a divan. It's bright turquoise velvet, and I kind of love it, though it has seen better days. It's more shabby than chic.

I settle on the divan, taking time to look around. The inside of the house is in much better shape than the outside. The floors are oak, and the ceiling is the same turquoise as the divan with a big fan. In the corner is an upright piano, the top of it covered in a Victorian fringed scarf and a Tiffany lamp. There are a series of framed photographs above the mantelpiece of the fireplace, which appears to still have its original Batchelder tile surround.

Next to the living room is a small dining room with a round oak table and four mismatched chairs. It's worn but cozy.

"What brings you by?" Misty takes the rocker across from me.

For the life of me, I don't have a good answer. But from the minute I woke up this morning, I knew I had to see her again. Perhaps it was the dream. All I know is that for some unfathomable reason, I'm drawn to this woman.

I decide to be honest. "I don't know."

"You must know something, or else you wouldn't be here."

I nod. "Can I be perfectly candid with you?"

"I wouldn't expect you to be anything less."

"I don't believe you can see into my future or my past. I don't believe any of this." I lift my arms in the air.

"Okay. The question still stands: What are you doing here, then?"

"I think I want to believe, so you can give me resolution. Absolve me of my guilt, like you did yesterday when you said my mother wasn't angry. It would be so easy if I could just believe."

"Then believe."

"But I can't. I'm a trained psychologist. We rely on data. Research. There's nothing metaphysical about it. It's sound science."

"Then use that science to absolve yourself."

"You don't understand."

"I understand more than you think," she says, and gets to her feet. "I'm going to pour myself a glass of wine. Would you like one?"

There's the drive down the mountain. The drive up nearly

killed me, but it's only one glass, and it might even steady my nerves. "Just a splash."

She heads to the dining room and disappears in what I presume is the kitchen. I get up to check out the pictures over the fireplace. A graduation photo of what I assume is Misty's nursing class. Various antique portraits of people, perhaps ancestors or pictures she found in a secondhand store. But the centerpiece is a smiling Misty with a group of women gathered in a circle in the middle of a golden field. All that's missing is a bubbling cauldron. Okay, that's uncalled for, but it's clear to me that these are her soothsayer friends or whatever you want to call them.

Misty returns with two glasses of wine and puts them down on the coffee table, a creation made of gnarled burlwood that is at odds with the antique pieces scattered throughout the room. I plop back down in the divan and take a generous sip. I'm not a day drinker, but between my strange dreams and the drive, the wine is good for taking the edge off.

"Why did you leave nursing?" I ask, because it seems like a good icebreaker.

"I was tired."

I peg her to be in her sixties, and nursing is indeed strenuous work.

"Tell me about the dreams," she says.

I strain to remember whether I mentioned my dreams when I came in, concluding that I must have. "I saw my deceased parents, and when I tried to follow them, I couldn't. It was as if I was weighted down with rocks."

"Why did you want to follow them?"

"I don't know. It was a nonsensical dream. Aren't you supposed to tell me why?"

Her lips curve up, and I'm struck by how striking she is, much more beautiful than she is in the graduation photo.

"Dreams aren't my specialty. But any well-trained psychologist could interpret why you wanted to follow them."

"They're my parents. I miss them."

"Hmm," she hums.

"What? You think I wanted to die, you think I wanted to follow them into the afterlife?"

"I don't know, did you?"

"No, of course not!" I'm angry because it's a ridiculous question, and I know what she's doing, because I do it every day. If I needed a therapist, I would've gone to one. "I wanted to know why?"

"Why what? Why your father killed your mother? Why he killed himself?"

My mouth falls open, because I know damned well I didn't tell her anything about my family's history. That's not to say that with a little research on the World Wide Web, she couldn't have read all about it. But why would she? She didn't even know I was coming here today.

I do my best to recover. Like I said, it's not something I talk about, especially with strangers. "I know why he killed her, and I know why he killed himself," I say, as calmly as I can.

"Okay. Then what did you want to know from them?"

"This is going to sound stupid, but I guess I want to know if she's forgiven him. If they're together . . . you know . . . in death or wherever."

"Yes."

"Yes what? She's forgiven him? They're together?"

"Yes, to all of it," Misty says. "This is the problem, though. No matter what I tell you, you're preconditioned to disbelieve me. So this whole endeavor is fruitless."

I sigh because she's right, though I desperately want to believe her. She's told me exactly what I want to hear, what will finally give me comfort. The conundrum is that not only don't I believe in fortune tellers, I don't believe dead people talk. Or have feelings. Or kiss and make up with their killers.

"So my mother is not angry that Lolly and I had them buried together?" I ask anyway.

"I already told you that." Misty takes a sip of her wine.

I stare at the lipstick stain she's left on her glass. "Why do you think my father was wearing his police uniform in my dream? What do you think that means?"

"I already told you my work doesn't involve dreams. You're much better equipped to interpret them than I am. My best guess, though, is that's how you want to remember him. As a hero."

I nod, because that makes sense.

"But you didn't need me to tell you that," Misty says.

"What's going to happen with Lolly and me? Will we find our way back to each other, to being real sisters again? It seems like we've made a dent since the accident, but it also feels tenuous, fleeting. Almost as if it's not real."

Misty takes another sip of wine, then reaches for my hands. Clutching them, she closes her eyes and reenacts the same routine as the one she did at the farmers' market.

I smirk. *It's showtime, folks.*

But if I'm going to make fun of it, of Misty, why the hell did I come here in the first place? I tell myself that I'm bored and it's something to do, but deep down inside I know it's not true. Since the accident, I've been on a mission to search for answers. Who knows? Maybe I've been on that mission my entire adult life and just didn't realize it.

"She misses you." Misty is in a trancelike state. "She's stubborn, though. Holds a grudge. She's hurt. Scared. Lonely. I see a desert. It's flat and isolated."

"It's probably Palm Springs." I snort. "She stays at the Ritz-Carlton at Rancho Mirage every chance she gets."

"No, it's not Palm Springs," Misty says. "It's fear. Separation anxiety. Desertion. That's it, desertion. Your sister has fears of abandonment."

Thanks, Captain Obvious.

"I know that."

"She blames you for something in her past." Misty squeezes my hands. She's focused, frustrated. "I can't see it. It's not coming to me."

"For leaving her when I went away to boarding school?"

"Yes. But it's something else, something more significant," Misty says.

"For her marriage? For the record, I thought her marrying Brent was a terrible idea. A disaster waiting to happen."

"Maybe her marriage . . . or her divorce. It's there . . . right in front of me . . . I just can't see it. Give me a second."

"Does it have something to do with Uncle Sylvester?"

"Shush."

My palms are sweaty from Misty holding them so tightly, but I don't dare pull them away. I can feel each second tick away in the pit of my stomach.

"Ugh, I still don't see it." Misty loosens her grip.

"Well, don't give up."

Misty opens her eyes. "You put up a lot of blocks. It's like concrete inside of you. It's hard to get through." She lets go of my hands. "I need a break."

She stands up and paces the living room. "I think we're done for today."

"But we were so close."

She pins me with a look and shakes her head. "I'll give you some exercises to do, stuff that will help you let down your guard. Because until you get rid of the concrete, I can't get through. And it's exhausting."

"Sorry." I don't fully understand what I'm apologizing for, but it seems like the right thing to say.

She goes off through a hallway, leaving me alone, only to return a few minutes later with a packet of papers that she hands to me. "Follow these instructions every night before you go to sleep and come back in a week."

"I don't have a week. I'm leaving on Friday to go back to

San Francisco. Then I have a speaking engagement in New Mexico."

"Can't you postpone it?"

"It's sold out. I can't just not show up. It would be the height of irresponsibility."

"Okay. Come on Friday before you leave. But there's no guarantees. You're a tough nut to crack."

I reach for my purse and rifle around inside the front compartment for my wallet. "How much do I owe you?"

She waves her hand at me. "I'll bill you at the end."

I drive down the mountain, going fifteen miles an hour with my heart in my mouth.

Chapter 11

The first thing I do when I get inside the cabin is call Lolly. I'll just ask her myself. *What's been eating you these past few years? What did I do besides leave for boarding school to make you hate me?*

We would've gotten it all out in the open if she hadn't been rushed away over Taylor's pukefest, anyway. I can persuade her to meet me in New Mexico. Santa Fe. We can go to a luxurious resort in Santa Fe after my lecture. My treat. And talk until the cows come home.

But after five rings and Lolly's voice telling me to leave a message, I say, "Call me," and hang up. It's almost five o'clock; she's probably at one of the kids' soccer games or at happy hour with some of her Malibu Barbie friends. For the record, that's what she calls them, not me.

I guess I should think about dinner, but I'm still recovering from the drive down the mountain, which was somewhat better than the drive up. Still, my stomach didn't like either.

Just the same, I pop my head inside the fridge. It looks like Knox made a good start on the leftover pasta. When I feel like it, I'll eat the rest. For now, though, just another glass of wine. There's a bottle of white from the other night in the door, and I pour myself a healthy serving.

I remember the wreath that's still in my back seat and go

outside to get it. Somewhere in the junk drawer, there's one of those adhesive hooks that advertises that it won't leave a mark. I stick it to the front door and hang my new wreath with its miniature orange and white pumpkins and inhale the fresh scent of juniper. Voila. Eat your heart out, Martha Stewart.

My phone rings, and I race inside, hoping it's Lolly. Not Lolly, Austin. I don't know how I feel about him calling again, but I answer it anyway.

"Hey."

"Why are you out of breath?"

"I was outside and ran in to get the phone." I hastily add, "I thought you were my sister. What can I do for you?"

"No need to be hostile, Chelsea. I was just calling to check in. No one's heard from you, and I was getting worried."

No one? It's not like we have anyone in common. The only person I'm regularly in touch with is Ronnie, and she hasn't been responding to me. I highly doubt she's been talking to Austin.

"I'm fine. Great, actually." *And I've met someone. Knox.*

"How's your head?"

"It's all good, Austin. Don't you have a wedding to plan or a marriage to break up?" It's a low blow; there's nothing wrong with being a divorce attorney. It's a necessary, even noble (okay, that's taking it too far), profession. But for whatever reason, I feel like poking the bear, maybe even drawing a little blood.

"What the hell crawled up your ass? I mean, here I am, worried about you, making sure you're okay. I don't know what you're so angry about."

Can he really be this obtuse? I'm about to say, think about it, Austin, but figure it's not worth arguing over.

"I appreciate your continued concern," I say, trying to keep any hint of hostility out of my voice. "Everything is wonderful here. I'm relaxing, enjoying the lake, and taking trips to town. I finally made it to the parade and was sorry I missed it all these years, because it was fantastic."

"Really?" He sounds doubtful.

"Really. You and Mary should try to make it next year." I can't help myself.

"Yeah, about that."

He stops, and I hold my breath, fantasizing that he'll say Mary's out of the picture, that he can't live without me, even though I've been living without him like a champ. It's true. Since I've come to the cabin, I rarely think about him.

"I was hoping you'd reconsider Christmas," he continues. "At the risk of sounding like a jerk, this week was my week. But you needed it, Chels. And I can't tell you how relieved I am that you've been able to recuperate there. All I want is for you to be healthy." He says it like a) he's a saint, and b) I'm two seconds away from being committed to a cuckoo farm. "But I think it's only fair that we make up for the week I lost."

"No problem," I say. "You can have the cabin my week in January." It's arguably the worst month in Ghost. Cold, foggy, and often rainy.

"That's not a fair trade. But we can talk about it another time. I didn't call to fight."

"Why again did you call?"

"I'm going to go now," Austin says. "And I love you, Chelsea. I only wish you the best."

He hangs up before I can say, *Fuck you, Austin.*

I'm sitting on the sofa, watching my third episode of *Curb Your Enthusiasm*, afraid to go to sleep. While I wouldn't call last night's dreams nightmares, they were discombobulating, even disturbing. I can't take a repeat performance. But the thing is, I'm having trouble keeping my eyes open. Every time they fall shut, I jolt upright, gulping in air as if I'm suffocating, and force myself to stay awake. I don't know how much longer I can keep this up without crashing.

That's when I make a split-second decision to go for a drive. It's not the least bit rational, but these days, I'm trying to be more spontaneous. Less myself, more Lolly.

It's not as dark as last night. There's a half-moon peeking down on me, lighting my way to the car. I roll down the window, figuring the cold air will give me a shot of adrenaline, or at the very least, keep me awake for hours to come.

It's a gorgeous night, clear and crisp, the cedar trees particularly pungent, reminding me that winter is just around the corner. I take the country road, avoiding the highway. The deer are out in droves tonight, their yellow eyes glowing in the dark, so I lighten my foot on the gas. Luckily, I have the road to myself and can take my time. It's a little eerie out here alone. But so calm and peaceful that there's no reason to be frightened.

I drive without a destination in mind, going wherever the road leads me. It looks different at night. Less like bucolic farmland and more like enchanted forest. Different, but lovely.

I hang a right on a road I've never been before. It's paved, and I believe if I follow it long enough, it'll take me to a sandy beach on the banks of Bear Creek, just outside of town. It's the right direction.

The beach is popular with locals and tourists alike because of its accessibility. Most of the river's shoreline is rocky and rugged. Still, the rocks don't stop the hardcore river rats from diving off the boulders into the clear, icy water below. As Uncle Sylvester says, "Some people don't have the brains God gave them."

I pass an outcropping of homes, some modest, others large and extravagant, like the million-dollar houses you see in

Lake Tahoe faced in stone and glass. That's how I know I'm near the river. I stick my face out the window to see what my nose tells me, to see if it picks up the scent of fish and fir and muddy flats. But instead of smelling it, I hear the rush of water in the distance.

There's a green reflective sign up ahead. Bear Creek Beach. I follow the direction of the sign's arrow to find a large parking lot, public restrooms made of cinder block, and a row of picnic tables. There are a few parked cars and a group of kids playing loud music. A girl is dancing in the back of a pickup truck, and the smell of pot is thick in the air.

I scrap my original plan to take a stroll on the beach but park on the far end of the lot. It's too dark to see anything other than the shimmer of the moon bouncing off the water. And the music seems to have gotten louder. More aggressive.

A few of the young people have spotted my car and are walking toward me. My intuition tells me to leave, but my car is now surrounded by them. I quickly roll up my window and try to come up with an escape route that doesn't involve mowing anyone down. For all I know, they're just being friendly. But my gut doesn't think so.

One of them, a young man with dirty blond hair and bedraggled clothes, is banging on my back window. He's at least six-two and outweighs me by sixty pounds. I take some solace in the fact that the other two people menacing me are female; then I remember the "Manson girls."

I tap on my horn, which comes out more as a soft toot than a muscular honk. One of the women holds up a joint and motions for me to unroll the window. I shake my head. The man has climbed onto my trunk and is jumping up and down, violently rocking my car, making me seasick.

I search the passenger seat for my phone and realize I forgot it. As a warning, I start my engine and slowly pull forward. Through my rearview, I see the man drop to his knees, then lie prone on my trunk, his arms dangling over the sides, his legs sprawled spread-eagle. He's laughing. Hysterically. The women, now flanking both sides of my car, are laughing, too.

I see no way out without flooring it. Panicked that I might kill someone in the process, I weigh all my options, deciding that it's either them or me. Then someone across the parking lot lets out a shrill whistle. The guy hops off my trunk, and he and the two women run to a waiting SUV. Within seconds, the parking lot is empty with the exception of me.

I sit there for a while, trying to regain my breathing, because for a time there I'm pretty sure I'd stopped. Then I nose out of the lot, taking a different road than the one I came in on, a different road from the SUV.

A few miles later, I try to convince myself that the parking lot idiots were just a harmless bunch of local kids, probably stoned out of their minds but gentle lions just looking for attention. Still, I'm unsettled enough that I keep my eyes on all my mirrors, looking over my shoulder every few seconds.

I take the back roads on the outskirts of Ghost, avoiding downtown, passing sheep farms, cattle ranches, old barns, and garages big enough to house tractors and farm equipment. Here, the houses are utilitarian. The lights out. Early to bed, early to rise. But there's safety in knowing that I'm just a driveway away from help if I need it.

Subconsciously—but the psychologist in me believes it's probably more conscious than I want to acknowledge—I wind up on Old Ranch Road. This time around, the road doesn't feel as long. And in no time at all, I'm sitting in Knox's driveway with the engine running, wondering what to do next. The porch light is on, so I turn off the car and climb the stairs.

As if he's been expecting me, Knox opens the door, then his arms, and takes me in.

He doesn't ask why I'm here so late or interrogate me about why I'm not home, safe in my bed. He just wordlessly holds me, and I'm no longer afraid of bad dreams or hoodlums in an empty parking lot. It's the most generous thing anyone has ever done for me.

"You hungry?"

"I never ate dinner, but it's got to be after midnight."

"So? Kitchen is always open here." With his arms still wrapped around me, he walks me across the house.

"I'm going to let you go now," he says, because I'm still clinging to him. Then he moves to the refrigerator and sticks his head in. "Soup or a sandwich? Or both?"

"Both, please." I didn't realize how hungry I was until now.

By the time Knox has the bacon sizzling in a frypan on top of the stove, I'm ravenous. The smell alone is making my stomach rumble. When he finishes building a perfect BLT, the microwave dings with the soup. Tomato. I don't know if it's homemade or store-bought. And frankly, I don't care. It looks delicious.

He serves me at the table and takes the chair across from me.

"You're not eating?"

"I ate already." Of course he did. The entire state of California is asleep by now.

"Thank you," I say in between bites. "It's so good." I can't remember anything tasting this wonderful.

"So you were just driving around and decided to stop by?" he says, trying to make it sound casual, but I can see he's concerned, possibly even thinks I lost my mind.

"Something like that."

He holds my gaze, willing me to tell the truth.

"I was afraid to sleep. Last night, I was besieged by weird dreams. I thought if I took a drive, it would clear my head. And I wound up here. Were you writing?"

"Nope. Done for the night. The odd thing is, I had a premonition you'd show up. When I heard Bailey barking . . . well, I knew."

I can't tell if he's playing around with me, joking. "What kind of premonition?"

"Just a feeling that you'd wind up at my front door."

"Hmm. I hope it's okay."

"Why? You planning on leaving if it isn't?" He reaches over and lightly touches my arm, a signal that this time, he really is joking. "I'll make you up a bed."

"You don't have to." All at once, I'm embarrassed to be here. Embarrassed that I intruded on this man I barely know in the middle of the night. Or rather, morning. Because by now it must be past midnight. "I can take this to go"—I hold up the sandwich—"and head home. I'm good now, honest."

"Nah, you're here. You may as well stay."

"You sure?"

"I wouldn't offer if I wasn't. I can't guarantee a good night's sleep, but I can guarantee a good breakfast in the morning. I make a hell of a chicken-fried steak. Country gravy, biscuits, the whole nine yards."

"Well in that case, I'll stay. I mean, who can pass up chicken-fried steak?" I'm so relieved I could cry. I don't think after the night I've had I could get back on the road and return to an empty house.

And I think Knox's hospitality is genuine and not made because of any false sense of obligation. He doesn't strike me as the kind of guy who stands on ceremony.

I finish my soup and sandwich and clean up while Knox makes me up a bed. It's a big house, and I presume there is more than one bedroom. When he doesn't return, I go in search of him. Mainly it's an excuse to have a look around, because on my previous visit I only saw the front rooms.

The main floor is a bit of a warren, a lot of chopped-up spaces with no rhyme or reason. But there is a certain charm to it. A certain symmetry. I can see kids growing up here, a family. It's so much different from the house Lolly and I grew up in. Not the first one with my parents, which was a tidy ranch in a leafy neighborhood in the San Fernando Valley, where kids rode their bikes on the street and played hopscotch on the sidewalk. Where neighbors looked out for one another, and everyone gathered for barbecues at the one house on the block with a swimming pool.

Not that one.

The house where Lolly and I spent our formative years was not really a house at all. It was a penthouse in the tallest building in Century City with sweeping views of Los Angeles. It was three times the size of our plain-Jane ranch, yet there was no place to play, no place to ride a bike, and no place for hopscotch on the sidewalk. A communal roof deck with an Olympic-size pool was our substitute for a backyard. Occasionally, our babysitter would succumb to our pleading requests to take us swimming. Then she would withstand the withering glares from the other residents, who didn't want splashing kids to get in the way of their rigorous aquatic workouts.

It's hard, even beyond privileged, to call the lap of luxury hell. But to Lolly and me, it felt that way. It felt like a gilded cage, even though we were lucky to have a roof over our heads.

This house, Knox's house, would've been heaven. Large and lived-in, like Mom's secondhand sofa. I can just imagine all the places we would've played hide-and-seek or built pillow forts on the floor. All the outside space we would've had to run and play.

I take the stairs to the second floor, peeking in the open doors. There's a big den up here, which looks as if it's used as a TV room with overstuffed couches, a couple of recliners, and a huge flat-screen. There's a wall of windows that probably showcases a view of the mountains. It's too hard to tell in the dark.

Down the hall is an office. Judging by the messy desk, it's where Knox writes. I go in and study the spines of all the books on the shelves, most of them academic tomes about science, biophysics, and agriculture. But plenty of fiction, too. There's also a collection of wooden mallard duck decoys, some that appear to be fairly old. Despite the clutter, it's a handsome room. Cozy, yet spacious, and like the rest of the house, has a warmth about it. It hugs you like a strong embrace is the best way to describe it.

Knox comes in to find me thumbing through one of the books. "I gave you Katie's room and put fresh sheets on the bed. You can have the bathroom next to it."

"This is a great house." I nudge my head at the decoys. "Are you a duck hunter?"

"Nope. Those were my dad's."

I'm secretly relieved. Shooting cute little ducks seems medieval.

"When did your parents pass?"

"My dad six years ago. My mom a year after my dad. He had non-Hodgkin's lymphoma but put up a good fight. Lasted two years longer than the doctors said he would. My mom, on the other hand, was in good health. But after Dad died, she just seemed to deteriorate. I figure she didn't want to go on without him."

"That's sad. I'm sorry."

"It's the cycle of life," he says, hitching his shoulders. "Let me show you your digs for the night."

Katie's room is unexpected and completely the opposite of the tattooed bartender with the flaming red hair. It's ultra girly and old-fashioned, with yellowed cabbage rose wallpaper, a pink canopy bed, and matching dresser and desk. I can't see her picking out this stuff, though tastes change as people get older.

"This okay?" Knox asks.

"It's perfect. Thank you."

"Feel free to scrounge through Katie's drawers for a nightshirt or whatever."

"I hope she doesn't mind."

"Nah," he says, and jams his hands in his pockets. "Help yourself."

We stand there awkwardly.

"Well, goodnight then," Knox says, but lingers.

I think maybe he's going to kiss me, and I want him to. Really badly. I'd like to say that it's because it's been so long since a man besides Austin has kissed me, and I'm curious how it would be with someone else. But that's not it. It's simply Knox. I want him to kiss me.

He doesn't, of course. He rocks on his heels with his hands still shoved in his pockets and walks out of the room.

Chapter 12

I'm awakened by two things: The morning light streaming through the window, hitting me straight in the eyes. And Knox humming "I've Got You Under My Skin." I recognize it, because Uncle Sylvester is a huge Cole Porter fan.

Besides humming, Knox is making a racket in the kitchen. I can hear pots and pans clanging and something that sounds a lot like a coffee grinder. Yuban, my ass.

I check the clock on the bedside table. It's only seven. I try to remember what day it is. Since I've been here, the days are a blur. Without having to go to work every morning, it may as well be a perpetual weekend.

Tuesday.

I'm pretty certain it's Tuesday, because the farmers' market was on Sunday. Of this I'm sure.

I throw my feet off the side of the bed and force myself to get up when what I'd rather do is stay in bed. In this room with the faded cabbage rose wallpaper and pink canopy bed. I kind of love it here.

Something crashes—it sounds like shattered glass—and a shout of "Shit!" echoes through the floorboards. I find a robe in the closet and go downstairs to see what the commotion is.

Knox is sweeping up the remnants of a Pyrex dish when I find him.

"Mornin'."

"Good morning. What's going on? It sounds like World War III down here."

"I had a battle with the cupboard. And the cupboard won." He starts putting away the bowls that are now spread out across the floor.

"You want some help?"

"It was only a minor setback. I've got it from here. Grab yourself a cup of coffee, sit back, and watch the master of breakfast."

There's a hutch with mugs hanging from hooks in one of the Hoosiers. Each cup has a map of a state. Arizona, Nevada, Wyoming, Michigan, Rhode Island, Vermont. It's not all fifty, but a good showing just the same. I take Minnesota.

The coffee maker is on the other side of the kitchen. I have to walk around some of the broken glass to get there to fill my cup.

"You sure you don't want me to get this?" I point to the floor.

"I got it." Knox sweeps the rest of the pile of glass into a dustpan and dumps it in the trash. "Watch your feet until I vacuum."

I have on socks that I borrowed from Katie's drawer, as well as her pajamas.

"So, chicken-fried steak, huh?" I'm watching him bread ground beef. "I must admit, I've never had it before. Why do they call it steak if it's really hamburger meat?"

A car pulls up just as he starts to answer, and we both look outside the window as a willowy blonde alights from the vehicle. She's tall, maybe five-eight or five-nine, and looks a little like Gwyneth Paltrow. Very glamorous and sure of herself.

"Do you know her?" I ask.

"Uh-huh."

I wait for him to tell me who she is, but he goes back to breading his beef, dredging handmade patties through flour, egg, and panko. I've been a psychologist long enough to read a room, and it's there, a soft pull of tension around Knox's mouth.

The doorbell rings, and his mouth pulls even tighter.

"Yoo-hoo, anyone home?"

"We're in the kitchen," he says.

She, the woman, sweeps in, clearly familiar with the layout of the house. She's fifteen times prettier than I thought she was when I first saw her through the window. It's safe to say she's supermodel material. Actually, more beautiful than a supermodel, who truth be told are usually a little odd-looking. Gangly and like their faces aren't quite right.

"Hello, Sienna," Knox says.

"Oh, I'm sorry." Sienna looks straight at me. "I didn't mean to interrupt anything?"

I start to tell her she isn't, but Knox says, "If you were really worried about it, you wouldn't have shown up without calling first."

She laughs, but it's an embarrassed laugh. A laugh meant to cover up the fact that she's been called out in front of a stranger.

"Katie said it was okay for me to borrow her ski pants," Sienna says.

"Katie doesn't live here anymore."

"I know that, Knox." Her voice is tight. "I'll just grab the pants and be on my way." She starts for the staircase.

"Now is not a good time," Knox says, stopping her in her tracks. "If you'd like to come back, three would be better."

I don't understand why he's making such a big deal about it, why she can't run upstairs, grab the pants, and be on her way. Why be such a jerk about it? It's unlike him.

And then it hits me who she is. Who Sienna, of the blond hair and blue eyes, of the supermodel beauty, is. Who she was to Knox.

"Seriously?" Sienna may as well stamp her feet on the floor. "It'll take all of five minutes, Knox. And I'm already here."

"I'm sorry, but this is an inconvenient time." He passes a pointed glance my way. "You'll have to come back."

"You're an asshole!" She marches off, slamming the door behind her.

The sound of Sienna starting her engine, and then her tires on the gravel road, fills the room as I watch through the window as the back of her car jackknifes down the driveway.

"So that was her, huh? The ex-fiancée," I say.

"That was her."

"May I say something?"

"Knock yourself out."

"It doesn't seem like you're over her."

"You can be over someone and still be angry with them."

I stop to mull that over, because he makes a valid point. I may or may not be over Austin, but there's no question that I'm pissed as hell at him. Love and anger can be mutually exclusive of each other, but I'm not altogether sure that's what I heard a few minutes ago.

"Why?" I ask.

"Why am I still angry at my ex? Because she did a shitty thing. She betrayed my trust. And worse, she took away my best friend."

Ahh, now we're getting somewhere. "Are you angry with her for that? Or the best friend? Because from where I'm sitting, he's equally responsible."

"You're doing it again. You're shrinking me. Aren't you supposed to be on vacation?"

"Yes. But friends and family get me twenty-four/seven."

He laughs. "Thanks, but no thanks. And as for him, the

best friend, he's more than equally responsible. He violated the guy code, which in my book is unforgivable. But it doesn't mean I don't miss him. And right or wrong, fair or unfair, I take it out on Sienna."

"Do you miss Sienna, too?"

He drops two pieces of his breaded meat into a pan of sizzling oil. "I thought I would, but the sad thing is I don't."

"Why is it sad?"

"You spend nearly a decade with a person, shouldn't you miss them when they're gone? And what does it say about me that I don't?"

"I guess it says that it was over even before she left."

"She says I was only staying with her out of loyalty. I never could figure out if she said that to ease her conscience or mine."

"Perhaps it was to ease both of yours. She's very beautiful, Sienna is."

He nods. "She's very beautiful. But so are you."

It's not until I get home that I realize why Ronnie hasn't responded to any of my emails. She never got them. I find them in my outbox, sitting there like they're waiting to be called into the doctor's office, but no one has come for them.

There must be something wrong with either my laptop or my Gmail. Unfortunately, my computer savvy is limited to hitting the control-alt-delete buttons when something goes wrong, or rebooting. It's always Ronnie who deals with these malfunctions.

There's a big box computer store in the neighboring town, so I pack up and hit the road. On my way, I call Ronnie, but as usual, get no answer. This is becoming a habit with her. I leave what is now my fifth message and pull off the highway to join the line at the drive-through coffee place right before town.

Austin and I used to come here on the way to the cabin.

The coffee is not great. It's one of those places where they put the cream and sugar in the drink for you and the coffee is inevitably too sweet. But it was our thing, a routine I'd come to associate with the start of a weekend in the mountains. Happiness.

I suppose the only reason I'm here, waiting in the long queue, is out of habit, sort of a Pavlov's dog. I see the coffee drive-through; therefore, I want coffee, even though I had three cups this morning at Knox's. The man makes a really good cup. Now, his chicken-fried steak is another story. I wasn't too crazy about it.

But it seems that I might be crazy about him.

Isn't it weird how life works? That saying—when one door closes, another one opens—always seemed like a throwaway line to me, like something designed to make you feel better when life goes to shit, even if it's not true. I've been guilty of using the cliché a time or two myself with despondent patients, knowing full well it's a phony platitude. Most of the time, the door just closes. Parents die, and you leave your happy home to live in a soulless apartment in the sky where you can't jump on the couch or touch the knickknacks. Or your husband leaves you with no warning and a year later is engaged to a woman named Mary.

But this time, another door has opened. Knox.

I get my overly sweet coffee and start again for the computer store. It's in a large strip mall that's anchored on one side by a Target store and the other side by the aforementioned electronics mecca. This is the town where Ghost residents go to do their real shopping. While it's not as charming as our small town, it has every big box store known to mankind, including two do-it-yourself emporiums.

Parking is plentiful, and I slide into a space right in front of the store, grab my laptop, and go inside. Surprisingly, it's crowded. I traverse the computer aisles, looking for someone to help me, but everyone seems to be in either the appliance or electronics departments. There are a few kids playing with the video game testers, and I wonder why they're not in school.

"Excuse me," I say, trying to hail an employee, but he gives me the five-minute sign and breezes past me.

I wander around for another ten minutes before finding someone else with a name tag, wearing what appears to be the store employee's uniform of khakis and a white polo shirt. He directs me to an empty counter, where I wait for another ten minutes for someone to actually notice me and come out from whatever back room she was hiding in.

"How can I help you?" she asks.

I wait for her to look up from her phone, but she doesn't.

"I'm having problems sending email. I was hoping someone could look at the issue." I push my laptop toward her on the counter, which finally gets her attention.

"Maybe it's your Wi-Fi. Did you try sending the email from here? Our signal is strong. Let me give you the password." She hands me a laminated sheet on a chain that says "Serendipity" and goes back to her phone.

I find their network, plug in the password, go to my outbox, and try to send Ronnie's emails again. Nothing happens. "Nope. It's not working."

She slides me a glance and lets out a put-upon sigh. "What email service do you use?"

"Gmail."

"It's probably a problem with it, not your computer." She crosses her arms over her white-polo chest and stares down her pug nose at me.

"I don't think so," I say, because even if it is, I don't have the first clue how to solve it. And it's not like Gmail has a customer service line. Like I said, Ronnie always takes care of my technical problems.

"I guess we could look at it for you, but you'll have to leave it. We're slammed today and it's first come, first serve."

I want to say it's *served*, not *serve*, but I doubt that would ingratiate me to her, and I'd really like to get this resolved, though I'm not thrilled about separating myself from my laptop.

"You're sure no one can look at it today? I can pay extra for the rush."

She scowls at me like she's a cop to whom I've just offered a bribe. "That wouldn't be fair to our other customers."

"When will it be ready then?"

"It's hard to say." With her dagger-long nails painted a bright purple, she taps out a series of keys on the counter's computer. "There are five people ahead of you, so it could be a couple of days. It's up to you."

I'm tempted to look for another computer place, but who knows if it'll be any different there? And I really need to be able to send emails, so I reluctantly leave my laptop with the hope that it'll be fixed no later than tomorrow.

On the way home, I stop at the fancy grocery store in the strip mall next to the one with the computer store. It's one of those co-op deals that looks a lot like Whole Foods but is even more expensive. Their cheese section, though, is unrivaled, and their organic produce is marvelous. Since I won't be here for the next farmers' market, I stock up.

Knox is on the roof when I get to the cabin. The roof, it seems, has become a full-time job. He waves down to me, and I yell for him to come in for lunch. It's more like an early dinner, but I'm starved.

I decide to make a charcuterie board with all the cheeses I've bought and try to copy a picture of one I find on my phone. Whoever did it makes it look easy, effortless, like they blindly threw cheeses, meats, olives, grapes, and veggies together on a platter and *voilà,* an Impressionist painting. Whereas mine looks like vomit—literally, like someone threw up.

I set the board, a wedding gift that has never been used, on the table anyway and find a bottle of red hiding in the back of the pantry.

Knox comes in and washes his hands in the kitchen sink. "Kind of late for lunch, don't you think?"

"Probably. But aren't you hungry?"

"I'm always hungry," he says, then looks at the table, or more accurately, my poor attempt at charcuterie. "Nice. Fancy."

I laugh, despite myself. "Don't be shy, dig in."

He opens the wine and pours us each a glass.

I clink my goblet against his. "After this, I don't think you should get back on the roof."

"I'm officially done. Your roof, I'm proud to say, is as good as new."

This announcement of his should be great news, yet all I can think is now Knox won't have a reason to come around anymore. And I'll miss him. I'll miss our morning coffee and our impromptu meals. I'll miss our conversations and our stories. I'll miss going to sleep at night, looking forward to seeing him in the morning.

"So I guess you can focus full time on your book now."

He nods. "The deadline is looming."

And suddenly I have this very odd sense that our—his and my—deadline is also looming.

Chapter 13

The Ghost Inn is packed this evening, but Katie has saved us a table at the back of the bar. It's Sadie, Ginger, the woman I have since learned is Amanda, and me. Tonight, at least until seven o'clock, Ghost Ghouls are half price, and it's five bucks for anything on the happy hour menu, including their famous smoked chicken wings.

We get a round of drinks for the table and order enough five-buck bites to count as dinner. Ginger is still talking about the boy who saved the dog, calling it "the height of stupidity."

And I tell everyone about my scary encounter with the kids at Bear Creek Beach.

"People think small towns are these safe little islands," Sadie says. "Well, let me tell you, we've got bigger drug problems here than they do in the big cities. OxyContin, fentanyl, methamphetamine, we've got 'em all."

"I think these kids were just smoking pot," I say.

"I doubt it." Ginger passes the basket of chips around the table. "Sounds to me like they were a bunch of juvenile delinquents, high on God knows what. Probably homeless."

"One of them had a fairly expensive SUV. They didn't appear homeless to me, just bored, and out for a good time, even if it was at my expense."

"Probably stole that SUV," Ginger says. "Did you check the police blotter today?"

I hadn't. I didn't even know there was one.

"Give it a rest, Ginger." This from Amanda, who looks from Ginger to Sadie. "You two make it sound like we're living in a hellhole, which we're not. Not once have I ever been afraid to walk around here at night, except for maybe the bears. Or a wolf. They're back, you know? There's a whole pack roaming the Sierra. Anyway, I wouldn't trade this place for anywhere in the world, not even a beach in Mexico, which would be my dream vacation if I ever got one."

Sadie is no longer paying attention; something across the bar has her distracted. We follow her line of sight and see it. *Her*. Sienna. She's sitting up on a stool, talking across the bar with Katie.

"I heard she moved to Truckee," Ginger says. "And yet, she's always here. I think that stool has a permanent imprint of her ass."

"I wouldn't mind having her ass." Amanda tilts her head to the side, literally eyeing Sienna's ass, or at least what she can see of it. "I mean . . . since we're talking about asses."

"It doesn't say a lot for her marriage that she's always here." Sadie takes a big gulp of her Ghost Ghoul and shudders. "Katie doesn't go light on the alcohol, does she?"

"That's why I keep coming back." Amanda holds up her drink and smiles. "What do you think is going on with her?" She points her chin in Sienna's direction.

"What I think is she backed the wrong horse. If she'd chosen Knox, she wouldn't be spending so much time in bars. Alone."

"Sadie's right," Ginger says. "Anyone who knows Brody could've seen this a mile coming. The man just isn't husband material. In fact, I wouldn't be surprised if he had himself a little side dish."

"Who has a side dish when they can have Sienna Bates?"

Amanda goes in for a smoked wing. "If I had her body, I'd never worry about my husband looking at other women."

"Have you seen Christie Brinkley?" Ginger looks at Amanda pointedly. "All her husbands cheated. Every single one."

"Men don't cheat because their wives aren't beautiful enough," I say, and find three pairs of eyes focused on me. "Just saying."

"Why do they cheat, then?" Amanda is working her way to the stuffed mushrooms.

"There's a multitude of reasons. Insecurity, boredom, sex, love, selfishness, just to name a few. Rarely is it *flaming locks of auburn hair* and *eyes of emerald green.*" The "Jolene" reference is not lost on this crowd.

"Is that what your patients say?" Sadie is keenly interested, and there's a sadness in her expression that wasn't there before.

"Some. Look, every case is different. But what I've found is that it's usually more about the cheater than the cheated. A seismic shift in his or her world, something that makes them want to compensate for whatever they've lost. A job, youth, their hair"—I try for a weak smile—"you get the idea."

Sadie nods, but it's still there, that sadness. She'd already alluded that her marriage was bad, but now I know why.

We circle back around to Sienna, and when the opportunity presents itself, I whisper in Sadie's ear, "We can talk about it later if you want, in private."

She pretends she doesn't hear me, but I know she does.

"All I'm saying is that if she'd stuck with Knox, she wouldn't be here tonight, looking lonelier than anyone should."

"Why did she choose Brody?" Until now, I've stayed out of it, but in this moment feel emboldened. Or nosy, depending on how you look at it.

"Well . . . he's Brody." Amanda laughs, and the other two join in.

I am, of course, lost, having never met Brody.

Amanda reaches for her purse and fishes out her phone, scrolling until there's a picture of a man filling her screen. He is, by all universal standards, a knockout. Dazzling in all his manly glory. And judging by the gear he's got on in the photo, a firefighter.

I'm still slightly starstruck when I ask the obvious question: "Why do you have a picture of him in your phone?"

"He's my first cousin."

"I can certainly see his appeal." It's an understatement. "But you know what they say, beauty is only skin deep."

"Clearly not to Sienna," Ginger says. "They're like freaking Ken and Barbie."

"It's not as if Knox isn't equally appealing." He may not be as beautiful as Brody, but in my opinion, he's a head-turner. "But that's beside the point. It all comes back to the fact that physical attributes actually have very little to do with chemistry."

"I beg to differ." Amanda's lips slide up. "I sure as hell wouldn't kick Bradley Cooper out of my bed, regardless of chemistry."

Our glasses are empty, and Katie is the only one working tonight, which is crazy with this crowd. I volunteer to get us a second round at the bar and manage to wedge myself between a plaid shirt—the half-price drinks and five-dollar bites bring in the locals—and Sienna, before getting Katie's attention. I hold up four fingers.

There's a football game on the television, but no one seems that interested. Maybe because it's not the 49ers. There's country-western music playing on the sound system, a definite switch from Miles Davis. I don't recognize the song, but unless it's a classic, I wouldn't.

"Have we met before?" Sienna says over the din. "I recognize you from somewhere."

My go-to would be the TED Talks or the books, but I know exactly where she knows me from. "We met, though not formally, at Knox's house the day you came to borrow Katie's ski pants." For some strange reason, I fixate on the fact that Katie's ski pants would be much too short for Sienna, but for all I know, she was borrowing them for someone else.

"Oh, that's right." She takes a good look at me. "You look different, though. The same but different."

I stare down at my jeans and sweater. "I wasn't dressed at the time. I mean, I was dressed but not dressed." I'm usually not so inarticulate. "I'd just gotten out of bed and was in a robe."

"Right." She nods, but I can see she's already thinking about something else. "Are you Knox's girlfriend?"

"No. We're friends."

"That makes sense. You don't at all seem like his type."

I wonder if I'm supposed to be offended. "What's his type?" I ask.

"Me."

This is where if I wanted to be a mean girl, a competitive girl, I would grin and say, "Not anymore." Instead, I successfully clutch all four drinks in my arms and walk away.

On my drive home, I get pulled over by a Ghost police officer. It's only the second time a cop has ever pulled me over. The first time was in college, when one of my taillights was out. He didn't even give me a fix-it ticket, just made me promise to have it repaired.

This is all to say that despite being a mature, professional, competent woman, I'm so flummoxed by the flashing lights that it takes me ten minutes to find a place to pull over. The crazy part is that I head in the direction of Misty's bungalow before I finally settle on a well-lit gas station. Because I am, or was, the daughter of a cop, I keep my hands on the steering wheel, even though my first impulse is to rifle through the glove box for my proof of insurance, then through my wallet for my license, so we can move this along. For the life of me, I don't know what I did wrong to get pulled over.

Then I remember the two drinks. While I'm nowhere near impaired, I'm petrified he'll give me a Breathalyzer test.

He's out of his car and motioning with his finger for me to unroll my window.

I crack it enough to have a conversation, letting in a rush of cold air. "Good evening, officer."

"Ma'am." He tips an imaginary hat. "License and registration, please."

I flip down my visor and hand him the registration, then slip my driver's license out of its plastic holder, debating with myself whether I should ask him why he stopped me. I opt to wait, preferring not to draw any more attention to my possible Ghost Ghoul breath than I have to.

He takes my information back to his patrol car, leaving me there to watch him in my rearview mirror and explore all the bad places this can go. At least I know a good lawyer. Unfortunately, Austin is the wrong kind of lawyer, and I'm not even sure we're still talking to each other anymore.

The police officer seems to be taking an inordinately long time. It's not as if I have any outstanding warrants or am on an FBI WANTED poster. My license, registration, and insurance are all up to date. I am a law-abiding citizen.

Finally, he comes wandering back, looking none too happy. But that might just be his natural demeanor. Who knows?

"I stopped you because you were weaving. Have you been drinking, ma'am?" He slides me back my stuff through the barely open window.

"I did have a drink at the Ghost Inn with some friends, officer. But I can assure you that I'm not the least bit impaired. Not even tipsy."

He illuminates my face with his flashlight, then sweeps it across the interior of my car. "Your daddy taught you better, girl."

At first, I don't think I hear him right. "Excuse me," I say.

"Drinking and driving. You know how many deaths result from drivers who swear they only had one drink? There were more than a thousand fatalities last year in this state alone."

"It's terrible, isn't it?"

He blinds me with his flashlight again. "And you, of all people, should know better."

I'm this close to saying, "Why?" Why me, of all people? But I'm not positive I wouldn't blow close to the legal limit if he were to test me. I've heard those Breathalyzers can be wildly inaccurate. So, I keep my mouth shut.

"Step out of the car, please."

This is when I know I'm in deep trouble. Even on a good day, I can't walk a straight line or touch my nose with my eyes closed. And the worst part of all, is the gas station where I've chosen to park is on top of a hill, a steep hill, where a person can get altitude sickness just from looking down at the twinkling lights of Ghost.

I do my best to make a graceful exit, which is instantly blown by the fact that my wallet, registration, and license are all in my lap. I quickly bend down to pick everything up off the pavement when I nearly topple headfirst over my feet.

"You should know that I'm afraid of heights," I tell the officer as I regain my balance.

"Right," he says. "And you should know that I've heard it all before."

"Look, I'm a licensed psychologist. Acrophobia is real. The DSM-5 defines it as an anxiety disorder. At least one in twenty people suffer from fear of heights; I happen to be one of them."

"We're not that high, Chelsea."

The use of my first name catches me off guard. How did we go from *ma'am* to *Chelsea* in under five minutes? I want to say, "We're not that familiar with each other," but decide it might antagonize him.

"Please take nine heel-to-toe steps, then turn around and come back to your starting point," he says.

"Like this?" I successfully complete the first few before getting tripped up on my number. I can't remember if I'm on four or five.

He stands there with his arms folded over his chest, no help at all. When I get back to my starting point, he asks, "Have you had any recent head injuries?"

"Why, yes, I have," I say almost gleefully. "I was hit by a cable car."

"Were you now?" He holds up a pen, taps the top, and starts moving it from side to side. "Follow the light, please."

I do it, though it hurts my eyes and seems like it should be illegal, like it might cause vision problems later on in life. "Don't I get a phone call or something?"

"For what?" he says, and sticks the pen in his uniform pocket. "Please raise one leg six inches off the ground and count in numerical order."

I try, but wind up grabbing onto his shoulder for support.

He softens. "This one is hard for everyone. Some people just have crappy balance."

"Don't forget, I also have head trauma."

"Yep, hit by a cable car. Where was that exactly?"

"San Francisco."

"Right."

"If you don't believe me, call San Francisco General. Even better, call the San Francisco Police Department."

"Leg, please." He points with his finger for me to raise it.

This time, I switch to my right leg, and am able to hold it up without falling. I manage to count to ten before he tells me to stop.

"How many drinks did you say you had?" He squints his eyes, closing in on me like we're in an interrogation room instead of a gas station on top of a hill.

"One," I say.

He gives me a hard look.

"Two, maybe."

"Is that such a good idea? You know, with your head trauma and all."

"Maybe not."

"I'm going to let you go this time. But I'm disappointed in you, Chels. I expected better. Your father expected better."

I don't understand why he keeps bringing my father into this. A man he doesn't even know. Then again, perhaps he's mistaken me for someone else.

"I appreciate it." It seems like a good thing to say to the person who stands between me and a jail cell. "I won't do it again, officer."

"I'm going to hold you to that," he says. "Now be careful when you pull out of here. I'll follow you down the hill." He waits for me to get in the car, then leans into my window with his arm resting on the roof. "Tell your dad hello from me."

The hairs on the back of my neck stand up. If he knows my father, there is only one way he can mean that. There's only one way I can tell Dad hello.

It's ridiculous, of course. And by the time I get to the highway, I decide that the officer thinks I'm someone else. Another Chelsea.

Chapter 14

From everything I can remember about my father, he was a good man. He loved us, Lolly and me. No matter what came later, I always knew that. I always knew that he loved us more than anything else in the world.

When we were little, three or four, he used to bounce us on his knee and sing, "Pony boy, pony boy, won't you be my pony boy. Don't say no, here we go, ride away with me. Giddy up! Giddy up! Pony my boy, hey." Then he'd throw us in the air to fits of giggles.

When we were a little older, he would make us elaborate pancakes for breakfast. Mickey Mouse, puppy dogs, gingerbread men, and big flowers decorated with icing.

As I got older and more independent, he let me cross the street to my friend's house by myself but would stand at the corner, watching me until I was safely at the door.

No one made us feel more secure than Dad, not even Mom. Part of it, I'm sure, was that he was a cop. A big, tall, handsome hero, who left home every day to fight the bad guys. He was the one we ran to after a bad dream. He's the one who would check for monsters under our beds, making a thorough sweep with his flashlight, shouting, "All clear" to prove it was safe.

He was the one no other man could live up to, not even Big Al Rosario.

Big Al was Dad's partner and the second most important man in our lives. Big Al could brighten a room just with his smile. It was electric, Mom used to say.

We loved him almost as much as we loved Dad.

I can still remember the days when Dad and Al would come home for lunch. Al tucking Lolly and me under each of his arms and carrying us across the living room, sideways, then dropping us on the sofa, making us laugh so hard, we'd pee our pants. Mom yelling at Al to knock it off, but she was laughing, too.

Al and his wife, Gloria, didn't have kids of their own, so Lolly and I became his surrogate ones. On our birthdays and Christmas, he'd buy out the toy store with gifts. My first Easy-Bake Oven, my third or fourth American Girl doll, and more electronics than I knew what to do with. The man would've bought me a pony if we'd had the room for it.

But for Mom, he gave her the biggest gift of all.

"I know you're safe out there," I once heard her telling Dad as she stood at the door, kissing him goodbye before he started his shift. "I know Big Al will never let anything happen to you. He loves you like a brother, Chris."

And even now, I know he did.

Once, they foiled a liquor store robbery. It was on Ventura Boulevard near Woodland Hills in broad daylight. A man, strung out on meth, went into the store and at gunpoint ordered the cashier to give him all his money. Luckily, the liquor store owner had recently installed a panic button under the counter and had trained all his employees how to use it. This particular cashier was the first to put the new panic button to the test.

When the call went out for a 211, Dad and Big Al responded. Dad liked to tell how he and Al were just two blocks away, eating hoagies outside the best sandwich shop in the valley. They'd put their soft drinks on the top of their patrol car and left so fast that when they got to the liquor store, the cups were still there; not a drop of soda had spilled. I doubt it really went down that way, but Dad never let the facts get in the way of a good story.

Inside, the robber had forced two customers behind the counter while he held the gun to the cashier's head as the poor man tried to open the safe. Dad and Al were supposed to wait for backup.

According to Dad and Al's version of the story, they rushed in anyway, entering from an alleyway at the rear of the store and using a small storage room for cover. It was a tricky operation. With hostages, anything can happen, and Dad and Al weren't exactly a SWAT team. And neither of them had hostage negotiation training.

As Dad liked to tell it, they'd just gone in, "guns blazing with their heads so far up their asses, they didn't stop to think about the ramifications."

What happened after that isn't completely clear, as Dad and Al changed the story so many times—with each new telling, they got more and more daring, more and more clever—that we'll never know for sure how it really happened. But by the time the cavalry showed up, Dad and Al had successfully handcuffed the robber without firing a shot, according to the official record. No one was hurt, everyone lived happily ever after, and Dad and Al got commendations.

That night, Mom and Gloria threw a big barbecue at our house, and all the families on the block came to give Dad and Al a hero's welcome. I remember Lolly and I being so proud that we took turns sitting on Dad's and Al's laps for the entire party.

It was after that that Al started coming around even when Dad wasn't home. I remember, even at eleven and twelve, wondering if things weren't good with him and Aunt Gloria.

Gloria was the opposite of Mom, who stayed at home, always baking cookies and volunteering at Lolly's and my school. Even back then, it was a novelty to have a stay-at-home mom. Most moms worked. Los Angeles is an expensive place to live, and one salary isn't usually enough to cut it.

Sometimes, to add a little to the coffers, Mom would freelance for a neighbor who had her own organization business. Together, they would go to people's homes and whip messy garages into shape or reorganize closets and storage sheds. Once, they even did a hoarder's house, Mom regaling us with stories about how the woman had taken over an entire bedroom with shipping pallets of every shape and size. She told Mom that she couldn't stand the thought of throwing away perfectly good wood.

But the organization jobs were few and far between. And Mom liked it that way, because she wanted to be home for Lolly, Dad, and me.

Aunt Gloria, on the other hand, owned her own hair salon. Lolly and I loved sitting in the swivel hair chairs and spinning around until we were dizzy. The shop had six stations and a waiting area with cheetah-print couches and every fashion magazine under the sun. Before she got famous, Charlize Theron used to go there.

Where Mom was traditional—always in jeans and a crisp white blouse—Aunt Gloria liked to push the limits. Red leather pants, cropped tops, high-heeled shoes, and big hoop earrings. Her hair color changed with the seasons. Platinum-blond in summer, auburn red in fall, inky black in winter, and chestnut brown in spring.

I once heard Big Al tell Mom that he wished Aunt Gloria wouldn't dress that way. That it embarrassed him. I loved it, though. She was brash and bold and, in my eyes, glamorous.

Every Easter, she would do Lolly's and my hair. First, she'd shampoo us in the sink bowls in the back of the salon, then take an inch or two off our long locks and add in a few layers. She spent at least forty-five minutes blowing each of us out with a large round brush that made our hair big and fluffy. No one did it like Aunt Gloria.

But even to a little girl, it was clear that Al and Gloria were on the rocks, their marriage on life support. The thing was, Big Al loved her. Even to a little girl, that was clear, too. He used to follow her with his eyes wherever she went and brag about her accomplishments to my parents.

That's why it was doubly sad when we'd find him sleeping on our couch on a random morning or find him scrounging through our refrigerator when Lolly and I got home from school. Dad had been promoted to sergeant and was home less and less, whereas Big Al was there more and more.

As I remember everything, or at least everything a twelve-year-old has the capacity to understand or process, I think about Knox. I think about Knox and Brody and Sienna. I think about Austin and me. Mary. I think about Sadie. I think about the countless couples I've counseled. About all the love triangles I've seen in my practice, none of them ending as tragically as the way it did with my parents.

Mom had taken Lolly and me to visit Uncle Sylvester. He and the show's developers had just finished a teen television series, and we were getting to meet the cast. Afterward, Uncle Sylvester was taking us out for a fancy dinner to celebrate, and we were staying the night with him in his Century City apartment. Dad couldn't come because he had to work.

It was an exciting day, our first time on a Hollywood set—at least, Lolly's and mine. Mom had been to others with Uncle Sylvester. Although the actors weren't on our radar at the time, the idea of meeting famous people, movie stars, put us over the moon. I'd changed my outfit for the big occasion at least three times. Even the dinner was magical. Uncle Sylvester let us order anything we wanted, and Mom even let us have small sips of her champagne.

We were outside the restaurant, waiting for the valet to bring around Uncle Sylvester's car, when Mom got the phone call. Big Al had been injured on duty, and no one could find Aunt Gloria. Could Mom come to the hospital?

We raced across the Westside, taking Laurel Canyon to the valley, where Mom dropped us home in Porter Ranch, asking a neighbor to watch us while she went to Sherman Oaks Hospital. She couldn't find Dad, but that wasn't unusual. He worked the night shift, often supervising arrest scenes where he was unreachable to anyone outside of the department.

Only through my own memories and police reports have I been able to piece together the sequence of events that led to what happened in our family home the next day. What led to the shootings of both my parents.

Big Al had ripped his calf open and hit his head on a cement bollard while trying to jump a chain-link fence during a foot chase in Canoga Park. Apparently, there'd been a string of break-ins there, and Al wanted to relive his glory days from when he and Dad had busted the liquor store robber. The hospital was keeping him overnight for observation.

He was expected to make a full recovery. And he eventually did, at least for the torn calf and concussion.

After a long visit with Al, my mother went to his house. Her mission was twofold. Find Gloria and pick up clothes for Al, so he'd have something to wear home from the hospital. No one was there when she got to Al and Gloria's, but she had a key. We took care of the Rosarios' cat, Tweety, when they went on vacations. They in turn watered our plants and picked up our mail when we went out of town.

We were two families that shared everything, and that was our undoing.

My mother made her way up the staircase to Al's bedroom. And when she opened the door, she found my father in bed with Gloria.

Lolly and I were asleep when Mom got home, but in the middle of the night, we were awakened by yelling. I remember Lolly getting out of her bed and climbing in with me.

Mom was shouting at Dad that she was going to tell Al everything and that she wanted a divorce. I heard the front door slam. And when I ran to the window, Dad was driving away.

But when Lolly and I woke up Sunday morning, he was there, in the kitchen, ready to make his famous pancakes. Mom hadn't gotten up yet, so we had breakfast without her. Dad said he'd clean up and told Lolly and me to go outside and play.

Then Dad shot Mom in their bed. Even from the sidewalk, we could hear the gunfire. Three loud pops . . . then a fourth one. When the police arrived, they found Dad lying next to Mom, with his service weapon still in his mouth.

Later, Gloria told investigators that she and Dad had been involved for more than a year. The night I saw him drive away, he'd gone to Gloria's to end it. To end it for good.

Neither Al nor Gloria came to the funeral. I remember waiting for him. I remember hoping he would take Lolly and me, that we could live with him in our house instead of going to Uncle Sylvester's. Not that we didn't love our uncle; we just loved Al more.

But we never saw Big Al Rosario again.

Last I heard, he and Gloria were divorced, and Al retired from LAPD and was living near Reno, Nevada, in a gated community.

I think back on that day with so many *what if*s. And so many questions. Ultimately, I could never understand why he'd done it. Why Dad took Mom's life.

Knowing my father the way I did, I can see his shame, his abject misery. I can see how he believed there was no coming back from his infidelity with Gloria. Maybe from my mother. Maybe with time, she would forgive him for the affair.

But Al never would. And he couldn't live with that.

I like to think that he couldn't live without my mother, either, and he knew that she couldn't live without him. So in those final minutes, with his finger on the trigger, he committed the ultimate act of love. The ultimate act of sacrifice.

But I keep coming back to the same brutal truth. It may have been love, it may have been sacrifice, but ultimately, it was an extreme act of selfishness. And no matter how much I try to romanticize it or even exonerate my father for what he did, every fiber of me knows it was warped and unforgivable.

Chapter 15

My laptop will be ready at noon, so I decide to kill time by having breakfast in Ghost. There's a cute café around the corner from Main Street. Austin and I used to talk about trying it, because every time we walked by, it smelled so enticing. Like fresh baked bread. We were also taken with the name. Hugs with Mugs. But we never made it past the door. The wait was always too long.

Today is no different. The place is swamped, with a line out the door. It's a sea of plaid shirts. Who knew everyone in this town loved breakfast so much? I write my name on the list and find an unoccupied corner in which to wait, because it's too cold to stand outside.

The restaurant is larger than it looks from the street. There's a to-go counter where customers can pick up a coffee drink and a pastry. Everything looks so mouthwatering; I'm tempted to try one of the cinnamon rolls or a morning bun while I wait for my name to be called. But the line at the to-go counter is also insane.

The Hugs with Mugs theme is everywhere in the form of giant hearts painted on the walls and rows of mugs hanging from hooks on the wainscoting chair rail. The idea being to choose one before being served. There's no rhyme or reason to the mugs, just a random collection of cups in various colors, shapes, and sizes. Some of them have names on them, and I wonder if they're reserved for regulars.

The hostess, a young woman with a pierced eyebrow and dreadlocks, says there's a seat available at the counter if I don't want to wait. It's a cramped spot in the corner. but I take it, grabbing a mug with a bright yellow smiley face on the way.

The proprietors haven't gotten around to taking down the Halloween decorations. There are still plastic cobwebs and fake bats and spiders above the backbar. The menu is huge, at least twelve pages, and I flip through it, trying to decide what to eat. A server fills my smiley-face cup, then dances away to fill a request for more syrup from a diner on the other end of the counter.

The elderly man next to me pays his bill and leaves. Next thing I know, Sadie's sitting beside me.

"Fancy meeting you here," she says. "Actually, I saw you through the window."

"Don't you have to open up Flower Power?"

"Not for another hour. But I thought I'd get a jump on things."

I hand her my menu, because she doesn't have one. "What's good here?"

"Everything. Well, not everything. Stay away from the black bean chili omelet, it'll give you the trots."

"Good to know," I say.

"The pancakes are out of this world and probably what they're most known for."

I'd noted that there were at least a dozen different versions on the menu.

"I'm getting a carrot-cake muffin and a side of scrambled eggs," Sadie says. "It's my go-to."

She does just that when the server comes to take our orders. Despite Sadie's recommendation, I get the cinnamon swirl French toast.

Since my last breakfast with Dad, I've never eaten pancakes again.

"You want to talk about it?" I cut to the chase, because I can sense it; a good therapist always can. She wants to finish what she started last night.

"Talk about what?"

I turn in my stool and hold eye contact with her. "Whatever's going on with you and your husband."

She takes a long sip of her coffee and stares at me over the rim of the cup. It's got a peace sign on it. "Oh, that." She lets out a long breath. "He's been seeing another woman for at least two years, as far as I can tell. Truthfully, I don't know why he hasn't left me yet. I guess it's the kids."

"How do you know this?" It's not really important how she knows, but to have the full picture, I need the backstory. The who, what, when, where, and why. It just makes it easier to put everything into perspective.

"What? That he's been seeing her for at least two years?" She shrugs. "I have the password to his phone. You'd think if a man was going to carry on a secret affair, he'd change his stupid password. But not Frank. Who knows, maybe he wanted me to find out?

"Anyway, his phone was going off one day like a rocket. Every five seconds or so, it would vibrate with a new incoming text. He's a Caltrans employee and works a lot of nights and was sleeping. I figured if someone needed to get a hold of him so badly that they were texting every few seconds, it had to be important.

"Instead of waking him up, I took the liberty of looking myself. It was her. She was pissed that he'd broken a date with her over the weekend. It had been our twentieth wedding anniversary, and I'd twisted his arm to take me out to a nice restaurant, a place where they didn't have chicken fingers on the menu. That's why he broke their date, because he was out with his wife. Can you imagine that she actually had the nerve to be angry about that?"

Sadie falls quiet as I'm served a heaping plate of French toast and she a plate of eggs. Her muffin is the size of a human head.

"They don't mess around here as far as portion sizes, do they?"

She nods.

"What happened then?" I ask. "Did you confront him?"

"No. I took his phone to the bathroom, locked the door, and read two years of texts. Two years of him lying to me."

"And how did that make you feel?" I realize I've slipped back into marriage-counselor mode and question whether Sadie just wants a friend. Because then the response should've simply been *I'm sorry.*

"A lot of things," she says, seemingly unoffended by my clinical approach. "Hate, betrayal, broken. But mostly fear. This is going to sound pathetic, absolutely pitiful, but I was afraid he was going to leave me."

"Because you love him?"

She lets out a raspy, bitter laugh. "I hate his guts. No, love has nothing to do with it. Do you know how much I make at Flower Power?"

I shake my head.

"A little more than minimum wage. Do you know how much it costs to raise a family, put a roof over your kids' heads, feed them, buy them expensive tennis shoes because that's what all their friends are wearing? Frank and I barely make it on both our salaries. How are we supposed to do it if we have to support two households instead of one? Add to that that I really love my life and don't want to lose it. My house, my neighborhood, my job, my friends. It's all I have, and if Frank leaves me, I can pretty much kiss it all goodbye."

Nothing Sadie has said surprises me. One of the top reasons unhappy couples stay together is for financial reasons.

"So how do you manage, knowing your husband is cheating?" I ask the question without judgment. Neutral.

"I pretend he's not and continue to live my beautiful life. That doesn't mean I don't fantasize that I'll win the lottery and leave him. Or that I don't wonder what it would be like to fall in love again, to be with someone who wants me as much as I want him." She takes a bite of her carrot-cake muffin. "Do you think it's wrong, like I'm living a lie and setting a bad example for my children?"

"There is no right or wrong, Sadie. Only you can know what's best for you. But has it ever occurred to you that it doesn't have to be all or nothing? In other words, there are other options besides staying with a cheating husband in exchange for the life you want, or leaving him and losing that life. For example, you could try to fix the marriage; you could both try to love each other again."

"How?" Her eyes flicker with something akin to hope.

"First, you can acknowledge to him that you know about this other woman. And then the two of you can get yourself to a good family therapist."

"You?" she says.

"I don't see patients anymore, Sadie. But I can recommend someone, someone really good."

"What if he doesn't want to stop seeing her? What if telling him I know gives him what he needs to leave me? Where would I be then?"

"I guess it's a chance you'll have to take if you want to save your marriage. Because, Sadie, make no mistake about it. What you have now is not a marriage."

I think about Sadie's dilemma for the rest of the day, about marriage, about how fragile relationships are, and the extraordinary lengths couples will go to save them, even when they're unsalvageable. I think about all the times couples came to me, fighting to stay together when it was plain to see that their expiration date was looming. I think about Austin and me, about how I thought he would give me security, and in the end, he pulled the rug right out from under me.

Yet, there's a part of me that still hasn't given up on love, even if Austin is out of the picture.

I take the long way back from the computer store and wind up at Knox's, telling myself that we still have an unresolved bill from the work he did. He greets me at the door, Bailey beside him, barking up a storm. All it takes is a brief sniff of my outreached hand for the dog to quiet down and wander back inside the house.

"We have to square up," I tell Knox, waving my checkbook in the air. "Or would you prefer Venmo?"

Knox scrubs his hands through his wet hair. "Do we have to do this now? I just woke up."

It's then that I notice that all he has on is a towel wrapped around his waist. I turn, so I'm not staring directly at his bare chest, even though that's all I want to do. Stare at his chest.

"And you're a farmer's son?" I say, hoping that if I talk, he won't see my reaction to his nearly naked body. "It's almost suppertime."

"I was writing all night and all morning. I have a full rough draft now."

"Seriously? That's fantastic, Knox." I brush past him, uninvited, and head to the kitchen. "I'll make you coffee."

"Let me get dressed." He climbs the stairs and vanishes down the hallway.

There's a bag of coffee beans on the kitchen counter, and I measure out enough for a full pot, then flip on the grinder. I should probably let Knox do it, because his coffee is better than mine. But he's done it for me so many times, it's only fair that I return the favor.

"If I'd known about your book, I would've brought a bottle of champagne to celebrate."

Knox is back and rummaging through the fridge. He holds up a bottle of prosecco. "Best I can do."

"It'll work," I say, finding two flutes in one of the cupboards and pouring us each a glass. "Prost!" I clink mine to his.

"Prost."

For the next sixty minutes, we drink prosecco and coffee and talk about his rough draft and all the ways he intends to massage it to make it his final draft. I don't know anything about plant-based biofuels, but Knox is apparently one of the foremost authorities on it in the country.

I get up to pour him another cup of coffee. "I saw your ex last night." I debate on how much to tell him and decide that in the short time I've known him, there have been no secrets between us. Why start now? "According to Sadie, Ginger, and Amanda, Sienna's marriage is on the rocks. Of course, that could just be idle gossip. No one knows the truth about a marriage except the two people in it."

"It's not just idle gossip," Knox says. "Sienna's miserable. And Brody is a son of a bitch."

"How do you know? I mean that Sienna is miserable. I assume Brody is just a son of a bitch in general."

Knox's lips hitch up. "Yeah, he is. I used to love that about him. Not so much in this context, though. Sienna told me herself."

"That she's miserable, or that Brody is a son of a bitch?"

"Both. But the latter went without saying."

"She just came over and told you that her marriage was in crisis and that she was miserable?" In my business, I don't find too many people willing to admit that they made a terrible mistake, that they chose the wrong partner. If anything, they fill Facebook and Instagram with false pictures of their so-called happy lives.

"We talk."

It's all I can do to stop myself from saying, "When?" But I'm afraid that it's overstepping. Or worse, that I sound jealous, even territorial. Instead, I ask, "Are you feeling a sense of schadenfreude?"

"Not really. I'm sorry she's unhappy. Does it change the fact that I'm still angry at her? No."

"No?" I hitch my brows.

He laughs. "Like I told you before, she and I were done even before we were done."

"So, you'd never take her back? You'd never try to make a go of it, even though you once loved her. And I'm assuming, judging by the fact that you listened to one of my TED Talks, that you loved her very much."

"I did, but I wouldn't," he says emphatically. "Sometimes it takes distance to see all the things you weren't getting from a person, all the things she wasn't giving. Sometimes it takes distance to even know you need those things to be happy. Healthy. And then it hits you. It wasn't her I wanted, it was the picture of the life I thought she represented."

"Do you still want that life?"

He nods. "The picture of that life never went away. Who I'm destined to share it with is the murky part." He looks at me, really looks. "If only we all had a crystal ball, right?"

"If only."

And then he does the last thing I expect him to.

He pulls me up from the kitchen chair, takes me in his arms, and kisses me, his lips moving over mine heatedly, desperately, more passionately than I've ever been kissed before. And as I stand there, wrapped in his arms, I can feel that the kiss is a prelude to something else. Something more meaningful than just sex and even more significant than his heart. It's a prelude to that picture, the picture of the life he wants.

Chapter 16

The next morning—strong coffee running through my veins—I do what I said I'd never do again. I drive up the mountain to Misty's bungalow, holding my breath the whole way. I swear that by the time I reach her driveway, I'll either asphyxiate or pee my pants.

Possibly both.

As per her instructions, I've tried her exercises, a bizarre series of puzzles that are supposed to unblock me. I have no idea whether they're working.

I went so far as to Google them on my now-fixed computer to see if they're even legit. But I couldn't find anything about them on the Internet. Not surprising. And while it should make me even more skeptical—and I'm already pretty damned skeptical—it only adds to Misty's mystique. And my deep-rooted desire to get to the truth, even if it means driving straight up a mountain for some Kabuki theater.

As I pull into Misty's driveway, my cotton shirt is sticking to my back, and my sweat has turned cold. But I'm here now; the worst is over. I gather up my purse and put on my coat, struggling with getting it on in the tight confines of my car. When I left the cabin, it was forty-two degrees.

I'm just about to exit the car when I get a text from Austin. My initial instinct is to ignore it. It's probably another plea for me to give up Christmas at the cabin. Why give myself something to get worked up over? Something more to "block me." But despite myself, I take a peek anyway.

Chelsea,

No one has heard from you since the last time we talked, and we continue to worry about you. Ronnie says you haven't been in touch with her in days. She says you're not responding to any of her emails, texts, or phone calls. I'm not trying to pressure you. If you need a break after everything that you've been through that's understandable. I know how badly you were in need of a vacation (you work too hard) and if this is your way of checking out, I get it. I really do. But please drop her a quick line (or me for that matter) to let us know that everything is okay.

Yours,

Austin

I don't know why he sends texts as if they're letters. But for as long as I've known him, he writes them formally that way. Like he's an old man.

I quickly tap out a message to Ronnie.

Austin says you've been trying to reach me. My email wasn't working for a while, but I've since had it fixed. Hopefully by now you've received the email I sent you this morning. I don't know why we haven't been able to reach each other by phone. I've tried you repeatedly but you don't answer. I'm leaving tonight to make my flight to Albuquerque in the morning. We'll touch base then. All is well on my end. Hope the same for you.

I hit the send button and get out of the car, taking the stairs to Misty's front porch. She opens the door before I can knock.

"Come in." She moves aside.

I'm hit with a rush of warm air. As we enter the living room, I see she has a big fire going. There's a plate of cheese and crackers on the burlwood table and a carafe of wine, like we're having a picnic. It was only about an hour ago that I had breakfast.

"This is lovely," I say.

"Did you do the exercises?"

"Yes. But I don't understand. How is doing a word puzzle going to unblock me?"

"It's not the puzzle. It's the words. We'll see if it makes a difference. Is there anything to report?"

"Like what?" The question throws me. It's almost as if she knows all the things that have happened since I left here five days ago, and she's testing me.

"Like anything illuminating or confusing or just plain wonderful."

Yes, to all of the above.

"There was this one thing. A police officer pulled me over the other night." This is how I start, because I'm not sure I want to get into the others. I especially don't want to tell her about Knox's kiss, because it's still too fresh, too new, too wonderful. And I want to preserve it all for myself. "The cop said I was weaving, which I wasn't. In any event, he kept referencing my father. Stuff like 'Your daddy taught you better, girl.' And 'You of all people should know better.' It was as if he knew my late father was a cop, like he was intimately familiar with my family. When he sent me on my way, he told me to say hello to my father for him, which is impossible, because my father is deceased. Dead. Besides, there's no way he could possibly know my father."

"Are you sure?"

"Positive."

"Hmm. What do you think?" Misty asks.

"I think it was probably a case of mistaken identity. But it was . . . eerie just the same."

"Why?"

"I don't know. I suppose if I believed in the . . . supernatural"—I hesitate to use the word *woo-woo* as not to offend her—"it would be a message of some sort, foreshadowing."

"As far as the *supernatural*, you're here, aren't you?" She fills two glasses with a heavy pour of wine and hands me one. It's only ten. I'm starting to think Misty might have a drinking problem.

"Foreshadowing of what?" she wants to know.

"Aren't you supposed to tell me?" I can analyze myself till the cows come home; I don't need Misty for that.

She takes both my hands and closes her eyes, like she did the last two times, then does her concentration thing. Whether it's real or not . . . well, who can say?

"I'm seeing a gas station," she says, pushing her face forward like she's there. Like she's at the gas station. "The one at the top of Cascade Road, not far from here. You're anxious." Her eyes pop open. "I wasn't aware you were afraid of heights."

I nod, stunned. I never told her that.

She closes her eyes again. "He's there with you. Lights. I see shining lights. You're walking." She shakes her head. "Give me a second. I've lost it. Wait, wait, it's back. He calls you by name."

"He did. But so what? He saw my license. My name is printed right there on the front."

Misty ignores me and continues to remain in her trancelike state or whatever she's doing. "The man, the police officer. He knows your father. Christopher. Is that the officer's name?"

"No, it was something that started with a *J*. J. Toomey." I remember, because I looked at the brass plate on his uniform. "My father's name is Christopher. Chris. He went by Chris."

"Ahh. Well, they know each other. Or knew."

"How?" What are the chances that a cop in Ghost would know my late father, a former LAPD sergeant?

"I don't know," Misty says. She releases my hands and opens her eyes.

"If he knew my father, knew he was dead, why would he tell me to pass on my regards to him? It seems cruel, or at the very least, insensitive." I'm still not buying it.

"He may not know that your father died." She passes me the cheese platter, but who can eat at a time like this?

"I still believe it was a case of mistaken identity," I say. "He thought I was a different Chelsea and mistook my dead father for the other Chelsea's living one."

"Perhaps." But she's just appeasing me, I can see it in her eyes, in her body language.

Yet, there's the whole Christopher thing to work out. How would Misty know my father's name, other than to have done a full vetting of me beforehand? Which is highly possible, but also highly unlikely.

"Shall we move on?" she says.

"Yes, let's do Lolly now." Because that's what I really came for.

Misty swirls her wineglass and takes a sip. "I'll see how far I get. But your sister is a puzzler. You, on the other hand, have opened up some. It's the exercises. I'm sure of it."

I'm not, but it won't help my cause to contradict her, so I flash a wan smile.

She sees right through it, because she shakes her head. "I can tell you think so, too. Give me a little time to recuperate before we start in on your sister. Unfortunately, I'm not a machine."

She gets up and begins doing these weird squats in the middle of the living room. Then ballet pliés. They're rather good. Graceful.

"Did you used to be a dancer?" I ask.

"Not professionally. But I took a lot of classes."

It's then that I notice her flowy, stretchy yoga pants. For reasons I can't pin down, they look familiar, like I've seen the print—a succession of dog paws—a dozen times before. Which is strange, because it's not at all a common pattern.

"Where did you get those?" I point to her pants.

"I made them. Why?"

"They're lovely. Really different."

"I can make you a pair if you like."

I don't have a ready response. Really, as cheerful as the print is, I would have no place to wear something like that. But I don't want to hurt Misty's feelings. She's obviously proud of the pants, and she probably put a lot of work into making them.

"Then they wouldn't be one of a kind," I say.

"No, that's true, they wouldn't be."

I can see she's giving her offer second thoughts. "I can make you a different pair."

"That's very generous of you. Thank you."

"Okay, let's try this again." She achieves the fifth position, arms en haut, and I'm unsure if she's talking about ballet or Lolly.

Which is when she sits down across from me again and does her thing of holding my hands and closing her eyes. I immediately flash to Knox and his comment about crystal balls, about the desire to conquer our present fears by seeing the future. By knowing that whatever bad thing is happening now, there's proof of something great right around the corner.

And then I realize I've been going about this all wrong. That I have been asking for the answers to the wrong questions.

"Never mind about Lolly," I say. "What's my future?"

Misty sighs, long and hard. Apparently, it's a standard request, the garage band's equivalent of "Sweet Home Alabama" for psychics. "You sure you want to do this? You may not like what I see."

"Yes, I'm sure." Whatever she sees can't be worse than losing my parents at the tender age of twelve or my husband's love at the fragile age of thirty-six or having a sister who barely speaks to me, lest I forget getting hit by a cable car.

Misty lets go of my hands and rises to her feet. "First, you'll have to sign a legal waiver." She makes her way across the room to a chest of drawers, and after some searching, finds what she's looking for and hands it to me with a Mont Blanc pen. "Right there at the bottom."

I skim the contract. Basically, it's a promissory note not to sue. People are so litigious these days. I sign with a flourish.

Chelsea Knight of sound mind and sound body hereby gives Misty (no last name) express permission to tell me my future.

Though I think for the waiver to be truly legal, it needs to be notarized.

Satisfied, Misty carefully slips the signed contract back inside the drawer, lights a circle of tea candles, and dims a few lights. I can't tell if it's for ambiance or part of the ritual.

Returning to her usual position, she says, "This is your last chance to back out."

"I'm good."

"That's what you say now." It should sound ominous, but I take it with a grain of salt.

I'm ready to see it, to see my future.

She bobs her head, silently acquiescing, then slips off into the land of the fortune tellers. "You're all in white," she says. "A wedding gown, maybe. No, no, it's a shroud. Wait a minute, I see both. Hmm."

"What? Is it bad? What does the white shroud mean?" I don't like the sound of it. I like the wedding gown better.

"I'm not sure. It's not always a literal translation; often it's a symbol for something else. Then again, sometimes a pickle is just a pickle." She laughs, which seems in bad taste, since a white shroud to me is synonymous with death.

"Am I going to die?"

"We're all going to die, sweetie."

"Like soon. Is that what you're seeing?"

"Shush." She's rocking back and forth, humming. "There's a man, a handsome man. He's by your side, he's crying."

"Who is he? Knox? Austin?"

"A tall man. Older. Your past. No, your future. Wait, there's two of them. Two men. No wait, three. The man in the tower, the same one on the street."

"What tower?"

"Is his name Mark?"

Oh, for goodness sake, could she please commit to at least one thing? And who the hell is Mark? "There is no Mark in my life."

"They're besides themselves with grief."

"Why are they grieving?"

"They love you. Yes, that's coming across strongly. I can feel it in the room. They're pleading with you. They want you back."

"Austin? Is it Austin?"

"Who's Austin?"

"My ex-husband?" I already told her this the last time. And she already went through the same song and dance about the three men. And yet, I'm hanging on her every word.

"I don't know," she says. "The older one feels more like a relative."

"That doesn't make sense. Why would a relative want me back?"

"Your father, maybe. You said his name is Christopher, right?"

"Right. Chris. Is it him?"

"I don't know. I feel his presence, but the older man . . . Ugh. It's frenetic. There's a lot happening around you. A lot to wade through. So many people."

"What about Knox? Do you see him, too?"

"Who's Knox?"

"My handyman," is all I say, because I don't know what he is, only that I'm falling for him.

"I see him," she says. "Plaid tie. No, it's a plaid shirt. He doesn't want you to leave. He's holding on, but you're slipping away from him. You won't take the jump. Wait . . . wait. Dammit!"

"What? What do you see?"

"I'm losing it. Everything has gone dark." Misty opens her eyes. "It was there, right in front of me, and then it disappeared, like a blank screen. We'll have to try again in the morning."

"But I can't, I'm leaving town. Can't we rest for a little while and do it again, like in an hour?"

"I'm sorry, I have another appointment. Your time is up."

"Seriously? It seems like we were making excellent progress. What about after your appointment? I can leave later, extend my time here."

"I'm booked solid today. I have time next week. Come back then."

Before I know it, she's pushing me toward the door. I'm not a paranoid person, but I'm getting the sense that Misty may have seen something she doesn't want to share with me. Something catastrophic.

I go over everything she said the whole way down the mountain, dissecting each one of her visions. I am so lost in my head, I forget my fear of heights and make it to the flats without hyperventilating. A small blessing. But I'm no further ahead than I was when I started. In fact, I'm more confused than ever.

So instead of focusing on myself, I swing by Flower Power. It's on my way out of town, and I've compiled a list of local marriage counselors for Sadie. I've checked out their credentials, and they're all top-notch.

I surreptitiously slide the list to Sadie when Ginger isn't looking.

"When will you be back?" Sadie says.

"Hopefully next weekend." But I know it's only wishful thinking. As soon as I return to work, it will suck me in and spin me out until I'm completely consumed by it again.

"We'll miss you for happy hour," Ginger says. "Can't you work remotely? It seems like that's what everyone is doing nowadays."

"I need to be based in San Francisco, near an airport." My stomach fills with dread. For the first time, I'm not so wowed by the idea of traipsing across the country, giving my spiels to sold-out rooms. It's probably just the accident. Once I get in the groove again, I'll remember all the reasons I loved it so much.

I move in to hug both women goodbye. In the short time we've been acquainted, it feels like I've known them my whole life. And like they know me, a different me than the one I really am, the me I wish I was.

"Let us know as soon as you're up again," Sadie says, and pushes a bouquet of pink stargazer lilies into my hand. "For the ride to the city. They'll make your car smell good."

She's not kidding. The flowers are incredibly fragrant, like perfume.

On my way to the car, I see Katie on Main Street, sitting on a bench, eating a sandwich. I wave and cross over.

"I heard you're going back to the city today," she says, and makes room for me on the bench.

"Yep. I'll be back, though. Next weekend or the weekend after."

"We'll miss you at happy hour." She wraps up the rest of her sandwich and sticks it in her backpack. "I've decided to go back to school."

"Really? That's great." I know Knox will be happy to hear the news, if he hasn't already. "Something for urban planning?"

"Nah, urban planning sounded interesting in the beginning, but I quickly figured out it wasn't for me. I've decided to teach high school. I'm going back to school for a teaching credential. Then I'll see if I can get a gig around here."

"Congratulations. Do you know where you're going yet?"

"I've applied to both UC Davis and Sacramento State. We'll see," she says.

"Well, I think it's wonderful, Katie."

"Knox about shit his pants when I told him. To tell you the truth, it was the last straw for him when my car died on me and he picked up the tab for a new one."

"He's just worried about you, Katie. He loves you and wants to know that you're taken care of."

"Yeah, the whole big sibling thing. I get it."

We spend a few more minutes talking about her plans for the future, how she wants to get a new place instead of the crappy studio she's renting, and how it won't be the same without me popping into the hotel when she's on bartending duty.

"Yeah," I say, "I'll miss it, too." But instead of dwelling on how sad it makes me, I hug Katie goodbye and promise to stop in at the bar the next time I'm here.

On the drive home, I let Katie's words sink in—*the whole big sibling thing*—and reflect on my relationship with Lolly. It's no secret that I wasn't there for her. After the situation with my parents, I wasn't even there for myself.

My mourning period lasted until I went away to boarding school in Santa Barbara. And even then, what transpired in our house in Porter Ranch never really went away. There are still times when a backfiring car or an explosion of fireworks can instantly transport me back to that day. To the gunshots, the chilling sound of sirens, and the swirl of chaos only found at a crime scene.

In certain ways, leaving Uncle Sylvester and Lolly was my salvation. Being in an unfamiliar place with unfamiliar people allowed me to reinvent my tragic history, or at least hide from it. And I took it, grabbed it with both hands, never stopping to consider that I was Lolly's sole support system. While Uncle Sylvester loved and provided for us, he was mostly an absentee guardian. Besides, he wasn't a survivor of a murder-suicide in the same way that we were. What should've bonded Lolly and me, tore us apart.

I remember one of my first cases, a couple who lost a child to crib death. It was one of those horrific, tragic, unexplained deaths that's a parent's worst nightmare. They came to see me because the death of their baby had understandably destroyed them. It had also destroyed their marriage.

For months, we worked on trying to separate their grief from the way they felt about each other. But no matter how hard they tried, they couldn't get back to where they started. The death of their baby had indelibly changed them. They were no longer the same people they were when they fell in love. They were no longer compatible.

I'm not saying that's what happened with Lolly and me. What I'm saying is that I ran away from the past, and anyone who reminded me of it, instead of confronting it head on.

And look where that got me.

Chapter 17

Knox is waiting for me when I get home. He let himself in and made a pot of coffee.

"For the road," he says, and holds up an insulated driving cup that he must've brought from home, because I don't own one.

"I saw Katie when I left town. She says she's going back to school to get her teaching credential. That's got to make you happy."

He rocks his hand from side to side. "Happier than her dedicating her life to working in a bar. But guess who'll wind up paying her tuition?" He snorts. "But I didn't come here to talk about Katie."

"Oh. What did you come to talk about?"

"I came to tell you that I don't want you to go." He holds up his hand. "Before you say anything, think about it."

"Think about me staying?"

"Or you leaving. It's a supremely bad idea."

"Not if I want to continue keeping a roof over my head and, you know, eat. But tell me why it's a supremely bad idea."

He locks eyes with me, his eyes sadder than I've ever seen them. "Because once you go, you won't come back."

"Of course I will. San Francisco is only two hours away. It's even closer to Davis. We can meet in the middle for coffee."

He turns away, but it's only for a moment. Just enough time so that I won't see the desolation there, the utter anguish. But I already have.

"Knox, what's going on here?"

"Let's go for a walk," he says out of the blue. Or perhaps it's a way to buy time so he can continue to try to persuade me to stay.

"I have to get on the road. It's getting late."

"It won't take long. I want to show you something."

I know it's a ploy, a stall tactic. It doesn't matter, because I'm already second-guessing myself for leaving, anyway. It's been so good for me here. Not only have Lolly and I made progress, but I've made so many friends in the last two weeks. And Knox. Not one day has gone by since I got here that it wasn't Knox instead of Austin.

"Let's go then."

He takes my hand, and the next thing I know, we're getting in his truck.

"Hey, what happened to a walk? This looks a lot like driving, Hart."

He grins. "We have to drive to get to the place where we walk. You'll see. I promise it'll be worth it."

Soon, we're driving up a steep grade, and I'm starting to question whether this is a good idea.

"Where is this place?" I ask as my ears pop.

"Not much farther. Trust me."

We pass a sign that says GHOST MINE HISTORIC STATE PARK, and Knox parks in a small gravel lot in front of the visitor center, a chalet-style wooden building with lush gardens. I hop out of his truck and read the historical marker at the tip of the parking lot.

"Ghost Mine State Historic Park was one of the oldest,

deepest and richest gold mines in California," the placard reads. "In operation for more than a century, miners here extracted more than seven million ounces of gold before the mine was shuttered in 1950. The park features many of the mine's original buildings, three hundred miles of abandoned mine shafts, and fifteen miles of trails."

The park is both beautiful and creepy, if a place can be both. I can sense death here. Both the miners, like the Ramsey family for whom the town was named Ghost, and the near genocide of the native Americans who lived here before the Forty-Niners came to reap their fortunes.

The other creepy thing about the park is that it's empty. Not a soul to see, a ghost town, if you will.

"Is this what you wanted to show me?" I shield my eyes with my hand and look out into the distance.

"Nope. It's up there." He points to a trailhead, then takes my hand.

I try to stop to read another marker, but he pulls me along. "You can read it later."

"What's the hurry?" I ask, then remember that I still have the two-hour drive to San Francisco. I'm already contemplating pushing the drive until tomorrow, but even if I left at the crack of dawn, it would be cutting it too close for my flight to Albuquerque.

"The light's just right," he says. "If we don't hurry, we'll miss it."

I try to match his long strides by speed-walking. What I don't account for is my shoes. They're slip-on loafers, and under regular circumstances are plenty sensible enough. But between the rugged terrain and the thistle, I'd be better off in hiking boots. Faster.

And then there is the small issue that I've never been terribly fit, catching only sporadic workouts in hotel gyms or walks from my condo to my office on the streets of San Francisco. Laughably, the route is flat as a pancake, not what you would expect from a city known for its hills. This is all to say that I'm winded.

"Can we slow down just a little bit?"

Knox stops, and I find a boulder to lean against to catch my breath.

"How much farther?"

"Not much, probably about a mile."

I drill him with a look. *Not much* is not a mile. To stall for time, I pretend to take in the view. Then I really take it in. "Wow!"

Knox breaks into a wide smile. "You ain't seen nothing yet."

Then it should really be something, because the sight before me, a series of red clay formations drenched in the afternoon sun, is beyond anything I've ever seen before. Ethereal and breathtaking.

"It's like something from another world," I say, awestruck.

"Yep." He meets my gaze and holds it.

"What?"

"It's nothing less than magic," he says, but I no longer think we're talking about the view.

"What is?"

"You asked me the other day what I'm looking for after Sienna, whether I still want the picture of the life I'd imagined with her. I told you I still did. What I didn't tell you, what I didn't know until today, is that I want this." His eyes never stop holding mine. "Magic. Nothing less than magic." He grabs my hand again. "Come on. I wasn't kidding about the light."

He pulls me halfway up the hill, giving me no time to parse what he's just said, no time to let it settle around me. But I'd be lying if I didn't admit it gave me chills. The magic part. Because I am feeling it, too.

We continue to trudge upward, my shoes rubbing my heels, leaving a blister. I clutch his hand, liking that it is larger than mine, liking the strength of it. And the warmth. It's cold outside. Colder than I had planned for, because I am only wearing a sweater.

"Almost there," he says, and slows his pace, giving me a moment to get my bearings.

This is when I see it. In the distance, an enormous waterfall cascading over a rocky ledge into a clear, deep pool. A fairy pool. Knox is right about the light; the sun is shining so bright, there's a rainbow in the fall's mist.

"Is that it?" I ask almost reverently.

"It's even better closer." He leads me down a narrow path to a wooden suspension bridge. "Come on. We can touch the water."

But I stop at the first rung, looking down at the rushing river below. "I can't. I'm afraid of heights."

"It's not that high. Only about forty feet. Besides, the bridge is safe. They wouldn't open it to the public if it wasn't."

I take a step, then pull my foot back, paralyzed with fear. "It looks rickety, like it's not strong enough to hold us."

"I've got you, Chelsea. I'll be with you every step of the way. But we need to get to the other side."

"Why can't we just enjoy it from here?"

He reaches out and brushes my face with the back of his hand, his eyes watery. "I wish we could, but it's time to cross over. We have to hurry, because we're running out of time."

"Okay," I say, and hold my breath. "You go first."

He takes five steps, then holds his hand out for me. "See, it's fine."

I miss his hand and grab onto his sleeve, gingerly testing the bridge with my foot. It swings under our weight, and I clutch Knox's arm tighter. "Is it supposed to do that?"

"Swing? That's the fun of it."

"Fun? I don't think so." I make the mistake of looking down. "Let's do it next time." I start to back up, but Knox pulls me forward.

"Chels, we're here now. Let's not blow this." But even he

seems ambivalent, reluctant. "I owe it to you, Chels. Your window of opportunity is closing. You'll see, it'll be fine. Scout's honor." He holds up three fingers and smiles.

"Okay. But you should know that there's a good chance I'll freak out in the middle. Then what will we do?"

"I'll go to the middle now. All you have to do is come to me, meet me halfway. We'll do the last part together."

I nod, doing my best not to look down at the swirling water below. Put one foot in front of the other, I tell myself.

"Stay there," I call to Knox over the cacophony of the river. "Don't move. Don't make the bridge swing."

"I'm right here." He holds his hand out, but it's too far to reach without me moving forward. "I promise, I won't move."

I take a baby step, testing the strength of my will, testing the strength of the bridge. Though wobbly, the bridge feels sound. Sturdy.

"Just a few more steps and you're here," Knox coaxes.

He's right, yet for me, it's a million miles away.

I consider turning around and running back to firm ground. "We can come tomorrow. I'll be better prepared tomorrow."

"You won't be here tomorrow. You're leaving, remember?"

"I've reconsidered," I say. "I'll cancel my lecture."

I can see he's exploring the idea, that it even appeals to him. But at the last minute, he insists, "As much as I want you to stay, it's a bad plan. It would be irresponsible to disappoint all those people. They're depending on you."

He's right. They're depending on me. And after Albuquerque, I could fly to LAX, finish what I started with Lolly. Convince her that it's different now, that I'm different. Tell her that I want to know my niece and nephew, really know them. And I should visit Uncle Sylvester, too, spend some quality time with him, because it's been too long. We hardly know each other anymore.

"Okay," I say. "You're right. But you'll have to be patient. This scares me to death."

Knox nods. "I know. But you're in good hands. I won't let anything happen to you."

I know this intrinsically, probably more than I've ever known anything before. Knox Hart won't let anything happen to me. More than anyone else in the world, I trust my safety—not just my safety, my everything—in his hands. And this is the sad thing—or maybe the best thing, depending on how you look at it—I can't remember the last time I felt safe in anyone's hands. Not even in Austin's.

"I'm going to do it," I say, taking a deep breath and another step forward. Then another one. But I'm still too far away to grab his outstretched hand.

My heart is beating so fast, I'm afraid it'll bounce right out of my chest. But I inch a little closer to Knox, to his hand, which is waving encouragingly to me.

"You've got this, Chels. Look how far you've come already."

"It's not that bad," I lie. It probably wouldn't be this terrifying if it wasn't for the river below us. The water is moving fast, deadly fast. And just looking at it, I can tell it's cold, hypothermic cold from the snow up in the mountains. Even a person without a fear of heights would be intimidated.

"Almost here," he says, and gives me a wide smile.

It's the smile that moves me to reach for his hand, to take the necessary last steps to grab it. And when I finally do, it's like something ruptures inside of me. Not relief, exactly; something more akin to an overwhelming rush of love.

"One more half to go." Knox pulls me to him and there, in the middle of the bridge, holds me like he never wants to let me go. "Ready?"

"I think so. But I'm still having second thoughts about leaving."

"Nah. It's time, Chels." He hugs me again, and I cling to him. "Let's do this."

"You go first." The bridge is narrow, and it makes me nervous to be so close to the edge.

"You sure? You don't want to do the last leg together?"

"It'll be better for me to do it the same way. With you going first and cheering me forward."

"You got it." He lets go of me and walks the final distance. He's so close to the waterfall that the mist shrouds him, making him look like an apparition.

"Are you getting wet?" I call.

"I can't hear you."

This time, I yell it. "Are you getting wet?"

"Yeah, a little. But it feels good. Come see."

It's then that I realize that it's equidistant from here to the end—or the beginning. In other words, there's no quitting now, because the only way off this bridge is to either move forward or backwards. And forward is where Knox is. And that beautiful waterfall.

"You do know we're going to have to do this all over again to get back to where we came from?" I shout over the gushing water.

He doesn't say anything, and I start to think he didn't hear me. But there's something in his face, at least what I can see of his face through the mist, that tells me he did. Something that tells me there's more that he's not saying.

"Stop stalling," he shouts back. "You came this far, you can do the rest."

I suck in my breath, put my arms out to my sides like a tightrope walker, and gingerly move toward him, forcing myself to keep from looking down.

The bridge sways, and I almost lose my footing, desperately reaching for the rope rails to steady me.

"You okay?"

"If having a heart attack atop a river on the world's ricketiest suspension bridge counts as okay."

Knox laughs. "You're doing fine. Better than fine. In fact, I wish I could take a picture of you, so I can remember you just like this."

"You mean about to crap my pants?"

He laughs again. "Facing your fears. Beautifully brave. A goddess."

"You need a good therapist, Knox Hart. Hold out your hand, because I'm getting the hell off this thing."

"That's the spirit." He reaches out for me, but I'm still holding onto the rope rails, frozen in place. "Want me to come get you to go the rest of the way?"

I consider the offer but shake my head. "Just give me a minute to regroup." I slowly take my hands away from the ropes and hold them out in front of me, like a ballast. Then I walk toward Knox, into the mist.

And that's when it happens, when against all statistical odds, the bridge breaks. It happens so fast, so violently, that I don't have time to think or even scream. I just hang onto one of the dangling wooden rungs for dear life, only feet above the rushing water.

"Knox! Knox!"

"I'm here. On shore. Can you see me?"

"I can't. I can't look." It's taking all my focus to maintain my remaining grip on the broken bridge.

"I'm coming to get you."

"How?" His only way to me no longer exists.

"Do you trust me?"

"Yes. But this is impossible. An impossible situation. And I don't think I can hold on much longer." The mere fact that I can even talk is astounding, astounding because I'm pretty sure I'm only seconds away from dropping to my death.

"Just a few minutes longer, just long enough until I can get to you. Whatever you do, don't let go. Chelsea, tell me you won't let go."

"Okay, I'll try. But hurry."

It's then that I let myself wonder whether it will be better, and by better, I mean less painful, to drown or to be crushed to death against the rocks.

I can feel my arms shaking from the strain of holding on so tight, and I can feel myself drifting away. From a distance, I hear Knox calling me, begging me to hold on just a few seconds longer.

It's already too late, I'm afraid. My left hand loses its grasp, and now I'm holding on with only my right one. I feel so heavy, just like the weightiness I felt in my dream. And I'm tired. I tell myself it's okay to close my eyes. To sleep. Even if it's only for a few minutes. Just long enough to gather my strength again. Or not. Because it would also be nice to sleep for a very long time.

"Chelsea! Chel . . . sea."

I feel the bridge shift, moving until I'm skimming the water, graceful, like a swan. Then I'm soaring only inches above the water's surface, like the geese on the lake at the cabin.

"Chelsea, Chelsea, hold on."

Strong arms wrap around me. Hoisting. Pulling. So warm. Knox. He's kissing my face, crying and begging.

But in my heart of hearts, I know I have to leave him now. That it's impossible for me to stay with him any longer.

The other side is calling.

Part 2

One who looks outside, dreams. One who looks inside, awakens.
—Carl Jung

Chapter 18

"Chelsea! Chelsea! Can you hear me?"

"If you can hear us, say something, honey."

The lights are so bright, they're blinding. I try to turn on my side, away from the glare, but there are wires in my arm.

Besides two voices, I hear the beeping and tapping of machines.

And my throat is so dry that I couldn't talk, even if I wanted to.

"Do you know where you are, Chelsea?" Make that a third voice.

I try to shake my head, but it hurts too much, so I hold up my hand instead.

Someone takes it and threads their warm fingers through mine. "We're so happy you're back. You had us worried there, sweetie."

It's Uncle Sylvester. Although I can't quite make out his face, I recognize the deep timbre of his voice. And the lemony scent of his aftershave.

"Can you give your uncle's hand a squeeze?" This from the third voice, the one I don't recognize.

I squeeze Uncle Sylvester's hand, but the effort leaves me exhausted.

"She squeezed it! Did you see that? She squeezed it."

"Hey, Chels, it's me, Austin. Boy, did you give us a scare."

I close my eyes, willing the bright lights and the voices to go away, wanting to sleep for a hundred years.

"Can you stay with us a few minutes longer? Just long enough for me to conduct a couple of brief tests."

I open my eyes again.

"Do you know where you are, Chelsea? If you can't talk or move your head, use your fingers. One for yes, two for no."

I hold out my index finger, pretty sure I'm in a hospital.

"Very good. Do you know why you're here?"

I make two.

"I'll explain that to you. But for now, just a couple more questions."

"Are you feeling any kind of pain?"

One finger.

"Can you show me where?"

I try to lift my hand, but I'm too weak. And frankly, too drained. I feel like I just ran a marathon with a vise grip clamped to my head.

"Your head?" he asks.

One finger.

"On a scale of one to ten, how bad is the pain?"

I hold out ten fingers, but at the last minute, fold one down, lest he think I have a low threshold for pain.

"We'll see if we can give you something for that."

"Anywhere else?"

One finger.

"Can you show me?"

I try to point to my shoulders, my arms, my hips, my legs, but can't manage it, so I extend two fingers.

"On a scale of one to ten, tell me the pain levels you're experiencing."

I hold out five fingers. It's more soreness than intense pain.

"Okay. We'll see about that, too. Would you like to rest now?"

One finger.

I wish I could ask him to turn out the light bearing down on me or turn off the machines making all the noise, but I can't seem to make myself talk. I would be deeply concerned about it if I wasn't so fatigued.

Someone is bathing my legs in warm water. When I manage to open my eyes to find the culprit, all I see are tiny paws.

"Good morning."

I follow the paws with my eyes to the voice and find a round open face with big blue eyes smiling down on me.

"It's good to have you back, Ms. Knight. How are you feeling?"

I make the okay sign with my fingers and try to reach for my mouth, but my arm isn't cooperating.

She seems to understand anyway, because she holds an ice chip to my lips and rubs it from side to side on my mouth. I'm too weak to suck on it or swallow, but the cold and wet feels good, though it doesn't quench my insatiable thirst. I point with one finger at the pitcher on the bed table, and she pushes it away.

"It's too soon for water," she says. "But we're giving you everything you need in there." She bobs her head at my IV drip.

I try to nod, but I can't lift my head. *How long?* I want to ask. *How long have I been here? And where's Knox?* I dare to let myself contemplate the unbearable.

What if I made it and he didn't?

I can't think about that now. I'm having trouble just keeping my eyes open. The woman, who I presume is a doctor or a nurse, is tending to the plastic bladders in the IV drip. Despite her smooth efficiency, the rustling noises of her moving around make my head hurt.

Her scrubs, printed with a loud pattern of bright orange

and purple animal paws, aren't helping either, though I have the strange sensation that I've seen them before. Could be that it's the theme of the room. I've spent a good amount of my awake time staring at a framed nature poster on the wall of a fox. A small red one, perched on top of a rock.

For the rest of the day, I drift in and out. There's a steady procession of people coming through the room. Some I recognize from voice or smell, while others are completely foreign to me.

The room is cold, so cold that I wish I could ask for more blankets but still can't seem to speak. I'm hoping that my inability to talk is only temporary. The fact that I'm not completely freaking out about it speaks to how out of it I am.

"Chelsea? Chelsea? This is Dr. Sadie. Can you hear me?"

I open my eyes, and with a great amount of effort, manage to move my head to indicate yes.

"Excellent," she says.

This is a different doctor than the one who had me respond by using my fingers.

"Are we feeling a little better today?"

I think so, but I don't know how to communicate it, so I hold out one finger.

A small voice that appears to be coming from the corner of the room says, "One finger means yes."

"Very good," Dr. Sadie says, and takes my hand in hers. It feels small and delicate. "Can you squeeze my hand, Chelsea?"

I squeeze it, but she doesn't seem to feel it, because she doesn't say anything and eventually removes her hand from mine.

"Can you blink your eyes?"

I blink and she smiles, clearly pleased. "You're doing quite well. As soon as you're up for it, we'll run some more tests. But this is good progress. Good progress indeed. Is there anything you need?"

Yeah, an extra blanket, more ice chips, and to know where

Knox is. But I can't say any of those things, not even a sound is able to escape my lips.

"I'll have one of the nurses bring you another blanket. Your hand is ice cold."

"Thank you, Doctor," the small voice says. Too few words for me to pin down who it is, and I can't lift my head enough to look.

I nod off, only to be jarred awake by a jumping motion and the loud thump of a bass. The music is coming from the ears of someone lifting and lowering my bed up and down. I should be alarmed, but it feels familiar, as if the sensation of being abruptly jostled has happened before. I'm automatically reminded of the young man with stringy blond hair and bedraggled clothes hopping around on the trunk of my car at Bear Creek Beach, making me seasick.

But I'm not in a car, and it's not the disheveled man. It's a clean-cut thirty-something with earbuds changing my sheets. Apparently, there's no rest for the weary in this joint. By the time I come to terms with the fact that I'm not in a parking lot, being besieged by young people, he's gone.

But now I'm wide awake in an empty room, with only my confusion for company. And the *click-clack*ing of the machines. There's also the smell of heavy perfume next to my bed. I take a few moments for my eyes to adjust to the darkness and spot the offender on the bed table next to me. A bouquet of pink stargazer lilies, pretty but cloying.

Next to the flowers is a smiley-face mug with a big helium pumpkin balloon and a collection of cards. I'd read them, but even the covers are fuzzy. I manage to prop myself up on my elbows, but only long enough to see the vacant chair in the corner of the tiny room.

There's no clock, at least none visible while I'm flat on the bed, and the one window, covered in a blackout shade, leaves no hint about the time of day. But judging from the relative quiet, it's night. Very late at night.

There's a nurse call button on the side of my bed. I'm tempted to push it just to make sure this is real and that I'm not dead. I try to roll onto my side and remember the IV. I'd move the tubes out of the way, but the effort is too exhausting, so I remain on my back, staring up at the ceiling, attempting to count the silver flecks in the acoustic tiles.

A short time later, a nurse cracks open the door to check on me, letting in a stream of light. But I feign sleep, hoping she'll leave me be instead of conducting what seems to be a bi-hourly routine of pinching and prodding.

I'm out of luck, though. She flips on the lamp, and it's like I just walked out of a darkened movie theater into broad daylight.

"You're awake." She sounds surprised.

She checks my IV, the liquids in the bags, and then the monitor making all the noise. "Are you comfortable?"

One finger.

She gently lifts my head and fluffs my pillow. With all the strength I can muster, I raise my hand and touch my lips. They're dry and cracked, and what I wouldn't do for another ice chip.

"Oh, you poor thing. Let me get some petroleum jelly, and I'll be right back."

True to her word, she returns a short time later with a tube of Vaseline and a handful of tiny samples that she piles on the table next to the sickeningly sweet flowers.

I extend my index finger toward the water pitcher.

"For your lips?"

One finger.

She disappears inside the bathroom and returns with a wet washcloth and uses it to wipe my lips. The water is lukewarm, not as good as the ice chip, but still, the moisture feels like heaven.

"Better?"

One finger.

"I'll leave the cloth here for you." She places it on top of my blanket, next to my hand, then reapplies the Vaseline.

She marks something in my chart and closes the door behind her, once again plunging my room in near darkness.

I've never felt so helpless in my life. And for the first time since I found myself here, I cry a pool of silent tears that soak my cheeks and neck and drip onto my hospital gown.

The final humiliation comes the next morning when an orderly comes around to empty my catheter bag.

Chapter 19

Dr. Sadie is back.

She is a leading neurologist on the West Coast, and I'm fortunate to have her on my team, according to Austin. I'm still not sure what constitutes a team or why I have one. Or how I got here. Very little has been said about the situation, only that confusion and short-term memory loss is normal.

Each day—I think it's been four now—is a new mountain to climb. Today, I reached the tiny tube of Vaseline and was able to apply it to my lips by myself. Yesterday, it was sipping water from a straw. I nearly wept with gratitude. Tuesday, it was being able to hold my head up long enough to see Lolly silently slip out of my room. She hasn't returned since. And Monday, I croaked my first word, "Help." Slowly but surely, my speech has returned, and I'm speaking in full sentences now.

"Hello, Chelsea. You look exceptionally well this morning." Dr. Sadie beams at me while holding a chart in her hands. "Your brain function is good, exactly where we want it to be. It'll just take a little time for everything else to catch up. The key is not doing too much too fast. A trauma of the kind you've suffered takes a long time to recover from."

"What about Knox?" I manage in a scratchy, barely audible voice. It's the first time I've been able to ask about him, the first time I've been able to face the fear that I might've lost him.

"Knox?" She tilts her head to one side, as if I'm speaking a foreign language.

"Knox." This time my voice is strong. "He was with me on the bridge when it broke. He pulled me out of the river."

"River? You were hit by a cable car on California Street. As far as I know, you were the only pedestrian injured, but you should talk to the police. I'm sure there's a report."

"Wait," I say, completely befuddled. "How long have I been here?"

"Two weeks and four days."

"That's impossible. I was at the cabin in Ghost. My vacation cabin."

"You may have been there before the accident, and that's what you're remembering," she says. "It's not unusual for our brains to try to protect us from the memory of trauma."

"No, I was there after the accident. That's why I went there in the first place, to recuperate."

"Chelsea, you came straight here in an ambulance after suffering significant head trauma. You were put into a medically induced coma so that we could reduce the swelling and pressure in your brain." She pulls the chair in the corner of the room to the side of my bed. It's the first time I've ever seen Dr. Sadie sit. In all her visits, she's brisk and businesslike, in and out in record time.

"It's not at all uncommon for patients in induced comas to experience dreams and hallucinations, even nightmares," she continues. "I had one patient who swore he'd joined the circus and another who believed he'd passed the bar when he was still in his first year of law school."

"So, I'm not here because the suspension bridge at the Ghost Mine Historic State Park broke?" I'm having trouble processing that news. Maybe she's mistaken me for another patient. Or is confused.

"No. Let me ask you, do you remember getting hit by the streetcar?"

"Yes. But other than a minor headache, I walked away, then drove two hours into the mountains to stay at my lake cabin. That's what I remember."

"It was a dream, Chelsea."

"You don't understand. I went to the annual Halloween parade with my sister. Met with friends . . . went to the farmers' market . . . happy hour at the local inn. I had a life there . . . a good life. I had Knox."

I reach for my handbag for proof. Knox's number in my phone, texts from Austin. I paw through the contents, ultimately finding my check register to show the payment for my roof or the one hundred and fifty dollars to Misty. But the last check I wrote was to Corrie, my housecleaner, dated three weeks ago.

Dr. Sadie shrugs and plasters on a faint smile, her way of telling me that I'm not stark raving mad, but wrong just the same.

"Look at it this way," she says. "It sounds like it was a wonderful way to pass the time."

I've been moved to the west wing of the hospital, which I'm told is a good sign. According to my nurses, it means that if physical therapy goes well, I'll be leaving here soon.

It also means that I'll have one less visitor. Uncle Sylvester left for LA this morning to get back to his life but promises that he'll return as soon as possible.

I haven't seen or heard from Lolly since the day she walked out of my room without even a backwards smile or the decency of saying goodbye.

The one constant is Austin, who hasn't missed a day since I got here. The nurses have all told me that the only time he's left my side is to go home to sleep and shower.

But it's different in the west wing. For one, I'm sharing a room. And from what I've heard, the staff enforces strict visiting hours. Besides, Austin has a law practice that needs him and presumably a fiancée who's furious that he's neglected her for his ex-wife.

That's okay, because I can use the alone time to come to terms with what has happened—or rather, what didn't happen—in the last three weeks. Despite assurances from Austin that no one has been to the cabin in over a month, I'm having trouble separating fact from fiction.

Katie and her bright red hair and the bough of flowers tattooed across her chest, serving up Ghost Ghouls at a furious pace. Sadie and her cheating husband, whom she doesn't want to leave because she needs financial stability. Ginger talking endlessly about the boy who saved his dog from drowning. Amanda and her cousin, the firefighter who stole Sienna away only to make her miserable. Madam Misty, Universal Diviner.

And Knox.

Sweet, wonderful Knox and the countless times I start to call him to tell him about my day. About Dani, the former pediatric nurse who transferred to trauma but still wears her bright and festive kiddie scrubs. About Michael Hart, the ER doc who looks strikingly like Knox (the coincidence of that is not lost on me). And Rihanna Prince, the duty nurse who claims I saved her marriage (so take that, Mr. Naysayer).

How can there be a hole in my heart from missing all these people so much when they didn't even exist? The truly desperate part is that I sometimes wish I could've permanently stayed in my own hallucination. No matter how hard I try, I can't seem to come to terms with losing the life I had there. It's like waking up from a dream that you've won the lottery only to learn that your bank account is as empty as when you went to sleep.

I find myself crying a lot. The nurses say it's normal to be depressed after a long illness. How do I explain that it has nothing to do with my injuries and everything to do with all that I've lost? Or more accurately, all that I never had.

Ronnie visits me in the afternoon and brings me a new screen saver for my phone. The old one was cracked in the accident. But my actual phone, along with the rest of the contents of my purse, survived.

"I guess we'll have to reschedule all of November's lectures," I say.

"Don't worry about that now." Ronnie is removing my old screen saver and putting on the new one. "Just focus on getting well, and I'll take care of the rest."

I acquiesce, though the truth of the matter is, we'll probably have to reschedule the rest of the year. It's impractical to assume I'll be up and running full speed even by December. It's a light month anyway, with only a few appearances before the holidays start.

"Ronnie, did I have my laptop with me during the accident?" The question only occurs to me now, even though I distinctly remember having it in my dream.

"No. It's still in the office. Why?"

"Can you bring it to me tomorrow?"

"Not if you're going to work. Doctor's orders are that you rest."

She's right. But other than a few hours of tests and therapy, the days here are long and boring. "I won't. But I'd like to be able to email my uncle and sister. It's difficult on my phone," I say, which is the truth.

"Okay, but only if you promise that's all you'll use it for."

"Scout's honor." I give her a three-finger salute the same way Knox did on the bridge, except it never happened. And yet, everything about that day is still so vivid and clear.

"I have a little gossip if you're up for it," Ronnie says.

"Yeah?" Ronnie and I have always maintained a professional distance, a tone I set when she first came to work for me, so I'm somewhat surprised that she's willing to share gossip with me. And a little touched.

"Before you tell me, I just want you to know that I bought you a lovely handmade bar of basil soap at the farmers' market in Ghost during my coma-inspired hallucination."

"Uh . . . okay. Thanks, I guess."

I laugh, realizing how ridiculous I must sound, realizing that people are tired of constantly having to tell me that none of it was real. "So what's the gossip?"

"I met Mary, Austin's new fiancée. I didn't even know he was engaged until she came to the hospital that first day when you were brought in. At first, I thought it was really nice of her. I mean, we were so scared that we were going to lose you, and Austin was a mess. It was great that she was here to support him, right? Except, I've since come to learn that she's not as nice as she seems."

"How so?"

"Well, this is going to sound horrible, and maybe I shouldn't even tell you, but I actually think by the third or fourth day, she was hoping you would die, that she'd begun to realize alive you were a real threat to her and Austin's relationship."

This is the most personal Ronnie has ever gotten with me. But you can't work with a person, share an office with them, and travel together all over the country without gleaning some personal information. For instance, I know about her mooch of a roommate, that her cat died sixteen months ago and she's too grief-stricken even still to replace it, and that the last guy she dated stole fifteen hundred dollars from her. In return, Ronnie knows my sister and I have a complicated relationship, and that my divorce from Austin was extremely hard on me.

"Why did you get that impression?" Not that I doubt she's wrong. One of the characteristics I've come to rely on from my assistant is her deep insight. Sometimes I think Ronnie would've made a better psychologist than me.

"She still came with him every day that first week, but she was resentful. You could see it all over her face. She was bitchy to the staff and bitchy to Austin, even though he was going through hell. Quite frankly, that's the reason why. It wasn't that she hated that he was going through hell, it was that she hated that he was going through hell over you."

"This is going to sound warped, but I'm flattered." And I don't say this to Ronnie, but I'm also sort of vindicated that Austin's new fiancée isn't the second coming, though he'd certainly intimated that she was. Or maybe that was just my interpretation.

But this is petty stuff for someone who has just had a near-death experience, I remind myself.

"At the end of the day, I get the sense that Austin saw right through it," Ronnie says. "I wouldn't be surprised if he calls off the engagement. That last week you were out, Mary was nowhere to be found. My Spidey sense tells me that Austin told her not to come anymore. My Spidey sense tells me almost losing you made him see the light."

"The light of Mary's faults?" I ask.

"No, the light of what he gave up when he left you."

There was a time when the sentiment, if it's even true, would've thrilled me, but I'm too exhausted to care right now. Too messed up to think of anything other than getting well again.

"Can you do me a favor?" I ask.

"Sure, whatever you need."

"Could you see if there's a floral shop in Ghost called Flower Power?" I figure if I start small, I can retrace my steps and disseminate what is real and what isn't. Who actually exists and who doesn't. Because even if no one believes me, including Ronnie, I couldn't have built an entire world out of thin air.

"You sure that's such a good idea?" Ronnie says. "Even if I find it, it doesn't prove anything. You have a place up there, Chels. I'm sure a lot of your hallucination is based on real shops and real people."

"I know. But can you please just do this for me? I'd do it myself, but until I get my laptop, the strain of searching and reading on the small screen of my phone hurts my eyes."

"I will, but nothing good can come of it."

Chapter 20

My last day at San Francisco General is a mixed bag. On one hand, I'm ecstatic that I'm finally going home to my comfortable and quiet condo, where I won't have a roommate who snores or doctors and nurses who hover over my every move. On the other hand, I'm petrified to be on my own.

Though I'm markedly better than a couple of weeks ago, I'm still unable to do simple tasks, like tie my shoes. It's as if I'm five years old again and have to learn the steps. Yet, I have no trouble dialing a phone or typing an email.

While waiting for my doctor to give the final release, I fold and pack my things. In the short time I've been here, I've managed to accumulate quite a few nightgowns, robes, slippers, and various sundries. It's a little crazy, because before the coma, I don't believe I had this much sleepwear to my name. Austin brought me my favorite carry-on, and with all I've stuffed inside, I'll be lucky if I can zip it.

A number of the nurses and staff have popped in to say goodbye and bring me small tokens to remember them by, including a dozen Vaseline samples. My lips will forever thank them. Everyone here has been so kind.

At noon, Austin arrives to drive me home. I told him I could take an Uber, but it's against hospital policy, which makes me wonder what patients who don't have anyone do.

The question only adds to the emotional roller coaster I've been on ever since Dr. Sadie told me I was going home.

"You ready to go?" Austin grabs my suitcase.

"We have to wait for someone to get me in a wheelchair. I'm not allowed to leave on foot. I think it's a liability thing."

"Yep. That would be my guess. You hungry? I thought we could stop somewhere and grab something to eat. I figure you've had enough of hospital food."

I don't have the heart to tell him that I just want to go home and surround myself with familiarity before venturing out to sit-down restaurants. "Sounds good. But nothing too elaborate."

"We can get it to go if you'd like and eat at home."

There's something about the way that he says "home" that irks me. Like it's still the place we share together. I chide myself for being uncharitable. Throughout this entire ordeal, Austin has been my saving grace. The one steady constant in my life.

"That sounds perfect," I say. "What did you have in mind?"

"How about the sandwich shop you love on Market? The place with the homemade chips. Or if you'd rather, we could do pizza. Tony's, your favorite. Whatever you want, Chels. This is a big day; a celebration is in order."

"Pizza sounds good. What do you say we call ahead, so we don't have to wait too long?" My body is constantly reminding me that it wasn't just my head that was hurt in the accident. Most of the bruising on my legs, arms, and torso have either turned green or disappeared completely, but I'm still sore, as if it happened yesterday.

"You got it." Austin jumps on his phone just as my favorite orderly, Clyde, arrives with the wheelchair.

"You're leaving us, huh?" Clyde helps me get situated in the chair.

"I'm afraid so, Clyde." We both laugh. "And guess what

I'm having for lunch? Here's a hint, pizza. Real pizza, not the kind on an English muffin with melted American cheese and soggy tomatoes."

"I hear you, Ms. Knight. Be sure to have a slice for me. But I bet you'll miss the Jell-O." He winks, then wheels me down the long corridor, my exercise track for the last two weeks. I walked up and down that hallway more times than I can count, trying to regain my strength.

When we get to the large double glass doors, it's sprinkling outside. Austin dashes off to bring the car, which he's left in the visitor parking lot. Clyde and I make small talk until Austin pulls up in front of the doors in his BMW. I flash on Knox's dinged-up pickup truck, and a touch of melancholy sets in.

Clyde wheels me to the passenger seat, and although I can do it myself, he helps me into the car. Soon, Austin is battling midday traffic in the city.

"The pizza is coming at two. Hopefully, when Ronnie stocked your fridge, she remembered a couple of bottles of wine."

"You got one of those delivery companies?" I ask, surprised. Tony's doesn't deliver, and Austin doesn't believe in paying for anything he can do himself. When we were married, it was a constant source of disagreement. We both work hard, and for me, the small expense is worth the convenience.

"Yep. No sense having you sit in the car any longer than necessary." He puts his hand on my leg like it belongs there.

I quickly move it away.

"Sorry," Austin says. "Did that hurt?"

"No. But I doubt Mary would approve."

"Mary and I are no longer engaged, leaving me free to innocently touch my ex-wife, who also happens to be my best friend."

Hmm, Ronnie certainly called that one.

"What happened with you and Mary?" I try to sound nonchalant, like it would be rude of me not to ask after he volunteered the information that they'd broken up.

"It's a lot of things, too many to bore you with the details. But primarily it was you." He slants me a sideways glance. "Almost losing you made me reevaluate what's important. It made me reevaluate who I want to spend the rest of my life with."

I feel the weight of those words. But before I can press him on them, we're at my condo, and Austin is asking for the code to get into the underground parking structure. The password changes every month.

It's one of the reasons we bought the apartment. I much preferred an older building, something from the 1920s with original hardwood floors and crown moldings. But those typically don't come with parking. And this building came with two secure spots. A veritable gold mine in the city by the bay.

He slides into his old space and cuts the engine. "You ready to do this?"

At first, I'm not sure what *this* is. But when he comes around the car to get me, I realize he's talking about resuming my old life, the time before the accident. He helps me out, then pops the trunk for my suitcase.

The other thing about this building is that it has an elevator. A few of them, actually. And in this moment, an elevator makes me even more happy than off-street parking.

I live on the sixth floor. It was the lowest floor we could get when condos in this building went on sale. The top floors with great city and bay views went first, of course. But because the bottom floors were the most affordable, there was a waiting list, leaving only condos on the middle floors. I let Austin convince me that six floors up wasn't high enough to trigger my acrophobia. But it took me three months before I could open the drapes. I still can't go out on the balcony, where I have a terrific view of the Bay Bridge.

Both Corrie and Ronnie have been here. I can tell because the house carries the faint smell of lemon polish and the organic cleanser Corrie uses to clean the floors. Ronnie has filled the house with all the flowers I received at the hospital and has left a stack of paperwork on the kitchen counter for me to sort through when I'm feeling up to it. For all intents and purposes, she's been running the business since my accident and has been paying the bills and keeping the lights on.

I'd forgotten how beautiful the apartment is. Austin and I hired a decorator shortly after we closed escrow to rid the place of its soulless white walls and builder-grade fixtures. She came highly recommended from one of Austin's coworkers and cost a pretty penny. But the end result is chic and luxurious, the kind of place where Uncle Sylvester would feel at home.

But seeing it today, the sleek white sofas, the abstract art, the miles of marble countertops, makes me wish I was at the cabin instead.

Austin flicks a switch, and the gas fireplace lights up. I used to think it was one of the best features of the apartment. But now, it just feels silly, like a pale imitation of the real thing. Something just for show.

He opens the fridge and peruses the shelves. "Ah-ha, Ronnie was thinking ahead." He pulls out a chilled bottle of Lambrusco and places it on the center island. "Go get comfortable while we wait for the pizza, Chels. You want me to unpack for you?"

"No thanks. If you could just leave the suitcase in the bedroom, I'll do it later." I have nothing but time on my hands.

The delivery person texts that he's here, and Austin buzzes him up to the apartment. "You want to eat on the couch or at the table?"

I have a strict policy against eating on my sofas. White, remember? But today, I'm going to break my self-imposed rule, because I don't have the energy to make it to the table. And maybe I'll get new couches anyway. Something cozy and comfortable that doesn't stain.

Austin sets me a place and joins me in front of the fire. "If you want, I can stay tonight."

Forty-five days ago, all I wanted was for Austin to return to the place he and I once made a home. But on my first day back, I need time to myself. To think. To contemplate all the things I've lost that it turns out I never really had.

"I'll be okay," I say. "But thank you for the offer."

"You sure? I can stay in the guest room." He's trying so hard.

"I need a little time, Austin."

"Gotcha."

I can't tell if he's hurt. But honestly, I don't have the bandwidth to be concerned with that now. I'm still reeling from almost dying. But that's not even the worst of it. To experience the greatest happiness you've ever known, only to realize it was all a dream, is . . . well, how does a person come back from that?

We eat and drink our Lambrusco in companionable silence, neither of us addressing the elephant in the room, otherwise known as Mary.

My eyes are bigger than my stomach, because I can barely finish one slice of pizza. Austin, on the other hand, has made a good dent on half the pie. Being in the apartment, eating a meal together, feels both familiar and foreign at the same time, but in a good way, like melding an old cherished story with a new one. A fresh start, I guess you can say.

And yet, I can't wait for him to leave. Like I'm literally counting the minutes until I can politely play the I'm-tired card, the I-have-to-go-to-bed card. Halfway through his second glass of Lambrusco, I let out a loud yawn.

"You've got to be bushed," he says. "I know it's a lot, Chels. I know the road looks long, but look how far you've already come." He waves his hand at the apartment as if to say, *You're home, and that's got to count for something*. And it does.

He starts to clean up. "I've been talking to a few of my colleagues at the firm, and they think you have a hell of a lawsuit against the city. These fucking cable car conductors are out of control."

"It was my fault, Austin. I wasn't looking where I was going. If I had, I would've seen the streetcar. I wouldn't have crossed when I did."

"Now is not the time to make any big decisions. All I'm saying is you shouldn't rule it out."

"Okay, I won't rule it out." But I already have. "If you don't mind, I think I'll take a nap. Will I see you tomorrow?"

"I've got a deposition in the morning but will swing by in the afternoon. Will you be okay until then?"

"Austin, I'll be fine. Thanks for being so attentive, but you don't have to worry." I join him in the kitchen to help with the rest of the cleanup.

"I know," he says. "You're the most capable person I know. But that's not the point."

"Then what is the point?"

"I don't want you to have to do this alone."

Long after he's gone, I consider his words. Am I truly alone? It didn't feel that way in Ghost, but here . . . I don't know.

I change into one of my new loungewear sets, a gift from Ronnie, and curl up on the sofa with the paperwork she's left me, so I can see what's gone on in my absence. It's mostly receipts, a few invoices, and a couple of get-well cards from strangers who have attended my seminars.

As I thumb through the stack, I see that Ronnie sent flowers to my parents' graves for the twenty-fourth anniversary of their deaths. I can't remember whether I'd asked her to do it or if she did it on her own because I was out of commission. Either way, I remind myself to thank her for it. She knew that it was an important day for me.

It appears she has everything well under control, including canceling all my upcoming speaking dates.

The rain has let up, and for a crazy minute I consider going outside to stand on the balcony for some fresh air and to stare out over the bay. It takes me less than a minute to completely reject that idea.

Instead, I wander into the bedroom and put away my things, a chore that takes a fraction of the time it took me to pack them. My phone rings, and when I dig it out of my purse, I see I have two missed calls—one from Uncle Sylvester, and another from a number I don't recognize.

"Hello," I say to Ronnie.

"Just checking in. You get home okay?"

"Yes, and it's good to be here. Thanks for stocking the fridge and for transporting the flowers. I don't know what I'd do without you. And, Ronnie, it means a lot that you remembered my parents and sent flowers."

"That's why you pay me the big bucks. You in the mood for company, or do you want some alone time while you settle in?"

"I'll probably just call it a night soon. Maybe tomorrow, though."

"I'll give you a buzz in the morning. But don't worry, I won't call too early. Sleep in, Chelsea."

I dial Uncle Sylvester's number and get his voicemail. "Hi, it's me. I'm home safe and sound. I'm turning in soon but will talk to you tomorrow."

I assume the other missed call is spam, which aggravates me, because it should've been Lolly. Everyone else had the decency to check in on me to make sure I've had a smooth transition from hospital to home. But not my sister, who apparently can't be bothered.

It doesn't pay for me to work myself up about it, not when I can pass the time noodling around on the Internet, trying to prove to myself that I'm not delusional. I carry my laptop into the living room and resume my spot on the sofa in front of the fire. I miss the crackling and woodsmoke smell of a real one, but at least it lends the room some air of coziness. Still, I can't help but imagine that Knox would hate it.

The first search I do is for Flower Power. Ronnie has already traveled this road and has reported that the floral shop did indeed exist. *Did* being the key word. According to her research, it closed two years ago.

The only evidence that it ever existed is an old weekly column in the *Ghost Advocate* that profiled local businesses, and a now-defunct website. The owner was someone named Gerald Mattson, not Ginger. And according to the pictures, it looked nothing like the shop I saw in my dreams.

I zoom in on Google Earth to find that the shop is now Gold Country Real Estate.

My next stop is the website for the Ghost Inn, which still exists and is an exact replica of the one I visited while in a coma. I click on the page for the Inn's restaurant and bar with no clear picture of what I'm looking for exactly. Eventually, I settle on the menu. The closest item they have to smoked chicken wings is "golden chicken nuggets" on the kid's page. They do, however, serve chips and salsa, as does pretty much every restaurant in California.

I click over to the drink menu and search for a Ghost Ghoul, only to come up empty. The most original cocktail on the list is a piña colada, circa 1954. I call the toll-free number on the homepage and ask the operator to transfer me to Katie Hart. If she's working today, she would be starting her shift right about now.

"I'm sorry, there's no Katie Hart here," the operator says.

"She's a bartender in the restaurant."

"Do you mean Cassie Reinhold? She's our only female bartender."

"This would've been a few weeks ago." Because Katie was going back to school. Maybe she'd already quit.

"Ma'am, I've been here for three years. We've never had an employee named Katie Hart."

"I'm sorry, I must have the wrong place." I hang up and cry.

Through tears, I search my texts for the dozenth time. But there's nothing from Austin during the two weeks I was in a coma. Just to be sure, I scroll through my call log. Again, nothing to indicate that any of the conversations I remember us having ever happened.

I don't know what I was expecting to find. It's clear I couldn't have been in two places at the same time, and yet, I was. Everything about those two weeks in Ghost was so real, so distinct. So life-changing.

I suppose I'm lucky. At least I didn't have nightmares while comatose, which, according to what I've read, is not uncommon. While I was recuperating in the west wing, I made a study of comas and dreams. Like the man who suffered from a high fever who kept dreaming that he was being burned alive. Or the woman who repeatedly dreamt she was drowning.

And then there are those whose experiences are not dissimilar from mine. For example, a man who hallucinated a whole new life while he was unconscious. In the span of only a few minutes, he met the love of his life, married, had two children, and then went crazy.

When he came to and realized that none of it was real, he went into a dark depression that lasted three years. He said he was grieving the loss of his nonexistent wife and children and thought he might be going insane.

This is what I'm up against.

Chapter 21

It's been five days since I came home, and I'm feeling a lot like my old self again. Not entirely ready to take on the world but strong enough to go into the office and do a little work. I call myself an Uber, because I'm still not ready to drive. And I don't want to zap my strength walking.

Ronnie's waiting for me with a cup of Peet's coffee. "You're sure you're up for this?"

"There's only one way to find out."

"Your agent called. The mockup for the new calendar is ready. I'll cue it up for you on the big monitor."

In September, I was beyond psyched for this calendar, a fun project that I thought could make a difference in the lives of couples working on their marriages. Now, it just seems . . . ridiculous. Like fodder for an *SNL* skit.

But I go through the motions, flipping through the months, reading the inspirational sayings at the top of each page, and trying to remember if the fonts match the ones I chose when we first started.

"What do you think?" Ronnie is looking over my shoulder.

"Yeah, I think it's good. What do you think?"

"It's great."

I turn to look at her. "It's a joke, isn't it? Like seriously mockable."

"What are you talking about? This is your baby, Chels. You worked so hard on this. And look at it"—she points at the screen—"it's a home run, a complete grand slam."

"Really? You don't think it's stupid? You don't think it's beneath my dignity? I have a doctorate degree in psychology, for God's sake, and here I am hawking calendars. What's next? Inspirational bookmarks? Charm bracelets?"

Ronnie laughs. "You think you might be overreacting just a little? So it's not the Stanford Prison Experiment. It's what you do. You make psychotherapy accessible to the masses. It's a good thing. What's with the sudden angst?" She gives me a soft appraisal. "Look, a lot has happened. You're finding your way after a significant injury; let's take it easy today. Not make any big decisions."

I get to my feet, go over to her, and lean my head on her shoulder. "What would I do without you?"

The rest of the day I dedicate to answering emails and posting on social media, though my heart isn't in it. My heart is in Ghost in a small cabin by the lake and a gold-country town where I had a life beyond work and Austin.

I can't help but wonder about Misty, about her odd and rather cryptic predictions, if you can even call them that. To be generous, she did sort of foreshadow my return to the real world. But the psychologist in me realizes that was merely my subconscious talking.

Still, I hop on the World Wide Web and search for her. Madam Misty, Universal Diviner. Much to my surprise, I get more than a dozen hits. She even has a website, which I immediately click on, then navigate straight to her bio. Her picture looks nothing like my Misty. This one is cherubic with short gray hair and resembles someone's sweet, round grandmother. Not the lithe Stevie Nicks, ballet-dancing figure in my dream.

According to her bio, she's had the "sight" since childhood and by the time she was a young adult, police departments around the state were using her "supernatural powers" to solve crimes. She lists several missing-person cases, including one I'm familiar with because it was headline news a few summers ago.

I move over to her contact information, copy her address, and plug it into Google Maps. Madam Misty, Universal Diviner is located off a stretch of highway four miles from Ghost, not far from the drive-through coffee shop that always has a long line. According to Google Earth, it's a trailer park that I must've driven past at least a thousand times. In the image, her shingle—the same design as the one in my dream—hangs on a post on the dirt shoulder between the entrance to the park and the highway.

I'm absorbing the discovery when my phone rings. Same number as the one I didn't recognize from my missed call the other day. I consider letting it go to voicemail—I get a lot of nutty calls, as you can imagine—but at the last second pick up, hoping . . . I don't have a clue what I'm hoping exactly. And to add voice to it would only make it that much crazier. But this is the thing. While I don't recognize the number, I do recognize the area code.

"Hello."

"Hey, it's you. I mean, of course it's you. I just didn't think you'd answer."

"Who is this?" The voice isn't remotely familiar. It's distinctly male, but that's the only thing I can place about it.

"It's Leo Antonelli. I hope I'm not disturbing you, but Austin gave me your number and said it would be okay for me to call on your private line. I just wanted to see how you were doing."

I scramble my brain for a Leo. As far as I recall, I know of no Leos. "I'm sorry, but at the risk of sounding rude, do I know you?"

He chuckles. "You probably don't remember me, but I was the guy who called nine-one-one after your accident . . .

of course, I'm probably not the only one who called. There were a ton of people on that cable car, a ton of people on the street that night. But I happen to be an EMT and . . . Well, I guess it was just fate that I was in San Francisco to meet a friend. In any event, I was behind you when you crossed, saw what happened, and was the first to respond. You were pretty out of it. I was worried that you wouldn't make it, but it sounds like you pulled through like a champ. I won't keep you any longer. I just wanted to see how you're making out and say I'm glad you're okay."

"Wow," I say, stunned almost speechless. I'm sure there were a lot of heroes that night, anonymous heroes. So to speak to one, actually get to show my undying gratitude, is quite amazing. "I'm much better now. Thank you, Leo. Thank you for everything you did that night. I haven't read the police report yet. Honestly, I'm still getting my bearings and am not ready to relive the accident. But my medical team believes that it was the quick work of strangers that kept me from being crushed under the wheels of the cable car. They thought it was lucky that all I sustained was head trauma, no broken bones. Apparently, someone pushed me out of the way just in the nick of time . . . just before . . ."

"Yeah," he says. "That was me."

All the time you hear about acts of bravery that change the course of lives. The pilot who landed his plane on the Hudson River to avoid catastrophe. The father who pulled his child, alive, from the jaws of an alligator's mouth. Hikers who fought a grizzly with their bare hands to rescue a friend. Never once do you stop to think that this will be you. That because of the quick, brave work of a stranger, you're still walking this earth.

That's how I feel about Leo. That because of him, I'm still walking this earth.

"I don't know what to say," I tell him. Seriously, do I offer to buy him lunch, send his kids to college? What can I possibly give him that doesn't seem trivial compared to what he's given me?

"You don't have to say anything," he says. "I try to check up on all my patients. Look, I've got to go. But it sounds like you're doing great. Hopefully, I'll see you around soon."

And just like that, he's gone.

It's Sunday morning, and I'm on my way to LA. Dr. Sadie cleared me for flying but not yet driving.

Despite making great strides—yesterday, I walked all the way from my apartment to the Ferry Building without once getting out of breath—I occasionally experience fuzziness. I'm sure there's a medical term for it, but the bottom line is my brain hasn't completely healed.

In any event, as long as I'm a passenger and not the captain (God forbid), it's safe for me to cross the state in an airplane—or even a car, for that matter. I'm going to see Uncle Sylvester and let him fuss over me. It's not like I'm doing much here anyway. Most days, I sit in my office and stare at a blank screen or search Google in an effort to corroborate my coma dream.

Friday, I once again studied the faculty pages of UC Davis's website in case I missed something the first three times I did the search. There is no Knox Hart anywhere on its roster. The only Professor Hart I found is a sixty-year-old Karen Hart, who teaches medicine and epidemiology at the university's school of veterinary medicine.

Just to be sure, I cross-referenced every school and science department in Northern California. I even looked up Old Ranch Road to find Knox's farmhouse. The house is there. But according to a property records search, it belongs to a Desi and Maureen Coopman and is indeed a working goat farm.

The only logical explanation is that I came across the property pre-coma while driving around Ghost, and its bucolic charm left an indelible mark on my memory. As far as Knox himself, it's fairly obvious that Michael Hart, my emergency doc and the first one to lay hands on me in the hospital before they induced the coma, was the inspiration for Knox.

There is some evidence that patients can hear what's going on around them while in a coma, and some can even recover enough to regain a modicum of awareness. Who's to say whether this happened to me or whether I simply have a robust imagination?

But instead of dwelling on it, it'll be good to get out of Dodge and immerse myself in a new environment, far from the hospital and Ghost.

It's a full flight, even in first class, a perk of traveling for a living. I have so many frequent flyer miles that I'll never use them all.

I'm next to a guy who looks vaguely familiar, like I might've seen him on the news. Or for all I know, he's an actor. It wouldn't be unusual to share a flight from San Francisco to Los Angeles with someone famous. I once sat next to Jane Fonda. It surprised me that she flew commercial, but it's probably more convenient. Some of the airlines make the trip between SFO and LAX five times a day.

She was extremely nice, by the way. Offered me her airline snack mix and said she liked my scarf.

I'm not getting a nice vibe from the familiar guy, who has made it abundantly clear that he doesn't want anyone talking to him. I get it. As a career traveler, plane time is the best time to catch up on work or correspondence. I give him plenty of space.

As we prepare for takeoff, I check my phone one last time, just in case Ronnic or Austin have texted or called. Nothing from Ronnie. But Austin has sent a GIF of a hand waving at an airplane. He's been up to his ears in alligators these last few days, negotiating the divorce settlement of a high-profile couple. He won't tell me who it is, only that he's representing the husband. I am guessing the client is either in tech or venture capital. That's who our "high-profile" people are. Whoever he is, he has no boundaries, calling Austin after hours and even on weekends. I don't understand why Austin puts up with it. He has a stellar reputation in the legal community and has no shortage of clients.

The flight is too short for a movie, and I forgot to bring a book. I lift the flight magazine from the netting in front of my seat and flip through it. Familiar guy has his music on too loud. I can hear Leonard Cohen through his earbuds. At least it's good music.

He also has his window shade open, which I would like to close. Although I'm in an aisle seat, catching even a glimmer of the sky reminds me that we're forty-two thousand feet in the air. I tap him on the shoulder and motion for him to shut the shade.

He pops out one earbud. "You want it closed?"

"Yes, please. If you wouldn't mind? I have a thing about heights."

"Then why do you fly?"

"Because it's faster than walking."

"Good answer." He pushes down the shade and stuffs his bud in his ear again.

I nod off, and before I know it, the flight attendant is asking us to put our seats in an upright position and to fasten our belts for landing. It seems like just five minutes ago we were served drinks. The cups, cans, and bottles are quickly cleaned up, and in no time, I'm pushing my way through the airport terminal with my small carry-on.

It's a balmy seventy degrees outside, and the sun hurts my eyes. When I left San Francisco, it was drizzly and cold. I grab a taxi at the cab stand, because it's faster than Uber, and rattle off Uncle Sylvester's address in Century City. He still lives in the same penthouse, though he's remodeled it two or three times since Lolly and I left.

It takes us forty-two minutes to go ten miles. Welcome to

Hell A, though San Francisco isn't much better. The businesses on Santa Monica Boulevard are decked out for Christmas, and the trees are all strung with lights. I can barely remember Thanksgiving, which came and went while I was in the hospital. If it wasn't for the cafeteria turkey, stuffing, and soggy slice of pumpkin pie, I wouldn't remember it at all.

The neighborhood has changed a lot since I lived here. Many of the restaurants and shops from my time have been replaced with new ones, trendier ones. And Westfield Century City, a mega shopping mall, is like a city onto itself. It even has a gourmet supermarket.

In the 1980s, Uncle Sylvester used to commute from Century City to Culver Studios, one of Los Angeles's most iconic studios. It is where *Gone with the Wind*, *A Star Is Born*, *Rebecca*, *Citizen Kane*, and *E.T.* were filmed. Last I heard, Amazon Studios had taken over a portion of the campus. Uncle Sylvester still makes the ten-mile commute (thirty minutes in traffic), but he's at Sony Pictures now.

We pull up in front of Uncle Sylvester's high-rise, and the cab driver helps me to the door with my carry-on. There's a new doorman, or at least new for me, who ushers me inside the lobby, then sends me up to the penthouse in Uncle Sylvester's private elevator. Like the neighborhood, the elevator has also gotten a facelift since the last time I was here. Grass cloth covers the walls where there once was chinoiserie wallpaper. The mirrors, though, are still here. Lolly and I used to try to outdo each other, making funny faces in them when we were kids.

The door slides open into a grand foyer, which I no longer recognize. It has the same grass cloth wall coverings as the elevator and new herringbone wood floors. There's a huge abstract painting on one of the walls.

"Hello, hello, hello." Wallace sweeps into the entrance and wraps me in a bear hug. "Look at you." He steps back a foot or two and gives me a full appraisal. "You look wonderful, my girl. Let me take this." He grabs the handle of my suitcase and wheels it into Lolly's and my old bedroom off the hallway. "You'll unpack later."

He takes my hand and pulls me through the apartment into the kitchen, where a stunning charcuterie board is waiting. It's much better than the one I made in my dream. Then again, Wallace owned a catering company for twenty-plus years, so I shouldn't be so hard on myself.

"Sly won't be home for another hour." Wallace is the only one who calls my uncle "Sly." He's the only one who has lasted more than five years. All of Uncle Sylvester's other boyfriends had an expiration date of around three years, except David, a perpetually out-of-work actor who lasted a little more than four.

I'm pretty sure Wallace is the love of Uncle Sylvester's life. And I'm pretty sure that if Wallace had been here twenty-four years ago, I never would have run off to boarding school.

"Tell me everything, little one." He pats one of the barstools and fixes me a plate from his charcuterie board.

"Where do you want me to start? Because I don't remember a whole lot of the accident."

"It was awful, I can tell you that. Sly and I caught the first flight out. By the time we got to the hospital, they'd already induced you."

I didn't know Wallace had been to the hospital, though I'm not surprised. One of the things I love best about him is how much of a family man he is. He has eight nieces and six nephews he dotes on, and two brothers and a sister, who are his best friends.

"You were so pale, Chelsea. Sly was beside himself. And Lolly . . . what can I say? You know how she is. Doesn't give anything away, that girl. But she was dying inside. No one could see that better than me. She's not the mystery she thinks she is."

I laugh, but I beg to differ. She's a complete mystery to me. She shows up at my bedside as if she cares, then leaves without ever saying goodbye. And never calls again. Who does that? Especially your own flesh and blood? I want the Lolly in my dream. At least there, she was willing to meet me halfway.

"Well, anyway, thank God you're here." He pulls me in for another hug, then points to the plate he's piled high with cheeses and fruit. "Now eat. You're wasting away."

I nibble on a piece of the Manchego, even though my stomach is still recovering from the stop-and-go of the cab ride. "The place looks great."

I note that the drapes have been drawn, hiding the view, and know instinctively that it's been done for my sake. Because of my fear of heights. This is where it started, where my acrophobia first took root when I was just twelve years old. No mystery why. No psychology degree needed.

Wallace glances around the apartment as if he's seeing it for the first time. "Doesn't it, though? It was six months of construction hell but worth it."

He stops hovering and sits down beside me. "Enough small talk. What's the deal with you and Austin? Sly says he never left your side at the hospital and has been there every day since."

"Yeah, he's been really good." I let out a long sigh. "Great, even."

He leans in. "And yet you sound miserable about it. Why is that?"

"I guess I'm waiting for the other shoe to drop. I mean, when he left, I had no warning. Nothing. One day we were this perfect couple, and the next, he was packing up and leaving. He didn't even give a good reason. Then he gets engaged to this woman Mary, who apparently he's no longer engaged to."

"People make mistakes, Chelsea. Maybe it took a crisis to see what he had in you, what he could've lost. Perhaps he's worth giving a second chance is all I'm saying. But I'm no marriage expert, not like you."

"I don't feel like much of an expert anymore. The coma really messed with my head." I laugh at my unintentional pun. "And now I'm all mixed up."

"How so, sweetheart?"

"Did Uncle Sylvester tell you about my dreams? While I was in the coma, I had this incredibly lifelike hallucination. I was myself, but at the same time, I was different. I had all these friends and social activities. I know that doesn't make sense, but it was as if I was living a completely new life. And this is the thing, Wallace. I liked that life better than my real one."

He rests his hand on top of mine. "Sly told me a little bit about it. This is what's important to remember. What happened to you is beyond traumatic. You almost died, Chelsea. Hallucination or no hallucination, you don't just automatically bounce back from that. It's a process. You give yourself time to heal physically—and mentally." He looks at me, really looks. "And you know, it might not be a bad idea to talk to someone . . . a professional."

"I am a professional."

"Of course you are." He waves his hand in the air. "But you know what they say. 'She who represents herself has a fool for a client.' "

"That's for lawyers, not psychologists." I stifle a laugh.

"You get the gist." He squeezes my shoulder. "You need someone who specializes in this sort of thing, someone who can be objective. Someone who understands these dreams you had. And let me just suggest this, if you loved the life you hallucinated, why not create it in your real life? A young woman like you shouldn't work so hard. You should have lots of friends and a calendar full of social events."

I don't know why, because I probably sound like a lunatic, but I blurt, "But there wouldn't be Knox Hart."

"Who's Knox Hart?"

"A man in my hallucination."

"Ah, the plot thickens, as your Uncle Sylvester would say."

Yes, the plot always thickens. Or as Uncle Sylvester's favorite screenplay writer Jim Thompson would say, "There is only one plot—things are not what they seem."

"And could this Knox fellow represent someone real in your life? Because it seems unlikely, at least from what I know about dreams, that you pulled him out of thin air. Austin maybe?"

"Not Austin, definitely not Austin. And I don't think so. Don't think I'm nuts, but I've done extensive research to track him down, and he simply doesn't exist." I tell Wallace about my ER doctor and the power of suggestion.

"Is the ER doc single?" Wallace waggles his brows.

"I don't think so. Ugh, what am I going to do?"

"You're going to keep on keeping on, that's what you're going to do. In the meantime, no big changes, just focus on you. By this time next year, we'll re-evaluate. Now come see our tree."

That evening, Uncle Sylvester and Wallace take me to a posh restaurant in Beverly Hills. We sit in a gorgeous solarium with a twelve-foot Christmas tree that's been decorated completely in fresh flowers. It's beyond impressive, though I can't help wondering how they keep the flowers from dying. Or do they change them out every few days? They're real, I know, because when no one was looking, I snuck a feel.

We order a bottle of French wine and then another. The food is so good that I'm stuffing myself. Had I known how delicious everything was going to be, I would've worn more stretchy pants. I see Uncle Sylvester and Wallace exchange gleeful glances. They're intent on fattening me up.

"Should we talk about Christmas?" Uncle Sylvester says. "In light of everything that has happened, I want us to make a concerted effort to spend it together. Lolly and the kids, too."

Since my sister and I flew the coop, Uncle Sylvester almost always spends Christmas abroad. Last year it was a villa in Greece. The year before, he and Wallace got an Airbnb in Portugal. The previous Christmas they spent in the Swiss Alps.

He pins me with his blue eyes, so much like my mother's that I feel a lump forming in my throat. "You girls need to work your stuff out. Life is too damned short to have all this pent-up animosity between you."

I'm too buzzed on French wine to get into it about Lolly. As far as Christmas, I can't imagine anything better than spending it with my uncle and Wallace.

"Where?" I say. "Where do you want to have it?"

"It makes the most sense to have it here. But if you'd prefer, we could all come to San Francisco. Whatever you want, Chelsea, as long as we do it."

Before we leave the restaurant, they have my firm commitment. At home, or rather Uncle Sylvester's penthouse, I change into lounge pants with a roomy elastic waist. Uncle and Wallace are night owls. I'll try to stay up with them but don't know how long I'll last. Between flying and all the wine, I can barely keep my eyes open.

The three of us sprawl on the sofas, sleek velvet numbers that are more about form than they are functional. This is to say, they're not very comfortable but look fantastic. The whole room looks like something out of *Architectural Digest*'s Christmas edition. Besides the tree with its delicate blown glass ornaments, there's an antique menorah (Wallace is half Jewish) on the sofa table that reminds me of a museum piece. Wallace says he got it at a garage sale in Brentwood. That's no garage sale I've ever been to.

"I'm turning in early." Wallace feigns a yawn, then kisses me sweetly on the cheek. "Sleep tight, sweetheart."

I know he's only leaving to give Uncle Sylvester and me time to talk alone.

The minute he's out of earshot, I say to Uncle Sylvester, "Don't you dare let that one get away."

"Nope. He's a keeper." He rises from the couch and pours us each a nightcap of cognac.

Tomorrow I'm going to have one hell of a headache.

"I meant what I said about you and Lolly," he starts, as I knew he would. "This has gone on long enough between you two."

"I have no idea what she's so angry about."

"Yes, you do, and you have to work it out, because you need each other. You need your sister as much as she needs you, even though neither of you will admit it."

I can't argue with that. I miss my sister. "Did she go to Mom and Dad's grave on the anniversary?" I don't tell him that she did in my dream, that we talked about it, and she said she'd forgiven them.

He shakes his head.

"Do you still hate him, Uncle Sylvester? Do you still hate my father?"

"I never hated him. I am . . . I was . . . just so angry. Angry as much for him taking his own life as I was for him taking my sister's."

"Was?" I ask, because he made a point of using the past tense. "You're not angry anymore?"

"At some point, you have to let the anger go, because it'll eat away at you like a cancer. I loved your father, Chelsea. I loved him like he was my own brother. What he did was unthinkable, abominable. But all the anger in the world isn't going to bring either of them back. The only thing I have left of them is my memories. To honor my sister, to honor all that she meant to me, I owe it to her and I owe it to myself to hold only the good memories dear and banish the bad ones forever."

"When I was in the coma, when I was having the weird dream, you told me that Mom and Dad loved each other.

Even in the very end, they loved each other. And that they would want to be buried together." I let that hang out there, waiting to see what he'll say in real life.

"In my heart of hearts, I believe that's true. I believe we did the right thing." He reaches out and takes my hand. "Despite everything that happened, they loved each other, but most of all, they loved you and Lolly more than anything else in the world. What I know above all else is that they wouldn't want you to worry about where they were buried. And I know this, they'd be so proud of you, Chelsea, they'd be so proud of all you've accomplished."

It's my so-called accomplishments that are my focus as I fly home. A baby cries. Fifty-six minutes of non-stop wailing, and it barely registers. I'm too in my head, wondering about my trajectory, how I went from having patients to having clients. It occurred to me last night, after my talk with Uncle Sylvester, that as I morphed from marriage therapist to inspirational speaker, the nomenclature for the people I supposedly help, changed. How did that happen? It's odd that it took me this long to notice it and for me to dislike it so.

Tomorrow is a workday, and I'm already dreading it. I tell myself it's only because I don't have much to do now that all my speaking engagements have been canceled. The days are spent posting inane inspirational sayings on my socials and deciding what Ronnie and I should eat for lunch. Austin calls four or five times a day, then winds up at my place, where we spend the evening deciding what we should eat for dinner.

It's a bumpy landing, and my stomach pitches as we speed down the runway. Mercy sakes alive, the baby stops crying. I can hear him cooing in economy as I reach up for my carry-on, only to have a tall gentleman wearing a UC Davis sweatshirt do it for me. I start to ask him if he knows a Professor Knox Hart, only to stop myself.

My phone rings the second I step inside the airport gate. Austin's timing is impeccable.

"I'm here, parked at the curb in arrivals until they order me to leave."

"You didn't have to come, Austin. I was planning to Uber home or take a cab."

"It was on my way," he lies.

I rush out into the cold, remembering that I'm no longer in LA, and scramble into the passenger seat before the surly cop walking up and down the sidewalk can tell Austin to move on.

"You have a good time?" he asks.

"I did."

We're quiet on the ride home. But I'm secretly delighted that he's chosen to pick me up at the airport. It feels good to be here with him, not alone in a cab on my way to an empty house.

"Should we pick something up for dinner or go out?"

"Let's go out," I say on a whim, the solarium restaurant in Beverly Hills and good French wine fresh on my mind.

Austin chooses a bistro not far from the condo. It's known for its fried green beans and butterscotch pudding. In all the time I've lived here, I've never eaten at this particular restaurant. It's a favorite with the ballpark crowd, and during home games, it's impossible to get in without a reservation. Tonight, though, it's nearly empty. There's only a group of dressed-up women in the corner near a window facing the street. Judging by the wrapped gifts piled on one end of the long table, they're here for an early Christmas celebration.

The host seats us as far away from them as she possibly can, but it's a small place. And sound carries. One of the women has an annoying, honking laugh that fills the entire room and echoes off the walls.

"We can go somewhere else if you want," Austin says.

"Nah, we're already here, and the food is supposed to be good."

My appetite is returning but only in fits and starts. I'd wager a guess that it has to do with the quality of the food. I peruse the menu and settle on the pork chops and braised greens. Austin gets the fried green beans to start us off. I'm anxious to see what all the hullabaloo is about.

As soon as our server leaves to put our orders in, Austin says, "I think I should move back in. My lease is up in January."

He's been staying nights at the condo but in the guest room. I don't know if it's to give me time to recuperate from my head injury or from him. But I think I'm ready to see where we go from here.

"That's something we can definitely talk about," I say, using my therapist voice. "I'm not going to lie, Austin, when it comes to you, I have trust issues. It's going to take a lot of work for me to get over that hurdle."

"I understand," he says, and hangs his head like he's ashamed of the way he walked out on me.

But I can tell it's an act. In his mind, we've already bridged the gap from divorced to reconciliation. In his mind, he's moving back in January.

In my mind, he may be right.

Chapter 22

The idea comes to me in the middle of the night, and the next day, I'm on a plane again. Ever since the accident and awakening from a coma, I've had this urge to tie up loose ends. And now seems like the time to tie up this particular loose end. To finally get closure.

It's only a week before Christmas, a week before I fly to Los Angeles to eat Wallace's perfect holiday turkey and open Uncle Sylvester's wildly extravagant gifts. And maybe see Lolly, if she deigns to be in the same room with me when I'm not dying.

The minute I land, I have regrets. First off, I have no idea where I'm going, and I haven't driven in months. At least the rental car is a Toyota. It's a different model than my Prius, but everything appears to work the same.

I set my GPS and take off for the wild blue yonder. Twenty minutes on the road, and I'm as comfortable behind the wheel as I was before the accident. What do they say? It's like riding a bicycle.

There is snow on the mountains and billboards for all-you-can-eat buffets and performances by has-been entertainers. A disembodied voice is telling me to take a series of turns until I'm breezing down a freeway entrance and driving across the desert, trying to get my bearings. It's difficult to know east from west without the Pacific Ocean as a guide.

I second-guess myself at least ten times, afraid that my reception will be anything but welcoming. It's been so long that I don't even know if I'll be recognized. But it feels like something I have to do, something that I should've done a long time ago.

My exit is less than two miles away, according to the map, and my pulse quickens. My palms sweat. At the exit, I pull into a Union 76 station just to get control of my erratic breathing.

It's there that I call Lolly, who surprisingly picks up.

"I'm in Reno." There's no need to elaborate, because she knows. She knows exactly why I'm here.

"Turn around, get back on the highway, and go home, Chelsea. Nothing good can come of it."

"I have to. For my own peace of mind."

"Then do it at your own peril." She hangs up.

Someone taps on my window, and I jump. It takes me a few seconds to disengage the child locks and crack the window.

"You're blocking the air compressor." He bobs his head at the tire inflator machine, which I am indeed blocking.

"Sorry." I watch him through my rearview mirror climb into a jacked-up truck, then move to a parking space in front of the tiny convenience store. I sit there, gathering my wits.

What's the worst that can happen? I ask myself, and nose the car back into traffic.

It's closing in on five, and commuters are clogging the four-lane boulevard on their way home from their workday in Reno. Congestion in the 'burbs. I pass a succession of strip malls, chain restaurants, and big-box stores, each one nearly identical. There's a megachurch that's as big as a city block and a high school with a jumbotron, promoting a winter formal.

I hang a right at the light, following the directions, and find myself traversing quiet residential streets. One-story stucco homes with red tile roofs and arched courtyards. Tidy rock gardens with succulent plants. Blow-up Santas and icicle lights.

By the fourth or fifth block, the houses start to get larger and the yards wider. There are more that butt up against a golf course with grass so green it looks like carpet against the desert sky.

"You have reached your destination," my GPS tells me. I park between two driveways and check the address on my phone. It's the two-story Mediterranean house with the wrought-iron balcony and the two-car garage.

I sit in the rental, gazing across the front yard, a drought-resistant garden of cacti and fake grass. There's a Mexican tile address sign that says THE ROSARIOS, the only clue that my father's oldest friend in the world lives here.

I flip down the visor and check my reflection in the mirror, wondering if Big Al will even recognize me. The last time he saw me, I was twelve years old.

I scoop up my purse, exit the car, and gird myself for a less-than-happy reunion.

A motion light flickers on as I make my way to the front door. A holiday wreath made of plastic poinsettias greets me, making it impossible for me to use the knocker without disrupting the wreath. I press the doorbell, instead, holding my breath.

A middle-aged woman in jeans and a turtleneck sweater swings opens the door as wide as the security chain will let it. A small barking dog tries to wriggle free through the narrow opening, and the woman pulls it back by its collar.

"Can I help you?" She looks behind me to see if I'm alone.

"I'm looking for Al Rosario. I was told he lives here."

She lifts the dog up into her arms and orders it to stop barking, which surprisingly works. The dog, some kind of terrier, nuzzles its face into the woman's neck. "What's this in regards to?"

I'm unprepared for the question. In all my plans for this

day, it was always Big Al opening the door. I suppose somewhere in the recesses of my brain, I made room for the possibility that he'd remarried. Even that he might be a grandfather by now. But I'm completely at a loss of how to answer.

"Who's at the door, Barbara?"

Now, Al is behind her, his eyes meeting mine, and it's as if I've gone back in time twenty-four years. His dark hair has turned gray, and he's carrying twenty extra pounds, but those sparkling brown eyes still light up a room.

"Chelsea? Well, I'll be goddamned." He undoes the chain, swings open the door, and reaches for me, pulling me into a warm embrace. All at once it's as if I'm surrounded by my father, my mother, and all those years of happiness. Of family.

"Let me look at you." He pulls back and gives me a warm assessment. "You're all grown up."

"It's been more than two decades." I don't mean it judgmentally, but I hear it come out that way. At least a little bit.

"It's been a long time," Al says. "Come on in. Barbara, this is Chelsea Knight. Chelsea, my wife, Barbara."

I reach out to shake her hand and really see her since she opened the door. Before, she was a faceless woman; now, she's Al's wife. The anti-Gloria. She's attractive in a quiet way with her neat brown bob, too-thin eyebrows, and warm hazel eyes. Her skin is flawless.

"It's a pleasure to meet you, Chelsea. Let me get the two of you something to drink. I'm sure you have a lot of catching up to do."

It's clear she knows who I am. What I represent. And yet, she is warm and welcoming without being ingratiating. And perhaps slightly distrustful. *Why has this young woman shown up after all these years? What does she want?*

I would be the same if I were in her place.

I follow Al through a hall of beige walls. There's a curio cabinet with carefully arranged ceramic figurines, like the kind you buy at Gump's or jewelry stores, and a console with a big pale pink vase of silk flowers. On the right is a sunken living room with more beige walls and matching carpet. But we keep going, winding up in a cramped den with too much furniture and dark paneled wood walls. It smells of cigar smoke, which surprisingly feels familiar. Al's man cave.

"You have a lovely home," I say to Barbara, who has been trailing behind us at a respectable distance. And it is.

"Thank you. We like it." She smiles at Al, proudly. "Coffee?"

"Coffee would be wonderful if it's not too much trouble."

She is gone, and it's just Al and me. He directs me to take one of the recliners, an oversized black padded chair with cup holders.

Al joins me in the chair's twin and a long, awkward silence stretches between us until finally he says, "I hear you're a psychologist now. A big deal with a talk show and books."

"Books, yes. But not a talk show, though I do a fair amount of lecturing. So, you're retired, huh?"

"It'll be six years in June." He repositions himself in the chair. "How is Lolly?"

"Divorced with two kids. She lives in Malibu now."

He nods, looking even more uncomfortable than when we first started.

"How did you meet Barbara?" I ask him, hoping it'll break the ice, hoping that the question won't somehow steer us to Gloria.

He brightens. "She was a court reporter in Van Nuys. I had a case before her judge, a burglary that went south when the perp interrupted a DV. The homeowner was beating the crap out of his wife. The burglar called nine-one-one. Craziest damn thing. Me and my partner caught the case. The jury convicted the husband, and I took Barbara out for sushi. The rest is history."

Al grins, and I get the sense that it's as much for his story as it is for the affection he feels for his wife. And yet I know. I know that Al will never love Barbara as much as he loved

Gloria. When he used to talk about Gloria, his whole body vibrated. And his eyes lit up like the sun. He used to watch her walk across a room, never taking his eyes off her.

Barbara brings our coffees and shuts the door on her way out. Al doesn't watch her go.

"You must think it's weird that I just showed up here today. No announcement. No nothing," I say.

He hitches his shoulders. "I'm glad you did."

I wonder.

"I was in a pretty significant accident not too long ago." I don't mention the cable car, because it's one of those things that people have trouble believing. Sort of like saying I was crushed by one of the toy boats in the "It's a Small World" ride in Disneyland. "It made me realize that I had unfinished business."

The expression on his face crumples. "Chelsea, you were twelve years old. If anyone has unfinished business, it's me. And I'm ashamed that it took you coming here for me to face it."

I surreptitiously wipe my eyes with the back of my hand.

"What happened?" he asks.

"A traffic accident. I was in the hospital for a month. But I'm good now."

"I'm sorry, honey. I'm sorry about everything."

"Me, too." It comes out hoarsely, and I have to wait to compose myself before I speak again. "I'm sorry about what my father did to you."

"Oh, sweet girl, now stop it. You didn't have a damned thing to do with that. None of you did. It was just one of those things."

I see the moment when he realizes what he's said, the way he's trivialized it.

"The affair was," he corrects himself. "The rest of it . . . Jesus." He scrubs his hand through his hair.

"Why didn't you ever talk to us again?" My voice is small, like I'm twelve again.

He palms his face. I've never seen Big Al cry, so I don't know what it looks like when he does but think this is probably it.

"I didn't know what to say to you girls. He was my best friend, and I was so angry at him for what he did to your mom, to you girls, to me . . . to himself . . ." He trails off and stares out the window. He's in his own world now, far away.

"It was wrong of me." He releases a breath. "You and your sister meant everything to me. But you've got to understand that for so long, I couldn't make sense of it. I couldn't make sense of any of it. The way he betrayed us, all of us. He wasn't the man I knew. He wasn't the man I loved like my own brother. It took me a long time to see clear of it. And when I finally did, you girls were in Los Angeles, living your own lives. I didn't want to bring any of it back to you. It was better that you moved on. And I knew your uncle loved you, that he'd take good care of you."

"He does and he did," I say. "But we loved you, too."

"I know, honey. I can't tell you how my heart ached losing the two of you. But you're a big girl now, a successful young woman, so you have to understand how much what happened messed me up. I lost the three most important people in my life that day."

Three? And then I realize he means Gloria, too.

"What happened to her, Al?" I don't even have to say her name.

"Last I heard, she married a chiropractor and moved to Tucson. That's all I know."

"I'm so sorry." I close my eyes, wishing I had something more constructive to say.

"It was a terrible situation. But this I can tell you with certainty, your father worshipped the ground you and Lolly walked on. Nothing made him happier than you two. He used to pass your pictures around the West Valley Division, brag about how smart you were, how you got straight As in school. No father was ever prouder of his kids."

I nod. Uncle Sylvester said the same thing in so many words. I have no reason to doubt it. I always felt my father's love. Growing up, it was all around me, pure and constant. I'm evolved enough to understand that my mother's murder, my father's suicide, had nothing to do with Lolly and me. We were just collateral damage.

"Have you forgiven him?" Al asks.

"I don't know." Because how do you forgive someone who took everything that ever mattered from you? "Have you?"

"I don't know that *forgiveness* is the right word." He sips his coffee, which until now neither of us has touched. "But I've made peace with it. It took a long time, but I have. Ultimately, I came to the conclusion that what happened couldn't diminish how much he loved us and how much we loved him."

"He did love you, Al. I may have only been a kid, but we all knew that you were everything to him." I turn to my coffee, which has already gone cold, and take a drink anyway.

"I wish it wasn't so complicated," I say.

"Don't we all, kiddo. Hang on a sec, I want to show you something." He gets up, goes to one of the built-in bookcases, plucks out a photo album, and motions for me to join him on the sofa while he flips through the pages. Pages and pages of pictures.

Dad and him leaning against their patrol car, laughing at the big box of donuts on the roof. Him and Dad in our old driveway, posing next to Al's new motorcycle. Mom sitting on Dad's lap in Al and Gloria's backyard. Lolly and me in a kiddie pool, splashing water at each other.

Gloria in a bikini, smiling at the person behind the camera. Probably Al.

I can't believe he kept this.

"It's part of my history," he says, sensing my surprise. "All of our history. The good history. I don't want to erase that."

He turns the page to a picture of my parents and Lolly and me, sitting around a cake on the dining room table at the house in Porter Ranch. "Was this my eighth birthday party?" I remember the dress. A frothy white confection that itched worse than poison ivy, but Mom made me wear it anyway, because it was a gift from Uncle Sylvester.

"Yep. I picked up the cake from that bakery on Ventura Boulevard. Went twenty minutes out of my way because you wanted their strawberry ice cream cake."

I don't remember the cake, but I smile, because I was picky like that.

In the next picture, it's Halloween, I'm dressed up like a fairy princess, holding Dad's hand. I trace the outline of his handsome face with my finger.

"Oh God." I tilt my head back in a useless attempt to keep the tears from dripping down my cheeks.

Al gets a box of tissues and pushes a wad into my hands. "These are the things I try to remember every time I think of him."

"I miss them so much." My voice trembles, and Al pulls me against him and lets me cry into his chest. "I'm sorry. I really need to pull myself together."

"I get a little misty myself when I look at them. Not a day goes by when I don't miss them, too, Chelsea."

"But you have this nice new life." I draw the tissue across my nose.

"Barbara's the best thing that ever happened to me. How about you? You have a nice guy in your life?"

I don't have the heart to tell him that I'm divorced, so I just say, "Yes. He's a divorce attorney, if you can believe that." But I almost say a biophysicist, who moonlights as a handyman.

"That's good. I know you said Lolly's divorced, but is she seeing someone? Someone solid? Reliable?"

I'm embarrassed to tell him that I'm clueless about my sister's life, that she doesn't let me in. Or worse, the truth. That for a long time, I didn't want in. That I've dedicated my life to fixing other people's problems but can't make room for my sister's.

"Not that I'm aware of." At least it isn't a lie. As far as I know, Lolly isn't dating. "It's tough with two kids. But she has a decent relationship with her ex."

"That's important," Al says.

"Did you and Barbara ever have children?" The world needs fathers like Big Al.

"Two steps from Barbara's previous marriage and three grands. Caleb and his family live in Maine, and Alexandra, her husband, and the twins in Reno. All good kids."

"I'm glad," I say, the words lodging in my throat. "You deserve the best, Al."

"Come here." He pulls me into another hug, and I linger there against his wide, warm chest and for a few seconds pretend he's my father. Pretend that my parents are still alive, and that Lolly and I are the best of friends, our babies the best of cousins.

Eventually, we come apart, and Al returns to the big book of photos. "Look at this one." It's a picture of Lolly and me eating ice cream on the Santa Monica Pier. We couldn't have been more than five and eight.

But it's not that photograph that catches my eye.

"Al, who's this?" I point to a picture on the next page of my dad, Al, and another man in Al and Gloria's backyard. The man is standing in front of a barbecue, holding a spatula. And Dad and Al are drinking cans of Budweiser Light, laughing, like someone just cracked a joke.

Al takes a closer look and breaks into a crazy grin. "That's Jimbo. You don't remember him?"

I shake my head.

"Jim Toomey. He used to be on the force with your Dad and me. Great guy. Did a tour in Desert Storm and joined the department around 1995. We used to razz him about his buzz cut. He married a friend of your mom's. Sandy, I think her name was."

I do remember Sandy. She was a petite lady with a voice like Minnie Mouse, who sometimes helped organize homes and garages with my mom and our neighbor. But I'm more interested in Jim Toomey.

"Is he retired?"

Al gives a lighthearted chuckle. "You can say that. He died eight years ago. Had a stroke on the job."

And yet, he was alive and well in my dream.

It's this, not my reunion with Big Al, that consumes me as I drive from the Rosarios' home to my hotel. And it's still Jim Toomey I'm consumed with as I fly home the next day.

Chapter 23

Austin is again talking about moving in. It's kind of become an obsession of his. I don't know why it matters, as he spends most nights here anyway. He has even graduated from the guest room to my room, which used to be our room. And despite everything we've been through these past fifteen months, it feels natural to be sleeping with him again.

Not just the sex part.

All of it. The snoring, the morning breath, even the late-night calls from his neurotic clients.

"You really think it's a good idea for me to come with you to Los Angeles?" He's lying on the bed, four pillows propped under his head, putting off taking a shower. It's Sunday. He's entitled to procrastinate.

"Of course I do. If we're going to do this"—*this* being us getting back together again—"let's do it right. I want to spend the holidays with you." Which isn't exactly true. It's more that I don't want him to spend Christmas alone.

Later, I'll parse the difference.

"Back to my dream," I say. "So, do you think Jim Toomey was my near-death experience? That I was on the cusp of death, and he was there to lead me into the great beyond? But at the last minute, I fought to live?"

"Jim Toomey?"

"The cop in my dream. The one who my father and Big Al worked with at LAPD. Come on, Austin, I've only been talking about him for days."

"Oh, right. I just forgot his name. No, I don't think he was your near-death experience, because there wasn't one. I believe whether you realize it or not, you remember him from your past. He was friends with your father, and you dreamt about him while you were in an induced coma, like you did everything else."

"How do you know I wasn't dying?"

"Because I was there. I was at the hospital by your bed, day in and day out. You never once coded, Chelsea. Never once."

"Maybe you don't code until you're actually gone."

"That's not how it works."

"How do you know?"

"Because I watch a lot of movies." His lips tip up.

"I still think it's weird that this guy I have absolutely no recollection of shows up in my dream."

"A lot of weird shit happens in the human mind. You of all people know that."

He's right. Look at déjà vu, the feeling that you've already experienced something that is happening in real time. Or déjà visité, having intimate knowledge of a place you've never been to before. Or apophenia, seeing patterns in things that don't exist, like a picture of Jesus in your toast. Or Cotard's delusion, the belief that you are already dead. Or hyperthymesia, the ability to remember every minute detail of every day of your life.

So, what's one coma-induced dream? But it feels like the dream was important, like the universe trying to tell me something. I just don't know what.

"The important thing is that you and Al are good," Austin says. "It was important that you made the trip, Chels. Closure."

That's the thing. I don't know if I'll ever have complete

closure or be able to rid myself of the fear of being abandoned. But seeing Al, feeling his love again, was a step in the right direction.

"Do you think you'll stay in touch?"

"I hope so," I say, but my sense is we won't. That no matter how good it was to see him again, it will always be painful, too. Like a million fragmented memories of my parents and Gloria stabbing me in the chest.

Austin slips one leg out from beneath the comforter. "Jesus, it's like fifty degrees in here." He rolls out of bed and crosses the floor to the thermostat in his underwear and cranks up the heat.

"Give me fifteen for a shower; then we'll grab breakfast."

While the shower is running, I jump on the Internet and take another peek at Misty's website, sorely tempted to book an appointment. I'm being crazy, I tell myself, and shut down my laptop before I talk myself into filling out her contact form and checking a box on her calendar.

The water stops, and Austin releases a cloud of steam when he opens the bathroom door. One of my white towels is wrapped around his waist. His chest is bare except for a few droplets of water, and I feel a surge of desire course through me.

The way it used to.

And for the first time since the accident, I'm overwhelmed by optimism.

Austin doesn't wind up coming with me to Los Angeles for Christmas.

His stepmother, who lives in Scottsdale, fell down a flight of steps. The two have never been close; in fact, they went a year and a half without talking after his father died and she sold off some of her husband's prized possessions, including a Masonic ring that belonged to Austin's grandfather that he wanted.

But she lives alone. So duty-bound, Austin went to take

care of her. That's what I love about him. He's a good person at his core, even if he sometimes makes lousy decisions.

Emboldened by my driving in Reno, I decide to make the 382-mile ride alone, instead of booking a last-minute flight. The original plan was for Austin to drive his car. I deliberate on whether to take Highway 101, the more scenic route, or Interstate 5, which is by far the quickest way, and opt for speed, anticipating Christmas Eve traffic.

It's a lonely stretch of road with not a lot to look at. Just a series of small towns with the requisite Starbucks, Economy Lodges, and Burger Kings. I don't plan to stop, unless it's to pee, and have packed plenty of snacks and a full thermos of coffee. Which makes me think of Knox and his ever-present insulated cup, always filled to the brim.

Will I ever stop thinking about him? About the man who doesn't exist.

By the time I reach Harris Ranch, I can't hold it any longer and exit the freeway. The parking lot is packed. There are rows of Teslas powering up at the electric charging stations and minivans filled to the windows with prettily wrapped gifts.

I slide into a spot a good distance from the restaurant and trot through the lot to find a bathroom. There's a line. When it's my turn and a stall finally opens up, I pee twice.

I'm in the gift shop, searching for a last-minute present for Wallace's dad, who is coming to dinner tomorrow night, when my phone rings. It's a familiar area code. Ghost. My pulse picks up.

"Hello." I step into a quiet corner and plug my non-phone ear with my finger. "Hello."

But there's no answer.

"Hello? Anyone there?"

I chalk it up to a butt-dial or a wrong number and hang up. It isn't until I'm on the forty-mile stretch of the Grapevine that it occurs to me that I don't have anyone in Ghost who could butt-dial me. No one but figments of my imagination.

Chapter 24

Lolly is pretending that I'm not sitting across from her at the table. She's spent all evening making small talk with Wallace's father. His name is Rudy, and he looks nothing like Wallacc. But he's a sweetheart like him and has a beautiful voice.

Before dinner, Uncle Sylvester played the piano, and Rudy sang "Angels We Have Heard on High," hitting all the high notes like an opera singer.

I caught Taylor and Luna laughing at his vibrato and had to cover my mouth so no one would see me laughing, too.

Austin has texted me three times. I don't think things are going well with him and his stepmother. But in a way, I'm relieved he didn't come. I haven't had a lot of time to myself since I left the hospital, and the six-hour drive was a nice break. Just me alone with my thoughts.

"The meal is amazing, Wallace." He's outdone himself.

The turkey looks like something out of a Julia Child cookbook, perfectly browned skin and cut in perfectly proportioned slices. There's at least a dozen sides, including homemade cranberry sauce with orange slices. Mom used to serve it from a can in one round block with the ridges still on it. After Mom, and before Wallace, Uncle Sylvester used to take us to the W Hotel.

"Before we dig in, I want to propose a special toast to my

niece, Chelsea." Uncle Sylvester raises his glass. "All I can say is thank God you're here." He chokes up before he can finish, and then in a last-ditch effort, concludes with, "Don't ever leave us again."

There's not a dry eye in the house, except, of course, for Lolly's.

Still, the evening is fantastic, the best Christmas I can remember in a long time. Uncle Sylvester is so at ease, so comfortable, which I attribute to Wallace, who makes everyone comfortable. And Taylor and Luna regale the table with funny stories about the screenplay they're writing. It's about a flea named Fly, who travels to Dubai on the back of a Weimaraner that's just won Best in Show at Westminster.

It sounds like a pretty original idea to me, and I wonder how they thought of it. I glance sideways at Lolly, but she's looking at her phone.

We spend the rest of the evening opening gifts and singing more carols around the piano. Rudy does a version of "Silent Night" that blows me away. And the kids insist on "Jingle Bells," which we all join in on.

I make my way around the room to Lolly's side, hoping that I can force her into a conversation. Or at least a few cordial words. Just something to open the doors of communication. But as soon as I inch closer, she heads toward the bathroom. I know it's a ploy to ditch me, but what am I supposed to do? Follow her into the loo and make a scene?

I linger in the hallway, waiting for her to come out, but Wallace asks me to help set the table for pie. And after dessert, Lolly announces that it's time for them to leave. Rudy takes her cue and packs up his gifts, and they all walk out together. It's just Uncle Sylvester, Wallace, and me.

I help clear the last of the dessert dishes, and the three of us clean the kitchen until it shines. Then we gather up all the torn wrapping paper and boxes and load it into a giant garbage bag, which Uncle Sylvester throws down the trash chute at the end of the hallway. It's only ten, but I can barely keep my eyes open.

When I turn in for bed, I see that I have two missed calls from Austin. I should call him, wish him a Merry Christmas. But I roll over and go to sleep.

The next morning, I shower, dress, and drive to Malibu.

Interstate 10 to Santa Monica is a zoo, a complete madhouse. You would think everyone would stay home the day after Christmas and play with their new toys. But apparently, everyone is headed to the beach. It's not even a good day for it. Windy and overcast. Though it'll likely burn off by late morning and turn out to be a beautiful day, as is usually the case in Southern California.

As soon as I'm on the Pacific Coast Highway, traffic starts to move again. It's one of the great mysteries of the world why everything comes to an abrupt halt and then, without reason, starts up again.

I've only been to Lolly's house a few times and hope I can remember how to get there. After a few false starts, I plug her address into my phone and let my GPS take me there. I should've done that in the first place, but I let my arrogance get the better of me.

She's not expecting me, and I have no idea if she'll even be home. The kids are with Brent today. I know this because I overheard her bitching to Uncle Sylvester about how the schedule screwed up any chances of her spending the rest of the week at their condo in Hawaii. Poor, poor, Lolly, so deprived.

I've forgotten how gorgeous Lolly's house is until I drive up her long, bougainvillea-lined driveway, and it takes my breath away. It's a 1920s Spanish colonial with a Saltillo tiled courtyard and an impressive fountain. The house is perched high enough on a hill and angled in such a way that there's a 180-degree unobstructed view of the Pacific Ocean.

I cut the engine and just stare at it for a while. She got the house in the divorce, because both she and Brent agreed that they shouldn't uproot the children. Otherwise, Lolly could never have afforded a home like this, even with her astronomical spousal support.

Brent is a Hollywood heavy hitter, who owns his own production and syndication company and is credited with launching *The Ellen DeGeneres Show* and distributing some of the top game shows on television, including *Wheel of Fortune* and *Jeopardy*. Lolly met him through Uncle Sylvester.

I get out of the car and walk through the lovely courtyard to get to the double-arched front doors that remind me of a medieval castle and ring the bell. Lolly's car is in the driveway. But no one answers, so I ring it again. It's a large house. Who knows if she can hear the ring if she's upstairs or in the kitchen?

I wait a few more minutes, then walk around to the back, where I find Lolly doing yoga by the pool. She doesn't seem surprised to see me, yet she doesn't acknowledge me, either. She just continues with her routine. In a pair of yoga pants and an exercise bra, my sister is in excellent shape. Then again, she has a lot of free time to work out.

The pool is a sparkling blue with an infinity edge that gives the illusion that the water is spilling over the edge into the ocean. I assume it's heated and gets used year-round. To check, I dip my hand in. It's about eighty degrees. I can only imagine the gas and electric bill. Just the thought of all those zeros makes me queasy. Another thing Brent is likely paying for.

I plop down into one of the lounge chairs, which is shaded by a giant umbrella. The sun is already peeking out from behind the clouds, and it's warmer than when I left Century City. The smell of chlorine is thick, and somewhere in the distance, a leaf blower or weed whacker rends the air. Still, it's peaceful here. Like a private resort above the beach.

I don't know why Lolly needs Hawaii.

She's winding down, I can tell, because she's sitting with the palms of her hands pressed together in front of her sternum in prayer position, her eyes closed, and her head bowed. I've taken enough yoga classes to recognize Anjali Mudra. That's about all I remember from the instruction, probably because it was my favorite point in the routine. In other words, over.

She sits there for a few minutes with her eyes closed, pretending to meditate. Or maybe she really is. But I doubt it. That's okay, because I'm feeling patient today.

"You look awful." It's the first words out of her mouth.

I look the same way I always do. Though perhaps a little thinner, because I haven't yet gained back my pre-accident weight. But I'm well on my way, considering my three helpings of potatoes and pie last night. I'm already thinking about having another slice of the pecan as soon as I get back to Uncle Sylvester's.

"I'm serious," she says. "You look like a bag of shit."

"That's lovely, Lolly. What a great thing to say to me after I almost died." I'm not above playing the death card when it comes to her.

"I'm just being honest."

"Well, you don't look so great, either," I lie.

"I look the best I've ever looked in my life. But you, on the other hand, look like a sad sack. Like that bitch, Mrs. Roberts, who used to yell at us for being too loud when she was trying to watch her programs." She accentuates the word *programs*, and I laugh.

Mrs. Roberts lived one floor down from Uncle Sylvester and was forever complaining that our footsteps were like a pack of elephants. No amount of rugs was ever good enough for her. She eventually died of a heart attack, and a young couple bought the apartment.

"Whatever, Lolly. Go ahead and get all the anger out of your system."

"Don't pull your psych shit on me. I'm not in the mood."

"I can see that." I shake my head. "You're in the mood to excoriate me. So have at it."

She gets up from her yoga mat in one fluid motion. It's graceful and at the same time aggressive. "I need a shower."

She leaves me sitting there while she goes inside the house. Despite not being invited, I tag along behind her and wind up in the kitchen. Five of my kitchens can fit in this room. The La Cornue stove alone would take up most of the floor space in my apartment.

I rummage through her built-in refrigerator for something to drink and help myself to a glass of orange juice. Then wait. I'm not going home until we do this, until we hash this out. I don't expect that it'll only take this once, but we have to start somewhere, right?

I pass the time snooping around her house. It's a long way from our humble beginnings at Porter Ranch, though I have no right to complain. While I don't have anything like this, I'm well taken care of.

"Stop pawing my furniture." Lolly sweeps down the wrought-iron staircase. "Why are you still here?"

"Can you just give it a rest already? All this feigned anger has got to be exhausting."

She surprises me by suppressing a laugh. "What makes you think it's feigned?"

"Because you're a very bad actress."

"Use a coaster." She points to the juice glass that I've put down on the mammoth wooden coffee table in her front room. "It'll leave a ring."

"Sorry," I say, and quickly pick up the glass. "Can we go in the kitchen?" I like that room the best. Even though it's ginormous, and the state-of-the-art appliances intimidate me, there's love there. I can feel it oozing from the walls.

She leads the way, motioning for me to take a seat at the

breakfast bar. "What happened at Big Al's? Did he tell you to leave?"

"He's remarried now. Her name is Barbara, and she loves him more than he loves her."

"How do you know? Did he tell you that?"

"He didn't have to; I could tell."

"Because you're psychic."

"Fuck you, Lolly."

This time, she really does laugh. "How was he?"

"Good. He has a nice house that backs onto a golf course and two stepkids and three grandkids. He seemed very content."

"Content?" she hitches a brow. "He wasn't angry that you just showed up unannounced, like the great white hope?"

I shrug. "He appeared genuinely happy to see me."

"Did he talk about Dad?"

"Yes, we talked about Dad. He says he made peace with . . . what he did."

Lolly doesn't say anything, just stares down at her manicured fingernails. "Why didn't he ever talk to us again?"

"He said he was grieving, that it was too difficult, but that he's sorry."

She snorts. "I guess his grief was more important than ours. What an asshole."

"Things aren't always black or white, Lolly. It was a terrible loss for him, too. He probably just didn't know what to say to us, how to react."

"What happened to Gloria?"

"He said last he heard, she'd married a chiropractor and moved to Tucson. That's all he knew."

"Weird."

I look at Lolly as if to say, *What's so weird about it?*

"Dad fucks her, blows Mom's heart out, then swallows his own gun, and she moves to Tucson. Don't you see the inequity in that?"

"I guess I never really thought of it that way. All my anger has been directed at Dad, not Gloria. What? You wanted her to die, too?"

"No, of course not. You're missing the point."

"What's the point then? Explain it to me."

"The point is that . . . oh, never mind." She waves me off, like I'm too stupid to understand.

I don't let it bother me, because frankly, I don't think Lolly even knows what she means. She's just angry. At me, at our parents, at the world.

"So while I was at Al's, he showed me this photo album he's kept all this time. It had pictures of you and me, Mom and Dad, and even Gloria. But there was one of this guy, Jim Toomey. Do you remember him?"

"No. Who is he?"

"He worked with Dad and Al at LAPD and died of a stroke. And this is the freaky part, he was in my dream when I was in the coma. He pulled me over for a DUI, made me take a sobriety test, then let me go with a stern warning. At the end, he told me to say hi to Dad, which even in my dream I found strange. Because how did he even know Dad? And if he did, he must've known he was dead." I look at Lolly to see if she's following me. "Do you see what I'm saying? It's as if he was telling me I would be seeing Dad because I was dead, too."

"Maybe you were and then by some miracle, you pulled through?"

"Do you really believe that?"

"No. I was there, Chelsea. You were in bad shape. Very bad shape. But you weren't at death's door."

"That's what Austin says. He says I would'vc coded if I died, even if it was only for a few seconds."

"It was just a stupid dream," Lolly says.

"But . . . Jim Toomey. I don't think I ever saw him before, and yet, in my dream, he looked exactly like the picture."

"You just forgot about him. It was a long time ago."

"Could be. I'll be honest with you, though, it's sort of shaken me. It's made me rethink everything."

"Like what?"

"Like the entire trajectory of my life."

"Is that why you're here? To make up for what a shitty sister you've been."

"Partially. You know you were in my dream, too? You came to my lake cabin, and we went to the annual Halloween parade together." I pause for a reaction, but Lolly is poker-faced. "It was nice, you and me spending time together."

"Hmm, that's funny. Apparently, I'm not fun in real life."

"You used to be," I say, but regret it. It was mean, and I'm here to patch us up, not out-cynical her.

"When? When I was twelve?"

The age is a thinly veiled cut. When she was twelve, I left for boarding school, in essence leaving her. "Let's not dance around, Lolly, let's just get it out in the open."

"What would you like to get out in the open?"

"Us." I wave my hand between us. "Why we don't work anymore. Because I would like us to. I miss you."

She pulls a bottle of pinot grigio from the refrigerator, pops the cork, and pours us each a glass. "Is this part of the new trajectory?"

"Perhaps. But even before the accident, I wanted to fix it. Fix us. I wanted to say I was sorry for leaving you when you needed me most."

"And when was that?" It's still there, that sting in her voice. The anger.

"When we were kids. I didn't mean to abandon you, Lolly. But . . . and this is the hard part . . . I think I was going a little crazy. I couldn't sleep. Every time I closed my eyes, I heard it. The gunshots. The moment Mom and Dad died. I got to the point where I thought there was something in the bed with me. The mattress would shake like there was an animal inside the coils and springs, running back and forth, as if it was trying to get out. I told Uncle Sylvester, and he took the whole bed apart while I watched. 'There's nothing here, Chelsea. See?'—he showed me. And then it happened at school. I was sitting on a wooden chair. At first, I thought we were having an earthquake. But when I looked around, nothing was moving. And that's when I realized it was me. I was the one shaking. My entire body was vibrating. And the only way to escape was to run. I ran as fast and as far as a fifteen-year-old could go. Santa Barbara. Boarding school."

"So basically, you're the kid version of Big Al."

Clearly, my story hasn't moved her.

"Yes," I admit. "I was the kid version of Big Al. We all have ways of taking care of ourselves. Ours, Al's and mine, was to run. And you got left behind. And for that, I'm eternally sorry."

"You don't get it, do you?" She peers at me with slatted eyes. "This isn't about what happened two decades ago, though I'm still pissed about that. I'm still angry that you left me here alone. But I'm not so selfish that I don't understand why. But this is about what happened three years ago."

I rack my brain to remember what happened three years ago, afraid that I'm missing something significant, and that if I admit I don't know what she's talking about, it will only infuriate her more.

"You have no freaking idea what I'm talking about, do you?" she says, and throws back half her glass of pinot grigio.

And then it comes to me. "Your divorce." But I say it more as a question than a statement, because I'm confused.

"You're a real piece of work, Chelsea. You know that?"

I want to say, *What did I do wrong?* Because I honestly have no idea.

"You divorced Brent." This time, I say it firmly, no wavering. I leave out that we knew she would. Brent is nearly thirty years older than Lolly. It doesn't take a psychology degree to know he was a replacement for Dad, and that it was only a matter of time before she realized she'd married him for all the wrong reasons.

"No one blames you, Lolly."

"Don't you get it? He divorced me. He left me for someone else. He's probably the only man in the entertainment industry who left his wife for an older woman. She's not even attractive." She tops off her glass with the bottle, and her hand is shaking. "I loved him. Do you understand that? I loved him, and he left me."

I'm speechless. "I didn't know that," I manage to say after a few minutes of absorbing what she just told me. "I'd always figured that you left him."

"You know why you didn't know he was the one who wanted a divorce? You know why? Because you didn't fucking ask. You jetted off to Boston or Memphis or Timbuktu, or wherever you go to help people you don't know to save their marriages. Yet you couldn't be bothered with mine. Or me."

"That's not true." But the thing is, it is. Everything she's said.

I try to remember three years ago. I try to remember where I was and what I was doing when Lolly told me she and Brent were breaking up. And nothing stands out. I have absolutely no recollection of us having any kind of momentous talk about it. Sure, there were conversations, snippets about custody of the children, who got what, where Brent would live. The logistics.

But nothing about *why*.

I'd always assumed it was Lolly who'd precipitated the dissolution of their marriage. That she'd married Brent for security and children. I suppose I never gave their divorce much weight because I never took their marriage seriously.

"Tell me what happened."

"There's nothing to tell. He met someone else. Someone who was his intellectual equivalent"—she makes quotes in the air with her fingers—"someone who knows the lyrics to

Beatles songs. He actually said that; can you believe it? He said he loved her in a way he could never love me. And then he left."

"I'm so sorry, Lolly. I had no idea."

"That might've been the worst part." She puts her glass down and locks eyes with me. "It was happening all over again. Mom and Dad dying, you leaving to go away to school, Uncle Sylvester always working. If it weren't for the kids, I'd be completely alone."

"You're not alone. You've got me. I know it hasn't seemed like that, but it's going to be different now."

"I loved him, Chelsea. I know it's hard for you to see that, but I loved him. I still love him." She crumples in my arms, sobbing.

I brush her hair with my hand like I used to do in that first year after Mom and Dad were gone. She would crawl into bed with me and cry, afraid that she was forgetting what they looked like, how they smelled, their voices. There was a box under my bed with their pictures, and we'd try to make out their faces in the dark. We'd try to inhale the lingering scent of them, even though it had already faded.

"It hurts so much," she says between her hiccupping sobs. "It's like a hole in my heart that never heals."

"It will," I say. "With time, it'll get better."

"But it's already been three years." She pulls away, and I instantly feel bereft of her weight, of her warmth. Of our impossible history together.

"I don't think you can measure grief in terms of years. I meant time in the abstract."

"Can you just speak English, please?"

"What I'm trying to say is that it won't hurt this way forever. You'll move past it. Maybe you'll fall in love again, maybe you won't. But you'll find something in your life that fills the hole. Something wonderful."

"How can you be so sure? There's no guarantee. For all

you know, I'll die a shriveled-up old lady with a broken heart. Taylor and Luna will have to send me away to a special home for sad, pathetic people."

"Now you're just being dramatic."

"Seriously, though, how do you know?"

It's the old crystal ball question. I remember something Knox told me in my dream about how in the long run, it wasn't Sienna he wanted, it was the picture of the life he thought she represented. Those words come back to me every time I'm with Austin. And I have to question if it's the same with Lolly and Brent. If he's merely a picture of the life she wants.

"No one knows anything for sure," I say. "But let me ask you something. Do you want to be happy and live your best life?"

"My best life?" She rolls her eyes. "You're an idiot. But yes, I want to be happy."

"Then let's make that your goal for the new year."

"Just like that." She snaps her fingers. "A New Year's resolution to be happy. Poof. It's that easy."

"I never said it was easy. In my experience, anything worth having is really, really hard."

My mind turns to the ridiculous mockups for the Chelsea Knight inspirational calendar sitting on my desk in San Francisco. The first thing I'm going to do when I get home is throw them in the trash.

"But I can help," I continue. "We can help each other."

"You don't have the greatest track record, Chels. You and Big Al are the cut-and-run brigade."

I let out a long breath. "Not anymore. No more running." I lean over and take her hand. "Will you do something with me tomorrow?"

"Probably not. What is it?"

"Mom and Dad's graves. I think it's time we said a proper goodbye."

Chapter 25

I stop and bend down to smell a bouquet of plastic flowers. They're everywhere at Forest Lawn. The practical side of me says, *why not*? They keep forever. And it would be a relief not to have to worry about clearing dead ones away. Or in my case, hiring someone to do it.

"Stop that. A dog probably peed on them." Lolly tugs my arm.

"At a cemetery?" I don't think dogs are allowed in cemeteries. But who knows? They seem to be allowed everywhere these days. Restaurants, grocery stores, hospitals. "But they're so pretty."

"They're disgusting and tacky." Lolly is done hearing me extol the virtues of plastic roses.

It's just the two of us, as Uncle Sylvester thought we needed to do this alone. We're walking down the rows of headstones, following a map given to us by a prim-looking man who punched our parents' names into a computer and within minutes could tell us the general location of their burial sites.

The last time I was here was for the funeral, a surreal event where no one spoke the unspeakable. Just a lot of eulogies about how my father was a cop's cop, a hero, and my mother, a friend to all. A young, beautiful couple that loved their family who were taken from us too early.

Lolly and I wore matching navy-blue dresses and sat in the first row as they lowered Mom and Dad's caskets into empty holes. Dad's brother, Jeb, sat next to us, drinking from a brown paper bag, mumbling expletives under his breath. Everyone pretended not to notice.

Grandma Josephine, my mother's mother, was there, too. I remember pushing one of the handles on her wheelchair while Lolly pushed the other. She died a year after my parents.

"According to this, it's the next row over." Lolly is holding the map, examining the red circle the man drew.

We veer off the trail, and our heels get caught in the wet grass.

"I should've wore flats," Lolly says.

It's one of those perfect Southern California days, if you like Santa Ana winds blowing in warm air. Everyone on the maintenance crew is wearing shorts. I, on the other hand, am in a sweater dress, the same one I wore on Christmas. It's all I brought that's appropriate for a graveyard visit, but I can't wait to get it off me. It's sticking to my skin.

"I think it's in this vicinity. Start looking for names," Lolly says.

It feels a little voyeuristic reading the names on the headstones, like we're invading a stranger's private nap. We walk in circles but can't find Christopher and Nancy Knight.

"I don't see it," I call to Lolly, who has skipped ahead. "Are you sure we're in the right place?"

"I can read a map, Chelsea. It's here somewhere. Keep looking."

I catch up to her and snatch the map out of her hand to study it. "It's three rows up."

"How do you get that?"

I start to show her, but she's already crossing the lawn, leaving divots in the sod with her stilettos. At least my heels are only two inches high. Besides a pair of tennis shoes, they are all I brought.

"Over here." She waves to me.

I quicken my pace and join her in a leafy spot under a mature oak tree. One of the few in this part of the cemetery. I suspect Uncle Sylvester greased some palms. My mother loved trees. There was a beautiful jacaranda tree in our backyard in Porter Ranch. Mom used to say that she always knew when winter was over, because the tree would bloom in a halo of glorious purple flowers, a stunning contrast against springtime's dreary gray skies.

I read Dad's headstone first. "Christopher Jacob Knight, 1957 to 1999. In Loving Memory." Then Mom's. "Nancy Gay Knight, 1958 to 1999. Loving wife, mother, daughter, sister, adored by all."

The contrast between the two is not lost on either of us.

"You know the 'in loving memory' part had to have killed Uncle Sylvester."

"I'm sure he did it for us." I trace the carved marble with my finger. "Besides, he did love Dad."

"We all did. I guess that's why it's so hard to understand." Lolly whispers the last part, even though there's no one around. The cemetery is eerily empty. "What do we do now?"

"Let them go." For me, that's forgiving my father and cease holding him accountable for everything bad that's ever happened to me since he took his own life.

Lolly surprises me by sitting down in the soggy grass at the foot of their headstones. She pats the space next to her, and I get down there with her.

"I'll go first," she says, and lays her hands on the cold marble. "Mom, Dad, we're here. I know it took us a while, but we're here now. Chelsea says we have to let you go. But I don't want to let you go. I want to remember you the way you were, the way Dad was when he taught me how to write my name one letter at a time. The way Mom always had a tissue rolled up in her sleeve to wipe our runny noses. That's what I want to remember. The rest . . . well, I'm going to blame that on Dad having a bad day."

I pierce her with a look. *A bad day?*

Okay, if it's her way of making peace, then so be it. And for the record, I know what she's doing. Her glib attitude doesn't fool me. I can see the tears behind her words. I can feel the hurt.

"It's your turn now, Chelsea."

I don't say anything at first. I underestimated how difficult this would be. Initially, I thought twenty-four years of pent-up anger, confusion, and heartache would tumble out of me like a storm, and the words would never stop. And somewhere between my pain and my love, I would find forgiveness.

"I don't know where to start," I say. "I guess anger is a good place. I don't know if I can ever stop being angry with you, Dad, for what you did. It was . . . it is . . . unforgivable. It's safe to say, and I say it with authority because I'm a psychologist now, that you're the reason for all of Lolly's and my abandonment issues. It's also safe to say that we don't know how we're supposed to feel about you. If we love you, we feel a deep abiding guilt, a betrayal of Mom and of ourselves. And if we hate you, we also feel a deep abiding guilt. It's a lose-lose situation. And frankly, it's exhausting.

"But like Lolly, I also can't stop remembering all the good. I know you loved us, which only makes it harder to understand why you did what you did. Having said that, the bad can't erase the good. And ultimately, all this anger and sadness isn't helping anyone. It's like a bag of weights dragging us to the bottom of an endless well. So, again, like Lolly, I'm letting the bad go and only embracing the positive. I love you, Daddy. I love you, Mom." I get to my feet and wrap my arms around both headstones. "Rest in peace."

Lolly and I are both crying our eyes out. Ugly, racking

sobs. When I try to hug her, she walks away. I go back to the car by myself. Then wait, because she's driven and has the keys. When she shows up ten minutes later, she acts like nothing has happened and everything is fine.

"What's going on with you?" I ask as she noses out of the parking lot.

"I need to clean the house before the kids get home tomorrow."

Since when does she clean? I don't say it, though, not even as a joke, because I'm back to walking on eggshells with her again. "Too bad. I thought we could go to lunch, just the two of us."

"No can do."

"Okay. It's too bad, though, I was looking forward to catching up."

Her response is to turn the radio on. It's talk radio, and they're playing a clip from one of my TED Talks. It's my lecture on visualization and how, if you train your mind to focus on something you want, the more likely it is to come true.

I reach forward and turn it off.

"Hey, I was listening to that."

"You don't have to listen to me on the radio, because I'm right here." My voice is raised, and I'm tired of holding back. "What the hell crawled up your ass?"

"What! It's been a very emotional day."

I can't disagree with that. I expected weightlessness to come from letting go, like my whole body would be purged of darkness and I would emerge into the light. Cleansed. Free. I feel all those things. But I also feel like there's a piece missing, like maybe Knox and Misty and Sadie and even Officer Toomey were trying to tell me something, something that could change the entire direction of my life.

Lolly pulls off PCH into a rutted dirt parking lot.

"What are you doing?" My voice is warbly from bouncing

up and down. Either the suspension on Lolly's car is shot, or it's about to be.

"You said you wanted lunch." She spreads her arms in front of her. "Come on." She's out and walking before I can say a word.

The restaurant is a cross between a dive bar and a hideaway for wayward surfers. Dick Dale's "Miserlou" is playing at an unhealthy volume. And fish netting, glass ball floats, and pictures of surfers covered in a thick layer of dust is the sole décor. While it may be kitschy enough, it's too clichéd to be cool—or even vintage surf culture. Even in Malibu. Which is all fine by me. But it's the last place I would expect Lolly to frequent, and judging by the friendly waves and shouts of "Hey, Lols" from the staff, she comes here a lot.

A guy with shaggy blond hair seats us by a window with a view of the beach. The tables are of the wooden picnic variety. To doll them up, someone pasted whimsical maps of the best surfing spots in America on the surface, then covered the top with clear resin. The blond-headed guy hands us two greasy menus and disappears.

"How'd you find this place?"

She pushes her menu to the edge of the table. "It's right off the road."

I don't remember seeing any signage, just a nondescript beach shack that could've just as easily been a bait shop. It seems like a strange place to break bread after the heaviness of the cemetery, especially because Lolly is always bragging on social media about the trendy, albeit expensive, restaurants she patronizes. But I don't say anything, just happy that she's changed her mind about having lunch.

"Do you come here often?"

"A few times a week."

I store this new revelation about my sister away for the moment, realizing that she has this whole life that I know nothing about. A whole life that isn't carefully curated for her public persona.

I flip open the menu and peruse the burger section, which is as tired as the décor. But hey, who doesn't love a good patty melt?

"What do you like here?" I ask her.

"The tuna salad sandwich and the potato salad."

My reaction is visceral. All at once, I'm back at our kitchen in Porter Ranch. My mother's favorite dishes (Franciscan Desert Rose) are on the table, scooped high with my father's homemade potato salad and a tuna salad sandwich that he cut into the shape of a fish. He made it specially for us.

"Don't," she says.

"I'm not." But I'm wiping my eyes with one of the restaurant's thin paper napkins. "Thank you for bringing me here."

She waves to get Shaggy Hair's attention and holds up two fingers.

"You're leaving tomorrow." She says it as an accusation rather than a statement of fact.

"I've put off work long enough. I had to cancel quite a few speaking engagements because of the accident. All of them need to be rescheduled. It's daunting, really."

"Don't you have people for that?"

"Just Ronnie, my assistant." I've always run a tight ship.

"So all that stuff you said about me finding happiness and you helping me was a load of crap."

"No, it wasn't. But it's not like I can stay here forever. I've got to work, Lolly. Unlike you, I have bills to pay."

"Unlike me? What's that supposed to mean?"

"Oh, for God's sake, you're just looking for ways to start a fight, aren't you? Let me point out that you're not exactly the sister of the year, either. You left me lying in a hospital bed without so much as a goodbye or even a get well soon."

"I came, which is more than I can say for you."

"I'm sorry I wasn't there for you during your divorce. I'm

deeply ashamed for that, Lolly. Can we please put this behind us and move forward?"

She doesn't commit one way or another, but I see cracks in her tough exterior. And that gives me hope.

"Would you and the kids like to come and stay with me at the lake cabin? It's in this great town called Ghost. You guys would get such a kick out of it."

Our food comes, giving her a temporary reprieve.

She points at my plate. "Taste it."

The sandwich is not cut in the shape of a fish, but it's made with the same kind of bread my father used to use. Thick slices of white. There's a pickle spear on the side of the plate that reminds me of the jarred dills Dad would slice in half to garnish our sandwiches.

I take a bite, my eyes close, and I'm instantly a child again.

Lolly smiles. "Now the potato salad."

I lift a forkful to my mouth, and I'm home again, with all the familiar sounds and smells of my childhood house. It's resonance. The phenomenon where something as simple as the taste of a tuna sandwich and a bite of potato salad triggers a memory that's been stored in the brain from the original experience, i.e. the first time Dad made us this meal. In other words, my neural pathways are going nuts.

Lolly won't say it, but I've already deduced that this is where she comes for comfort. This is where she comes to remember our parents. The good stuff, only the good stuff.

"I figured out the significance of that cop in your dream, the one Dad and Big Al worked with at LAPD," Lolly announces.

"Yeah? What's his significance?"

"He wasn't telling you to say hi to Dad for him because you were at death's door. He told you to say hi to him as a message."

"What's the message, then?"

"That you should go to Dad, that you should talk to him

and find whatever forgiveness you can muster. He was sending you to him. He was telling you to say goodbye and to extend an olive branch. To finish it, Chelsea, so you . . . we . . . could move on."

I take in what she's said, because it makes sense. "Like we did today?"

"Like we did today. I think subconsciously you knew that, and that's why the visit to their graves was so important to you, why you needed to do it."

"What about you?" I ask her. "Did it help?"

She nods. "I think so. It was this ugly thing that never went away. But maybe now we can just concentrate on the beauty. Because before Dad did what he did, we had a beautiful life."

"Yep." I reach for her hand. "And we're going to make it beautiful again. I promise."

We eat, our hearts full. And the lightness fills me again. For all its difficulty, today was a good day.

"What's going on with you and Austin?" Lolly breaks the silence.

"He wants to move in next year. January."

"Are you going to let him?"

She and I haven't discussed Austin since he left me—or anything, for that matter. But I assume she's gotten all the gory details from Uncle Sylvester.

I nod. "He loves me." But I know I'm saying it more for myself than I am for Lolly.

"He left you."

"Yes, he did. Brent left you. But if he wanted to come back, you would let him, wouldn't you?"

"First of all, it's different for me than it is for you," she says. "Brent and I have kids together. I have to think about my children. But even still, I wouldn't take him back. You know why? Because I'm sick the fuck of people always leaving."

I can't argue with that. Because I'm sick the fuck of it, too.

"So are you saying I shouldn't take Austin back?"

"I'm not saying anything of the sort. I'm saying you do you."

"That's helpful."

"You're the fancy, famous marriage expert. You figure it out."

"I already have. But thanks for your input, such as it is."

We finish lunch and drive to her house, where I've left my car. I still don't know where I stand with her. She's so unpredictable. But I get the sense that we've made inroads. Going to Forest Lawn together was a huge step. A small piece of closure.

Before I leave, I pull her in for a hug. She tries to pull away, but I won't let her.

"I love you, Lolly."

She doesn't say it back, and it hurts. It's like losing a part of yourself. It's like losing everything.

"Bye, bitch." She pulls away and starts walking to the house, then calls over her shoulder. "See ya in Ghost. Shitty name for a town, by the way."

And then she's gone, leaving me alone with a smile blooming in my chest.

Chapter 26

Last night, I tried to channel Knox in my dreams. I thought he'd fade with time, but it hasn't happened. There's not a day that goes by that I don't think of him. About his coffee, his unvarnished truths, and the closeness we shared.

It's crazy, irrational, but I can feel it in every fiber of my body. If Knox were real, he'd never leave. Ever. It's so instinctual that in moments of pure panic, I wonder if perhaps I'm the one who is in a dream. It's actually a thing. Depersonalization-derealization disorder, an out-of-body experience, or the sense that things aren't real around you. In layman's terminology, you feel like you're living in a dream. Except in this case, the dream is real.

Or is it?

I'm going to drive myself mad.

"Can you do February ninth for our makeup in Albuquerque?" Ronnie's got her hand over the phone's mouthpiece and motions to me that's it's my lecture coordinator.

"Uh, I don't know. Do we have to decide right now?"

"Kind of. That's the only day the room is available. Otherwise, we have to wait until August."

"Okay, book it for the ninth." But my heart isn't in it. I keep telling myself that once I get back on the road, everything will click in place. I just need to find my groove again.

"What about the sixteenth for Phoenix?"

"No, that's Taylor's birthday." Lolly sent me an invitation. She's hiring a mini circus to come to the house, which is so Lolly. I want to shock her by actually showing up. "What about LA—can we book there on the seventeenth?"

"You're in LA in March."

"March what? I've got Uncle Sylvester's and Wallace's anniversary in March. We're going out for dinner. I can't miss that."

"March twentieth." Ronnie is looking at my calendar. "Your dinner is on the fourteenth, so you're fine."

"Wait, March twentieth is the Western Days Festival in Ghost. I want to go to that. You know what? Let's put the bookings on hold for right now. I can't deal with this; I'm going home."

I slip my purse over my arm and walk out. It's so out of character for me that I almost turn around and go back in. Ronnie has to be sitting there, slack-jawed.

What if I don't want it anymore? Any of it. What if the picture of the life I thought I wanted looks different now?

I drive home in the pouring rain, making my way through the soggy city, pondering the idea of second chances. The days are supposed be getting longer, but except for the light coming from an occasional streetlamp or the headlights from the cars in front of me, it's already dark.

Austin won't be home for another few hours. He hasn't even moved in yet, but my house has become his again. We have morphed from *he and I* back to a *we*.

It's Wednesday, his night for dinner, which means he'll either get sandwiches at Whole Foods near his office or grab a pizza at Tony's. I used to like the constancy of it, how the routine made him feel reliable, like he was a sure thing.

But tonight, I'm in the mood for nachos and smoked chicken wings and a Ghost Ghoul. And a kiss that's a prelude to a new life. Maybe it's the one I've always wanted and just didn't know it until a streetcar knocked me on my head.

I punch the code into the gate, pull into the garage, and sit in the car, listening to the rain pelt the overhang outside. Then I call Lolly.

"What if I quit?"

"Quit what?" she says.

"Everything."

"Where are you?"

"In my car in the underground garage of my condo."

"Go upstairs, take a hot bath, and get a good night's sleep. You'll feel better in the morning."

"What if I don't?"

"Then welcome to Suckatopia, also known as the real world."

"You're not being a whole lot of help."

"Look, I don't have a PhD in psychology, but it doesn't take a genius to figure out that you're going through some shit after the accident. And it only stands to reason that you're evaluating your life. My suggestion to you is that you don't make any big decisions right now. Don't they say to wait a year? I'd wait a year."

She's right, that's what "they" say, though a year sounds so arbitrary. How will I be different in a year than I am now? What I learned most from the accident is that every day is precious and that you shouldn't waste a minute of it. But one bad decision, and I could be throwing away a career I worked hard to build. Lolly's right; I need to think about this long and hard.

"Are you still there?" she says.

I sigh, exhausted from thinking too much. "I'm here. I guess I should go up."

The rain seems to have tapered off. I can no longer hear it pounding the overhang.

"What are you planning to do?" she asks.

"What you said. Wait."

"It's probably the right decision. But hell, what do I know?"

"No, you're right. I've been through a traumatic experience. My mojo is off. I'll get it back," I say, hopeful.

"You will. I've got to go, so don't do anything stupid."

"Like what?"

"I don't know, run off with the mailman. Or give yourself bangs. You look awful with bangs."

"Thanks. You've been incredibly helpful," I tell her.

"I know. You're welcome."

I catch the elevator, which is empty and smells like Indian food. It stops in the lobby, and a young couple gets on. I can tell from their body language that they've been fighting. He's trying to hold her hand, and she keeps pulling it away. Her eyes are puffy like she's been crying, and his are pleading. And I wonder what he's done. Or what she thinks he's done.

The door slides open on my floor, and I squeeze by them to get out, though I'm tempted to slip them my business card. There was a time before best-selling books, TED Talks, and inspirational calendars, when my greatest joy was helping people fix what was broken in their relationships. One on one. Before it was one size fits all.

Despite the rain and the cold, the apartment feels stuffy. And claustrophobic. And although I have a spectacular view of the Bay Bridge, I miss looking out a window and seeing the lake. Or the geese. I miss the Canada geese that are supposed to fly south but never seem to leave. I miss watching them dabble in the shallow end of the water with their butts in the air.

I open the slider a crack for air and hear the rain hit the balcony. It's only spitting now, but the dampness feels good, like renewal.

There's a message on my phone. Probably Austin wanting me to choose between sandwiches and pizza. But when I play the message, it's Ronnie.

"Just checking to see how you're doing. You seemed . . . Call me."

I hit redial, and she answers on the second ring. "Sorry I rushed out like that. I didn't mean to leave you in the lurch. It just all became overwhelming."

"No worries," she says. "I just wanted to make sure everything is okay."

"Everything is fine." But the thing is, I don't think it is. It's like I'm stuck in a rut and can't get out. That every time I hit the pedal, my wheels keep spinning, but nothing happens.

"I know it's a lot. No one would blame you if you wanted to take a little more time. We can book in summer."

"No, no. It was just a moment of panic. I'm sure tomorrow will be better."

"All right," she says. "Hey, Chels, I hope you don't think this is out of line, but maybe you should see someone. I only say this because . . . never mind. I'm definitely out of line."

"Because why? Go ahead and say it. You won't offend me. You're worried that I'm a whack job now, sending you in search of people who don't exist, staring off into space because I'd rather be in a coma instead of here."

"Oh God, not a whack job. Come on. I just see you struggling, and who wouldn't after what you've been through? I'm sure you have a list of people, but if you'd like, I could make the appointment for you."

"Call JoAnn Sands," I say, because what kind of therapist would I be if I wasn't a proponent of therapy? And to say I'm struggling is an understatement. "My guess is she doesn't have an opening anytime in the near future, but it's worth a try."

"On it."

"And thank you, Ronnie. Thank you for all you do. I may not say it often enough, but you're appreciated." I sound like one of my self-help lectures, which makes me throw up a little in my mouth.

At seven, Austin comes through the door, surprising me with gyros from the Greek place on the corner. The restaurant is actually called Troy, but the entire time we've lived here, we've simply called it *the Greek place*.

"Wow, a little out of your comfort zone," I tease.

"I was in the mood for french fries." The Greek place makes incredible fries. Double-fried, with the exact right amount of salt and a healthy sprinkle of parmesan cheese.

He unpacks our food from a series of white greasy bags, while I set the table. It's been our ritual for as long as I can remember.

"What do you say we go out Saturday night?" He uncorks a bottle of white from the fridge.

"Sure," I say, though it's only Wednesday, and I am not thinking that far ahead. But Saturday date nights were also part of our routine on the rare occasions we could fit it into our schedules.

"Some place special." He squeezes my shoulder. "I'll make a reservation."

"Look at you." I smile at him, but I'm finding it difficult to breathe, like I'm on that mountainous road to Misty's house and I can't look down. It's just a nice dinner, I tell myself. Like dozens of other nice dinners with Austin.

"You okay? You look a little pale."

"I'm great," I say. At least the pressure in my chest is loosening.

"Good." He pulls me in for a quick kiss, then goes on to tell me about his day, specifically about a client who, against his counsel, has decided to give up everything. The house, the investments, spousal support, half her spouse's pension, all in exchange for the cat. She just wants the cat.

"These are not paltry assets," he says. "The house alone is probably worth two mil, and it's paid off. Between that and the investments and pension, she'd be set. But the fucking cat, yeah, that's an equitable trade." He shakes his head. "You can't fix stupid."

"Did you ever think that maybe the cat is her child, and without it, she'd be lost?"

"It's a cat, Chels. This is a woman in her late fifties, who works three days a week as a substitute teacher. How's she going to secure her retirement on a damned cat?"

"Did you ask her that? For all you know, she has a plan."

"I don't care if she has a plan. The husband's getting away with highway robbery."

"You're just mad that you're not getting to fight."

"What's that supposed to mean?"

"All it means is that it's not always about money or winning. Sometimes it's just about getting the life you wanted. In this case, the life is a cat."

"Whatever the hell that means." He takes a big bite out of his gyros and grins. "In other news, I booked us a trip to Bonaire this spring."

"What?"

"You said you always wanted to go, and after everything . . . us, the accident . . . well, we shouldn't put it off. Carpe diem, right?" I must look stunned (I am), because he quickly adds, "Don't worry, I checked your schedule with Ronnie, and everything lines up. No conflicts."

I'm at a loss for words. The best I can do is, "Bonaire, wow," hoping that it sounds enthusiastic enough.

He doesn't miss a beat. "You need this, babe. It makes me happy that I can give it to you."

"Thank you," I say, but I'm already dreading it.

Chapter 27

JoAnn Sands's office is in a bright yellow Victorian cottage in Berkeley, not far from campus. She specializes in trauma and is booked out until summer, but as a professional courtesy, she made a slot for me. Seven thirty in the morning.

The street is empty, and I have the added benefit that the meters don't start running until nine. I'm early because I thought there would be traffic, but it was smooth sailing on the bridge with the reverse commute.

The last time I saw a therapist was after my parents died. Uncle Sylvester booked us appointments with everyone from child psychiatrists to murder-suicide support groups.

The Victorian, which houses three psychologists' offices, is as cheery on the inside as it is on the outside. The shared waiting room has brightly colored walls and rugs and pictures of nature.

"Come on in." JoAnn is a tall woman, with steel gray hair with a blunt cut, who reminds me of Diane Keaton. She ushers me into her office, which is slightly more muted than the waiting room—a little less cheery—and motions for me to take a seat. "What brings you in?"

I tell her about the accident and what precipitated it, about my vivid dream and all the people in it, including Knox, and how I'm having trouble adjusting to the real world. I also tell her about my parents and Lolly.

"The accident, but mostly the dream, left me unsatisfied with my life," I say. "I realize that it's a phase, the aftermath of trauma, and I'm afraid I'll make decisions that I'll regret later on."

"Like what?"

"Quitting my job." I pause, then laugh. "Trading all of it, the condo, the ex-husband, the life I've built for a cat."

She smiles, but it's a quizzical smile. "A cat?"

"It's a long story, but I was just sort of using it as a symbol for the life I had in my dream. The cat is that life."

"But your dream wasn't real."

I nod and start to cry.

She hands me a box of tissues and tells me our time is up.

On our second appointment, I tell her about what Knox said about how we all have pictures in our heads of what the life we want should look like. But what if my original picture was molded by what happened to my parents and my new picture is based on an alternative reality?

"Neither seem very healthy, so where does that leave me?" I ask.

"What about either picture isn't healthy?"

"The first one is needy. It's all about security and safety."

"What's wrong with that?" She leans back in her chair. "What's wrong with wanting security and safety? Even putting aside what happened to your parents, security and safety seems like one of the basic food groups. But you tell me."

I don't have a ready answer. I want to scream *I'm here, so you can tell me*. "Are you saying that the first picture is the one I should choose?"

"I'm not saying that at all. What I'm saying is that the first and second pictures don't have to be mutually exclusive of each other."

"But the second picture is born out of a lie. Or not a lie,

but a fantasy. A hallucination. There is no Knox, there is no idyllic town where everyone knows me and wants to be my friend. Basically, I want to bury myself back in my dream, which is impossible."

"Did you ever consider that there may be a third picture?"

"And what would that be?"

"The whole kit and kaboodle. You get what's behind door number one, door number two, and door number three."

"Are you saying I keep my security and safety, quit my job, move to Ghost, and make real friends? Is that what's behind the three doors?"

"It's whatever you see behind them. It's your picture."

"That's the problem. I don't see anything clearly. Just confusion. Tell me what you see."

She fixes me with a long, hard look, then says, "Did you come here for a crystal ball or a therapist?"

I'm in the bathtub when Lolly calls.

"I have a date tonight," she says. "What should I wear?"

"Really? Who's the date with?"

"My mechanic, if you can believe it."

"Don't be so snobby," I tell her. "I think it's great. What's he like?"

"Well, he's not old, he's not in the entertainment business, and he's divorced with two kids. Winner, winner, chicken dinner."

"Is it possible that all that sarcasm masks deep insecurity?"

"Is it possible that you're a bitch?"

I laugh. "Where are you going?"

"Dinner and a movie. Very original."

"I'd go with something understated. A nice pair of jeans and a dressy blouse. But not too dressy."

"Flats or heels?"

"Boots."

"Because they're made for walking?"

"Yeah, something like that. How are the kids?"

"Luna is getting an F in PE, and Taylor has decided that he wants to be a garbage man when he grows up, because he likes the idea of hanging off the side of a truck. Tonight, they're with Brent and the Ancient One."

"You mean the woman who is Brent's age?"

"Who's being sarcastic now?"

"Does the mechanic stand a chance?" I ask.

There's a long stretch of silence, then, "I like him. And he's madly in love with me."

"I'm not surprised, but how do you know that?" I rise from the tub, letting the water sluice off me before toweling off.

"He told me."

"So this isn't your first date."

"Nope."

"You've been holding out on me."

"You held out on me for twenty-four years, so we're not even close to even," she says. "Gotta go."

Despite her surliness, I know she's close to forgiving me, or else she wouldn't have called in the first place.

I'm dressing when I hear Austin come through the door. For the last few weeks, all he's been talking about is Bonaire. I think he needs this vacation more than I do.

I should be more excited about it than I am and find myself going through the motions just to make him happy. I bought a new bathing suit, even though my old one is perfectly good. And I called the hotel to get activity recommendations, so we don't while away our time lying on the beach, getting skin cancer.

"Here you are." Austin throws his tie on the bed and starts taking off his shoes.

The move has been a slow process. He's been hammered at work, a lot of people getting divorced in this town. But most of his clothes are here, making me miss the extra space I had in the closet. He has a couple more weeks left on his lease, plenty of time, I keep telling him. Which in and of itself should be an ominous warning sign.

"Did you get that restaurant list I sent you?" he says.

"Uh, I'll check my email." I saw the list about an hour ago but want to talk about something else other than Bonaire. Anything else, actually.

"Want to go for a walk?"

I wave my hand over the pajamas I have on. "It's kind of late for a walk, don't you think?"

"It's only seven thirty. And it's a nice night."

"Aren't you hungry?" It is my night for dinner, and I have big plans to zap us frozen lasagna in the microwave.

"They sent out for pizza at the office. But if you're hungry, we can grab something on our walk. Come on, throw some clothes on. A little exercise will do us both good."

I don't want to, but I do it anyway, because it's better than talking about our trip to Bonaire.

On the street, Austin takes my hand, and we stroll in the direction of the ballpark. Austin was right, it's a perfect San Francisco night. Breezy but not too cold. And no fog in sight.

There's a man rolled up in a blanket, sleeping in a doorway. Across the street is the woman from our building, walking her cat. As strange as it is, I've grown accustomed to seeing the fluffy feline on a leash. I wave, but she's too busy scooping up cat poop with a plastic bag to see me.

The bars are doing a brisk business from the after-work crowd, reminding me of happy hour at the Ghost Inn. Half-priced drinks and five-dollar bites that don't exist.

The smell of greasy burgers fills the sidewalk, and my stomach growls.

"You want to get something here?" Austin says.

It's one of the few eateries left that we haven't tried.

"I don't want to eat alone."

"I'll get a milkshake or something."

We go inside, but the line is too long. "Let's find something else," I say.

We go back outside and head toward the bay.

Austin pulls me down onto a bench facing the shoreline, where we watch a flock of seagulls dip in and out of the water. There's just enough light from the restaurants and bars to make out the birds plunge-diving for prey.

"I want to talk to you about something."

The first thing that goes through my mind is that he's leaving again. The last time he did it, he sprung it on me just like this. One minute, we were this happy couple, and the next, he was feeling restless and unfulfilled. A wave of panic passes through me, making my stomach clench, then a strange calm.

He starts, "What do you say we renew our vows in Bonaire? Okay, *renew* isn't exactly the right word given our status, but you get the gist. I guess you'd call it a recommitment ceremony. Just the two of us. And later, when we come home, we could invite everyone and make it official."

I turn toward him on the bench, our knees now touching. "Are you asking me to marry you?"

His lips tip up in a huge grin, the same grin that used to turn me inside out. "Yeah, I was going to ask you tomorrow during our dinner date, do the whole down-on-one-knee thing, except we're beyond proposals, don't you think?"

"I don't know, Austin. A few months ago, you were engaged to someone else."

He's quiet at first, chewing on the revelation that I might not make this easy for him. I suspect he expected me to jump into his arms with joy, even gratitude.

"It was a mistake, Chelsea. I got caught up in the thrill of the new, I suppose. It's nothing I can explain with any kind of clarity; it's just something that happened. And when you almost died, when I almost lost you for good, it put everything in perspective for me. It made me see what I had given up. Because we were good together, Chels. We were a team, working toward a common goal. I guess I just got scared of that."

"Why?" I ask him. "Why were you scared?" Because it's the first time he's mentioned fear, and it seems significant.

He chuckles. "Okay, we're going to do this"—he waves his hands between us—"the therapist-client thing."

"Or how about the-woman-you-left-out-of-the-blue thing, who you're now asking to spend the rest of her life with you?"

"Fair enough," he says, contrite. "I suppose I was afraid that there was more out there."

"In other words, that you could do better."

"Don't say it like that, Chelsea. That's not what I meant."

Except it's exactly what he meant.

I return to that day at the gold mine museum, just before the bridge broke, and I died right before Knox saved me. Right before I returned to Planet Earth. He was saying something.

"*You asked me the other day what I'm looking for after Sienna, whether I still want the picture of the life I'd imagined with her. I told you I still did. What I didn't tell you, what I didn't know until today, is that I want this. Magic. Nothing less than magic.*"

At the time, his words were cryptic. But now they make sense.

I take Austin's hand and squeeze it. "You were looking for magic."

He chuckles again. "But there's no such thing. No one knows that better than a divorce attorney." He lifts his brows. "Or for that matter, a marriage counselor. But what we had, Chelsea, was good."

"You mean good enough."

"Why are you twisting my words?" he says. "I love you. I always have. And I always will. I merely got caught up in a moment of self-doubt. It's over now."

I start to respond, but he holds up his hand that he isn't finished.

"I know I hurt you. I know I have a lot of making up to do. But I also believe I've proven that I'm up to the task."

It's true that he's been by my side every day since the accident. Without him, I would've been even more lost than I am now. And I love him. I never stopped.

"Lolly says I was never near death after the accident," I say, and I can see that he's confused by the turn in the conversation. Even perturbed. He did just ask me to marry him, after all. But I'm getting to it. "Even so," I continue, "I feel like a part of me died. I feel like a part of me was reborn, too. And what I learned is good isn't enough. I want magic. Maybe you're right, and magic is setting my expectations too high. But I'm willing to take that chance."

His eyes are soft in the moonlight, and the way he's looking at me makes my heart fold in half.

"Then magic will be our motto." He holds me against him, and I can feel his heart beating in his chest. How easy it would be to stay this way forever.

"I'm sorry, Austin, I can't accept your proposal."

He pulls away and gently clasps my shoulders. "Come on, Chelsea, don't punish me for one mistake. If you need more time for me to prove myself, then we'll wait. But this is everything we always wanted."

"That's the thing; it's not. At least not for me. There was a time when I thought it was, but now everything is different." Which isn't strictly the truth. I still want some of the same things I once thought he gave me. Security, safety, love, and happiness.

But I want magic, too.

"Don't do this." His voice breaks.

I reach out and trace his face with my finger, feeling like I know what I'm doing for the first time since I took that long elevator ride to the Top of the Mark. "You're a good man,

Austin. You, too, deserve nothing less than magic. And I hope with all my heart that you get it."

The next day, I stop at the coffee place in the lobby of my office building, buy two coffees—one for me and one for Ronnie—bring them up to the second floor, and promptly quit.

"I'm going back to private practice," I tell Ronnie. "Cancel whatever lectures we have scheduled."

"Thank God." She collapses on the sofa and splays her arms wide. "I'm taking a job in Seattle and didn't know how to tell you."

"Really? Because I planned to keep you on. That is, if you still wanted to be my assistant."

"I don't think you can afford me anymore." Her entire face lights up. "MacKenzie Scott hired me to help her give away her billions. Okay, a bit of an exaggeration. But she needs an assistant, and Barbara from TED Talks put in a good word for me. She knows her through mutual associates." She waves her hand in the air. "Six degrees of separation and all that."

Excitement radiates off her in waves. And for a few seconds, I remember what it was like to be her, to be filled with the promise of new possibilities, like a whole new life is waiting around the corner.

"Wow, it sounds like quite a job. Are you okay with leaving San Francisco?"

"God, yes. Don't take this the wrong way, but I need a change in the worst way. I feel like nothing is happening for me here, like I'm standing still."

"No one understands that better than I do." I wrap my arms around her. "I'm so happy for you, Ronnie. I'm going to miss you like crazy, but I'm thrilled for you."

"And you," Ronnie says. "Private practice? When did this all come about?"

"When I realized I wasn't happy anymore. When I realized this"—I gaze around the office at the small empire I built—"isn't who I am anymore. I started out with the simple goal of helping people, and I believe I can do that better one on one."

She nods, a world of understanding in her eyes. "I don't think you've been that into it for a while. Even before the accident. Are you going to keep this office?" She takes a visual lap around the room. "You've got me for two more weeks. If you want, I can help you turn this into the waiting room, and we can tweak your office to better accommodate patients. Get some comfy sofas, that kind of thing."

"Thank you, Ronnie. But I've decided to start from scratch." I think about JoAnn Sands's cheery Victorian cottage, about the muted colors and nature pictures on her walls, how it felt more like a home than a therapist's office. "I'll start looking next week."

For now, I need a minute to breathe.

Part 3

Dreams are often the most profound when they seem the most crazy.
—Sigmund Freud

Chapter 28

"Hey, you'll get eaten alive out here."

I feel warm hands on my shoulders, shaking me. "What? Get off of me!" I'm startled awake, and my hammock sways, then pitches to one side before I right it without falling out.

"Whoa, whoa." The man holds his hands up in the air and backs away. "I come in peace."

It takes me a few seconds to get my bearings. Then it all rushes back to me in Technicolor. I've come to the cabin to regroup. To breathe before starting over. Lolly and the kids are coming for a whole weekend.

I pull myself up into a sitting position and stare at the man standing in front of me. He looks vaguely familiar, but in my hazy state, I can't place him. And we're here . . . alone. The nearest neighbor is a good half mile away.

"Do I know you?" I feel like I've been here before, like I had this same encounter just a day or so again, like I'm experiencing a severe case of déjà vu.

He tilts his head to the side and looks at me like I'm a little off my rocker before saying, "I'm Leo Antonelli. Austin hired me to fix your roof."

And then it hits me where I recognize him from. That strange plaid tie. "It's you! You're the guy from the Top of the Mark! The one sitting at the bar alone. The one with the . . . tie."

He's looking at me with a patient grin on his face, like maybe he thinks I've lost it.

"It was in October, right before Halloween," I try to explain, digging myself in deeper, making myself look even nuttier than he probably already thinks I am. "You were at the Mark Hopkins. I remember because Austin thought you looked familiar, and we kept glancing back at you to figure out why he thought he knew you."

"Yeah. Probably because I've been doing work on and off at the cabin for Austin over the last year. Didn't he tell you?" He's still grinning.

It's such a nice grin that I kind of get lost in it and forget my train of thought.

"You okay?" He crouches down until he's eye level with me.

"Yes, yes. Sorry. Tell me what?"

"That I'm the one who called nine-one-one, the one who resuscitated you after the cable car hit you. I just happened to be in San Francisco to meet a friend. Fate, I guess. You don't remember?"

"You're that Leo?" I do a double take. "I thought you said you're an EMT."

"EMT and part-time handyman and roofer."

I remember the area code when he called me. It's the same as Ghost's. At the time, I didn't put it together. "Austin never mentioned anything about it . . . or that he finally figured out how he knew you."

"He was probably distracted." Leo looks at me as if to say *You'd just gotten out of a coma, he had other things on his mind.*

"Yeah, probably," I say, still trying to piece out the missing parts. "Do you live around here?"

"Not too far. You know where Old Ranch Road is?"

I meet his gaze and stare, stunned. I can't help wondering

if I fell asleep in the hammock and am now lost in the dream again. The dream from my coma.

To test my theory, I get out of the hammock. Leo stands there, watching me, then follows me as I walk around the side of the house. There, in the driveway, I find a dinged-up pickup with a ladder strapped to the top of the truck's utility rack.

My gaze wanders to the front door. "It's red!" Just like in my dream, I almost say.

"Yeah, I changed it out a few weeks ago. A surprise from Austin. He said you hated the old one."

I can't believe my eyes, but the Halloween wreath from Flower Power is hanging there, too. The tiny orange and white pumpkins and the green juniper boughs are as fresh as the day I dreamt I bought it.

"Did you hang the wreath?" I ask, baffled at how it got there.

"Nope. I don't know where that came from." He shakes his head. "A little past its season, though."

I look at him, wondering if I'm imagining it all. Him, the red door, the Halloween wreath. Or is it magic? "Are you real? Is this real?"

"Excuse me?" He tilts his head to one side. "I think you got up a little too fast. You want to sit down? I could get you a glass of water. Maybe that'll help."

Before I can stop him, he's off to his truck, returning a few seconds later with one of those lunchbox-sized ice chests.

"Here, drink this." He hands me a bottle of water, then rummages through his cooler until he finds a package of vanilla wafers.

I stare at the familiar-looking cookies, dumbfounded.

"For sugar," he says. "Sometimes a jolt of sugar helps."

"Oh . . . right. Yeah, I get that." I blink a few times, making sure that I'm really seeing what I think I'm seeing, then point at the package. "Where did you get those?"

"Uh, the grocery store. Why?"

"It's just that I know someone . . . knew someone . . . that had a fondness for that particular brand of cookie." I look down at the wafer he's pushed into my hand, still trying to decide whether this is actually happening.

"They're good stuff, my favorite," he says. "Go ahead and take a bite. Hopefully it'll make you feel better, less disoriented."

"I'm fine . . . I think." But Leo has caught me off guard. Everything about him is foreign, yet completely familiar.

"It can take a while," he says.

"A while? For what?"

"To recuperate. You suffered a pretty serious head injury."

"Yes, I did. But I'm better now, better than I've been in a long time."

He gives me a long, assessing look and says, "You sure seem good to me," then flashes that wonderful grin again.

And there, in his shining, happy brown eyes, I see hope—and even traces of my future.

Acknowledgments

I have so many people to thank for this book. First, my dear friend and critique partner, Rebecca Ahlfeldt, who is always there to talk me off the ledge. This time was no different and I know you'll be there for the next one, too. Just know that your insight and feedback is always invaluable.

Thanks to Alexandra Nicolajsen for more reasons than I can count and especially for being my inspiration on this one. To Wendy Miller, who always helps me get that first chapter right. A special thanks goes to Jill Marsal for believing in me and being the best first reader an author can have. To John Scognamiglio, who gave my very first novel a home and continues to be my greatest cheerleader. It's a dream to be working with you. And to the rest of the Kensington team, especially Carly Sommerstein, Lauren Jernigan, Jane Nutter, and copy editor Scott Heim. My deepest gratitude for all that you do.

And last, but never least, my eternal thanks to my family. There are not enough words for how much I appreciate all of you.